"I don't kn
being a ho

"It's probably got being a policeman or fireman beat all to heck, though," Billy said earnestly.

Cosmo's eyebrows went up in surprise. "How so?"

"Men who are drawn to those jobs are attracted to danger."

Cosmo looked at her speculatively. There was so much he couldn't tell her. "Is that what your husband was like?"

"I suppose so. He probably would have changed when he got older. Maybe."

Cosmo shook his head. "People don't change as they get older, they just get more like themselves."

Billy gave him a long, considering look. Why was she so drawn to this man? First a jock, then a crooked intellectual, now a self-styled hobo. Maybe it was time to see an analyst. Or maybe it was just time to leave this island paradise and go home.

ABOUT THE AUTHOR

Bobby Hutchinson's books have touched and entertained countless readers all over the world. Like all of her books, *Vagabond Hearts* has drawn on an element of her personal experience.

Eight years ago, Bobby and her husband, Al, traveled across North America by motorcycle. For two months, they lived out of a pup tent. "In a strange way, we were vagabonds," Bobby says. "In living out this sort of fantasy, we came to understand ourselves and the things around us in a different way."

Although Bobby and Al now live more conventionally in Winfield, B.C., the experience was one she will never forget.

Books by Bobby Hutchinson

HARLEQUIN SUPERROMANCE
229–MEETING PLACE
253–DRAW DOWN THE MOON
284–NORTHERN KNIGHTS
337–A PATCH OF EARTH
376–REMEMBER ME
443–JOURNEY'S END

Vagabond Hearts

BOBBY HUTCHINSON

Harlequin Books

TORONTO • NEW YORK • LONDON
AMSTERDAM • PARIS • SYDNEY • HAMBURG
STOCKHOLM • ATHENS • TOKYO • MILAN
MADRID • WARSAW • BUDAPEST • AUCKLAND

Published March 1992

ISBN 0-373-70492-5

VAGABOND HEARTS

For Alan,
fellow vagabond and resident research department,
with gratitude and love

CHAPTER ONE

"THIS IS IT, ladies. The Kona Beach Apartments, Kailua-Kona town. Welcome to Hawaii, the Big Island. You're going to love it here."

The talkative taxi driver gave the words a lilting, exotic sound as he twisted around in the seat and grinned at them.

"The office is right over there, and there are elevators at the back to take your stuff up. I'll load it all on for you—you know which unit you're in? You got a key for the main door to the lobby?"

Billy was trying to look in every direction at once so as not to miss any part of the vista of green palm trees, crimson hedges and azure blue ocean. She turned her attention to the building where she and Amanda would be living for the next three weeks.

She had to admit it was a little disappointing at first glance, all boring cement and glass. She'd envisioned a little thatched-roof cottage on the beach, but this seven-story concrete structure would have been quite at home back in Vancouver.

Never mind. It was here in Hawaii, and that made all the difference. And the ocean was just across the road, impressive waves rolling onto a rocky beach, miles of water stretching out to meet a hazy blue horizon.

"We're in 410," she told the driver. "I've got a couple of keys—one of them must be for the entrance door." She turned to her mother-in-law. "Amanda, I'll just go over and tell the management we're here."

Billy swung her long legs out of the car and loped over to the office door. She tried it, but it was locked. She looked around her, but there was no one anywhere. The entire building seemed to slumber in the midday heat. Maybe they took siestas in Hawaii. She shrugged and hurried back to the car, where Amanda was waiting.

"Nobody home. We can always check in with them later, I guess. Let's get all this junk upstairs right now while this nice man is still offering to help."

Billy gave the "nice man" one of her best smiles, and the portly driver almost tripped over himself in his rush to unload their seven bulky pieces of mismatched luggage into the elevator. She also made sure she gave him a generous tip.

After effusive thank-yous, he pulled out several of his business cards and offered to take them on a guided tour of the island at rock-bottom rates. At last he stepped away and the elevator doors were allowed to close.

Billy rolled her eyes and blew out a long breath as she punched number four. "Nice guy, but kinda long-winded, huh, Amanda?"

Amanda laughed and agreed. "It always tickles me to watch you turn on the charm. Too bad you can't bottle it and sell it. You'd be rich."

"Don't I wish. But c'mon, I'm not that calculating, am I?" Billy gave her mother-in-law's arm a little poke, unable to contain her high spirits. Her heart was hammering with excitement, the way it had been off and on ever since they'd left Vancouver.

Could it have been only this morning? It felt as if days had passed since they'd left Vancouver's dismal November rain for Hawaii's tropical heat and glorious sunshine. She could hardly believe they were actually here at last, and as far as she was concerned, travel wasn't at all the tiring production it was purported to be. Far from exhausting her, the long flight to Honolulu and the short hop over to the Big Island had filled her with exhilaration.

Amanda was obviously feeling much the same way. Her mobile features reflected her awe and excitement, and she sounded a bit breathless.

"Smell, Billy. It smells different here, doesn't it? Sort of equatorial, perfumed and kind of... heavy. I noticed it the minute we stepped off the plane. It made me realize we truly are in a tropical country. Oh, I'll bet it's nice in the apartment. I can hardly wait to dump all our stuff and explore the town. Did you see those quaint little shops on our way in? Hardly any of them had walls or windows."

Billy shook her head. "I wasn't looking. I was busy counting restaurants. I'll bet there's one restaurant for every single resident of Kailua Village. It's like going straight to heaven. Did you smell all that divine food cooking? I'm starving—I can't believe they don't give you more to eat on airplanes."

Billy had eaten her own portions of everything the airline had offered, plus anything Amanda hadn't wanted. She'd also unashamedly accepted the bun, packaged cheese and rich dessert the old woman in the other seat had offered her.

Billy's appetite was phenomenal. It had been an embarrassment to her at times, but at twenty-eight, she felt she'd reached a point where she was more accepting of herself generally, and that included being comfortable with her eating habits. Miraculously, in spite of the amount she put away, she stayed lean and lanky.

Amanda always told her it was because she was so tall, adding wistfully how much she wished her own five foot four and plentiful curves could just once be stretched over a six-foot frame like Billy had. "Not that I'm unhappy about it," Amanda would declare stoutly, giving her daughter-in-law a lewd wink and a modified version of a bump-and-grind. "After forty-nine years of living inside here I'm rather fond of the old equipment. But just once it would be fun to see how it felt to be tall and svelte instead of short and . . . well, pleasantly plump."

The elevator, slow and stately, dinged now, and the doors opened onto the fourth floor. Billy fished out her keys and handed them to Amanda. "Here, you go open the door. I'll put a hold on this thing and unload our stuff. Gad, we've got tons. We didn't start off with this much, did we? Do you think these old bags reproduced on the way over?"

Amanda didn't answer. She was gazing, wide eyed, up and down the corridor. "Oh, look, Billy. Isn't this something?" Now that they were inside the building, it seemed more like what they'd hoped it would be. "I love it—it's so tropical. And no walls! I can't get over this idea of everything being open to the elements."

Billy pushed the Hold button and stepped out to see.

There was a waist-high barrier to the walkway that continued around all four sides of the building, hung at intervals with overflowing baskets of exotic flowers. It overlooked a large swimming pool in the enclosed courtyard four stories below. The turquoise water was undisturbed—it still seemed as if no one else was stirring in the entire complex.

After a false start in the wrong direction, Amanda located 410, but she didn't open the door. Instead she trotted back and helped Billy make trip after trip with the bags, dumping them on the coco matting just outside their door.

When they were finished, Billy reclaimed the keys, finally locating the one that fit the lock. The door opened. Billy stepped inside, hesitant, hopeful that the apartment would be all she'd imagined.

It smelled like toast. She was in a tiny hallway. On her left was a compact kitchen with bright yellow appliances, and beyond that was a roomy living-dining area decorated in bamboo, with plump cushions covered in a brown-and-white Polynesian design. On her left was a short hall leading to two bedrooms, and directly ahead was a closed door that must lead to a bathroom.

The dirty dishes on the table, the pile of books on the floor beside the desk didn't register at first.

"C'mon in, Amanda, it's—" Billy's sentence ended in a horrified yelp.

A tall, muscular man threw open the closed door a few yards in front of her, releasing billows of steam and the smell of soap and shampoo. He had a flimsy brown towel clutched around his loins. His thick white hair stood on end and drops of water ran down his broad shoulders into the corresponding mat of white hair that covered his chest.

He stared at the two women for a moment, then at the stack of luggage behind them.

"How the hell did you get in here?"

He sounded more puzzled than angry.

Billy held up the keys, speechless.

A wide, white-toothed grin split his bronzed features.

"Well, it's nice of you to drop in this way, but I'm afraid there's some mistake. As you can see, you've got the wrong unit. My name's Max—Max Caplin. I live here." His voice was deep and jovial, as if laughter lurked just behind the mock courtesy of his greeting.

Both women were stricken dumb. They stood rooted to the spot, unable to do anything but gape at him.

At last Billy found her voice. "What do you mean, you live here? This is the unit we were promised—you can see my keys just opened the door." She planted her fists on her hips.

The man's eyes were an amazing shade of turquoise that stood out against the deep tan of his skin... and every inch of his skin was tanned, Billy noted. He had thick white eyebrows, and they rose now in quizzical amusement.

"I suppose we could stand and argue about it," he drawled, "but I'm not dressed for it. Besides, I was here first, so obviously there's been a mistake."

He looked at Billy and then at Amanda, and the incredulous looks on their faces must have registered.

"Look, if you'll excuse me for just a moment while I slip into something more presentable, I'm sure we can sort it all out. Why not go on in and sit down?" He gestured toward the living room. "I won't be a moment."

Still holding the towel with one hand, he nonchalantly moved from the hall into the bedroom and shut the door. The toweling covered his muscular buttocks, but just barely. His legs were strong, long and well shaped. He was an older man, but he was definitely in good form.

Billy tore her gaze from his posterior and turned to stare at Amanda. Her own confusion and distress were mirrored in her mother-in-law's huge green eyes.

"Look at the key, Billy. Is there a number on it?"

With trembling fingers, Billy turned it over. She studied it and shook her head. "It's 410, all right, so what in blue bloody blazes is going on here? That woman from the symphony who told me I'd won this trip didn't say anything about somebody else living here, too. She just said one of the symphony patrons had donated the condo for three weeks to help with their raffle.

"I've got the official letter with all the conditions and things somewhere here in my bag." Billy opened her oversize handbag and started rummaging frantically through the contents.

"Never mind right now. I'm sure you're in the right, dear. There's probably some simple explanation for it all." Amanda's shoulders slumped, as if she didn't believe that any more than Billy did. "Let's just do what he said and sit down. I feel as if my legs are about to cave in, anyway. It must be this sudden heat."

Amanda did look pale. Billy took her arm and led the way into the living room.

The apartment faced west, and the hot Hawaiian sun was shining in through sliding-glass doors that covered the front wall. Beyond the doors was a narrow deck, enclosed on both ends with cement walls that afforded privacy from the unit on either side.

Nope, Billy amended silently, not a deck. Here it was called a lanai. She and Amanda had spent the past weeks reading everything they could find about Hawaii. Billy had had a hard time believing that she'd actually won this trip for two to a place she'd only dreamed of visiting some far-off day, when and if she got rich. And now... She swallowed hard. Instead of a dream come true, the Hawaiian trip was beginning to feel more like a rotten practical joke.

The lanai provided a breathtaking view of the ocean, across the road and beyond a row of tall palms. From up here, the Pacific sparkled like precious gems in the late-afternoon sunshine. The lanai's lounge chairs would provide first-class accommodation for one of the spectacles Amanda had been anticipating—her first Hawaiian sunset.

Even now, the fiery ball was sinking closer and closer to the western horizon, the blue-green water turning amazing shades of salmon and scarlet and gold.

"It's spectacular, isn't it?"

Amanda's voice was filled with awe. It was everything they'd hoped for and more, but an ominous feeling of foreboding spoiled Billy's appreciation of it. There was undoubtedly a serious mix-up over their accommodation.

Billy suddenly felt close to tears, and for all Amanda's show of bravado, she knew her mother-in-law was feeling every bit as let down as she was. Their wonderful windfall of a holiday was being ruined before it even had had a chance to begin.

Before they could sit down on the bamboo couches and matching armchairs, upholstered in the dramatic brown print Billy had first noticed, the bedroom door opened.

The man—Max?—was now clad in white shorts and a loose-fitting shirt patterned with startling blue-and-crimson flowers and yellow parrots. Again she noticed his impressive physique, as he came striding toward them. His blue eyes met Billy's, and she could see kindliness and humor there, as well as a spark that might just be mischief.

"Now, before we start discussing all this again, how about a cold drink, ladies?"

Without waiting for an answer, he went into the kitchen, opened the fridge and pulled out a carafe of orange juice. A moment later he came toward them balancing a tray with three tall glasses jingling with ice and filled to the brim.

Watching him, Billy could only marvel at the air of youthful energy he exuded. He had to be at least Amanda's age—fifty next July—or maybe even a few years older, but there was no sign of the all-too-familiar paunch and stooped shoulders middle age often bestowed.

There was a quiet moment while they all took long gulps of the icy-cold, refreshing juice. Then Billy set her glass down with a little thud on the low coffee table and said, "Now, Mr. Captain..."

"'Caplin,'" he corrected with a grin. "'Captain' does have a nice ring, though. But I suspect that like everything else there are disadvantages that go with the job."

"Mutiny for one," Amanda said unexpectedly.

Billy glanced at her in surprise.

"And I think you need a boat. Or is it a ship?"

"Well, that's out, then. I can't even row properly, and I never did figure out what 'fore' and 'aft' meant. Or 'starboard,' either."

He was looking across at Amanda, and his amazing blue eyes twinkled as if the two of them were alone, enjoying this inane banter. For the first time since they'd walked into the apartment, Amanda was smiling. Billy looked from one to the other as they grinned at each other like a pair of fools, and with an impatient frown, she took charge.

"So, Mr. Caplin. How come you're living in the apartment we've been told to move into?"

"Why not call me 'Max'? And you are...?" He raised a quizzical eyebrow not at Billy, but at Amanda.

"Oh. Of course, I beg your pardon, how rude of me. I'm Amanda Reece and this is my daughter-in-law, Billy Overton Reece."

"How do you do, Billy. Amanda, I'm delighted to meet you." He inclined his head in a courtly gesture to each of them, but his eyes returned to Amanda. "You're here in Hawaii on your own, then? Your husbands didn't come with you? Where are you from?"

"We're both widows, from Vancouver, Canada," Billy snapped impatiently.

"Really? What a coincidence. I'm from Vancouver myself. Lovely city, Vancouver."

He still seemed to be talking directly to Amanda, and she answered as if they were old friends.

"It is beautiful, but one tends to get moldy in all that rain."

"My feeling exactly. It takes me six months of Hawaiian sunshine a year to get the rust out of my joints." He beamed at her, and again she smiled back.

Billy was fast losing patience with both of them. She had to get this matter of accommodation settled, didn't they realize that?

"Look, here's the drill, Mr. . . . Max." She leaned forward on the soft cushions, punctuating her words with her hands. "I won a free trip for two, and three weeks' accommodation, starting today, in this suite, in this apartment building. I have letters stating all that, from both the symphony committee that sponsored the raffle and the owner of this unit. So what we need to know is, why are you living here and how soon can you move out?"

The best defense was a good offense, Graham used to say. Mind you, her husband had said it about football, but Billy felt it had good application here, as well.

Max didn't seem at all ruffled by her bluntness.

Billy glanced at Amanda. Her mother-in-law's face was aflame with embarrassment. Billy knew Amanda felt she was being a trifle more assertive than necessary, but what was she supposed to do? She felt responsible for bringing Amanda here and then getting her into a predicament like this.

"I'm afraid moving out is impossible," Max said in a gentle tone. "You see, among other things, I own this apartment. Jointly, that is. With my ex-wife. And I suspect that's where this mix-up originated. Is one of the letters you mentioned signed by Frances Grant, by any chance?"

Billy had the letter in her hand. She didn't need to look at the signature to be sure. She simply nodded and handed it over to him. Her stomach felt as if she were riding an elevator that was dropping far too fast.

He scanned it quickly and shook his head. "Well, Fran's gone and done it again. She's notoriously rattlebrained, you see, and she's forgotten that we switched our dates for the use of the place this year. Usually she has it from September to February. This year I wanted to be here at this time, and since she was going to Europe, anyway, she agreed to the change. A long time ago, I might add. Knowing Fran, she then promptly forgot all about our agreement and offered it to this symphony committee. That's the sort of thing she does all the time." A mixture of exasperation and impatience flitted across Max's face. "Scatty woman. But I do have a letter from her lawyer here somewhere confirming the change. . . .

Max walked over to a writing desk, opened it and found an envelope in one of the cubbyholes. He withdrew a sheet of paper and handed it to Billy. "I've learned the hard way to get everything in writing when dealing with Fran."

Billy took it, but she was loath to unfold it and confirm everything he was telling them. Maxwell Caplin was obviously well organized and sure of his ground. There was no doubt in her mind that what he'd said was exactly what had happened. She and Amanda were out on their ears.

The knowledge made her feel sick inside. She handed the folded paper to Amanda instead of reading it herself. Her suspicions were confirmed by the dejected expression on her mother-in-law's face.

Amanda offered Billy the paper, but when Billy shook her head, Amanda refolded the document and set it carefully down beside her juice glass.

"It's just as he says, Billy." Amanda's voice trembled a bit.

Well, that was that. Billy got to her feet and dusted off her hands in the unconscious gesture she always used to signify the end of something.

"Well, I'm sorry we've bothered you. It's not your fault, and it's not ours, either, but we'd better get cracking and find somewhere to stay tonight. Do you mind if we use your phone? We'll have to locate a hotel room."

"Go right ahead." Max waved a hand in the direction of the phone on the kitchen counter. "But why not wait fifteen minutes? The sun's about to set, and that's an event around here. I'll refill our glasses and we can sit out on the lanai and watch."

Billy shook her head, but Amanda said firmly, "I'd love that, thank you." Amanda gestured to Billy to come and sit down. "Why not, dear? I don't suppose it's going to make any difference whether we call now or a little later. And tonight might be our only chance to see a Hawaiian sunset, after all."

Max, in the process of refilling the glasses with orange juice, looked at her in surprise.

"But surely you aren't thinking of going home? I'm quite certain there'll be a vacancy at one of the hotels. In fact, I know the managers at several. I'll make some calls for you."

Amanda tried to smile at him, but Billy could tell it was difficult for her.

"Whether there's a vacancy or not won't really matter," Amanda said ruefully. "I'm sure we couldn't afford a hotel for longer than a night or two at the most. I know approximately what the rates are at this time of year. No, unfortunately we couldn't possibly stay on. Widows we are, but rich we ain't," she added in what she hoped was a lighter note.

Amanda's attempt at humor left Billy feeling worse than before, because what she'd said was the bald truth. She'd been mentally adding up the traveler's checks in her own wallet, along with the meager balance in her checking account back home. She knew Amanda wasn't any better off than she was. There wasn't any way they could stay.

Max didn't reply right away. Instead he handed them their glasses and led the way out the sliding doors, motioning for Amanda to take the most comfortable-looking lounge chair. Billy collapsed on a worn chaise a few feet away, wondering if she'd ever have the energy to move again.

In spite of her sagging spirits, the raw and spectacular glory of the Hawaiian sun sinking past the rim of the ocean gradually captivated her and held her enthralled. For a moment her problems took a back seat to nature's pageantry.

Max, too, was aware of the sunset—he'd never grown jaded about Hawaii's splendor—but there were other, more urgent matters racing through his mind. Rationally there was no need for it, but the fact was, he felt responsible for this mix-up Fran had perpetrated. God knows it wasn't the first time she'd landed him in an embarrassing situation or involved him in matters he would otherwise stay clear of. He suspected he had an overdeveloped sense of responsibility, and sometimes it proved to be a royal pain.

Such as this mess with the hoboes. He was involved in that now, up to his neck, and if he had any sense at all, he'd have ignored what Boxcar Charlie had told him and just stuck to getting the information he needed for his book. But how could a decent man ignore what sounded very much like murder? He'd felt obliged to go to the police when Charlie had disappeared a week ago and give them the scanty information he'd gleaned from Charlie. And he was aware the police thought he knew a lot more than he was telling, which wasn't the case at all.

By being honest, he'd ended up under suspicion, which should teach him once and for all to mind his own business. Still, that situation and this one were poles apart. This was a simple misunderstanding. And he wasn't responsible for other people's holidays, was he?

Nevertheless, the disappointment on Amanda's pretty face wasn't easy to dismiss... especially coupled with her ingenuous admission that she and the daughter-in-law couldn't afford to check into a hotel for the rest of their stay.

And despite his hard-earned education from Fran on how devious people could be, he had not a doubt in the world that Amanda was telling the truth. That open countenance must make lying impossible, because her every emotion was written all over her face. She had exceptional eyes, too—large, green, trusting. Innocent eyes. It was rare to find a lady of... a certain age... with that particular quality.

In today's world, it was rare at any age, he thought with a touch of sadness.

She was attractive; soft and rounded and feminine. She hadn't made the mistake of dying her hair some phony color, either. It was thick and curly and an honest nut brown, turning white in a dramatic strip above her forehead. And she had the greatest grin in the world—wide and crooked, filled with devilry, tilted up at one corner and down at the other. When she smiled her dimples gave her the look of an appealing, slightly wrinkled elf.

A sense of humor—that's what came with a grin like that. He'd bet she had the greatest sense of humor going. All the sexy women he'd ever met appreciated humor.

The best sex always came with lots of laughter.

Whoa, Max! Get hold of yourself. How did sex get into this, anyhow? There are far too many women in your life as it is, never mind getting involved with a thoroughly nice little lady whom life has obviously kicked around some.

They had no money. No place to stay. Unless...

Forget it, Max. It's not your problem, and it's certainly not one of your better ideas, especially not with that troop of questionable research sources traipsing in and out of here at a moment's notice.

Hoboes weren't everyone's cup of tea. Nope, it wouldn't do.

He shook his head with finality, but just then Amanda looked at him, still spellbound by the sunset. He caught his breath at the sight of her enraptured face. If one Hawaiian sunset could stir that depth of passion in her...

"I can't thank you enough for letting us share this with you, Max." Her husky voice had a catch in it. "It's everything the books said it would be, and that sort of accuracy is all too rare."

Her soft eyes reflected the glory of color beginning now to fade from the western horizon, and for a moment he wondered if he'd met her somewhere before. She struck an old and familiar chord deep inside of him, as if they'd been dear friends long ago, in a forgotten place and time.

She intrigued him.

The last lingering rays were spilling dusky gold and crimson on the water now, radiating out from the spot where the sun had slipped into the ocean. It was already dusk, and Max knew that in swift tropical fashion, full dark would soon fall.

Billy, too, had obviously been caught by the spell of the sunset, but she shook off its effects and got to her feet. "Time I started phoning around, so if you'll excuse me..."

"Look, hold it a minute, Billy, would you?" There was something in Max's voice that stopped her, made her turn and look at him.

"I've got a proposition for you. For both of you."

CHAPTER TWO

MAX REALIZED immediately that his choice of words hadn't been the best. "Proposition" had a sexual connotation he hadn't meant at all.

"I have an idea," he blundered on. "Why not stay here for the night? It's going to be dark soon, and there are two bedrooms with twin beds and en suite plumbing in each. There's also the main bathroom. Tomorrow we can scout around and see if there's a place in town you can afford for a week or two."

He knew even as he spoke that it was virtually impossible; every reasonable and available closet in this town had been rented for weeks already. It was November, the high season. But he'd deal with that tomorrow. This would give him time to think, to consider all the ramifications of letting them stay on here in the condo with him.

"Oh, that's very kind of you, but I really don't think we could possibly—" Amanda was shaking her head.

Billy interrupted her. "That's a generous offer, and we can't afford to turn it down."

She smiled for the first time since he'd met her, and Max realized that Amanda wasn't the only lovely woman in the room. This girl, with her short silver-blond hair and deep brown eyes, had a wide smile that lit up her whole face.

"Thanks a lot, Max," Billy confirmed enthusiastically. "We'll take you up on it—we don't have a whole lot of choice. And—" she turned and looked at Amanda for confirmation "—in return, we'll cook you dinner tonight. How's that?"

Max was in the habit of eating out or microwaving TV dinners. His cooking skills didn't go beyond opening boxes of dry cereal and boiling wieners. "That sounds fantastic," he agreed at once. "There's a grocery a couple of blocks away. Make a list and I'll get whatever you need."

"Nope, dinner's on us. I'll go do the shopping if you steer me in the right direction. I can handle shopping, and Amanda's a whiz at cooking. We're a winning team. Isn't that right, Amanda?"

Max watched Amanda as she looked from Billy's now-eager face over to him. He noted the uncertainty in her expression. Their eyes met and held, and he felt the same sense of familiarity and recognition he'd felt before. An invisible wave of reassurance went from him to her and was acknowledged and accepted.

"Go get the groceries, Billy." Amanda's frown disappeared and she headed toward the kitchen. "I'll just get on speaking terms with the stove, find out where the pots and pans are, how the oven operates and all that." She gave Max another anxious glance. "I do hope we're not upsetting any plans you had for the evening. Please don't feel you have to stay here and entertain us. We're certainly all right on our own."

"I didn't have anything important planned at all," he lied. "A...new friend, a fellow I just met, might be dropping by a bit later, but that's no problem. You can't imagine how much I'm looking forward to a home-cooked meal."

Not that the Matrimonial Brigade didn't cook for him. But the price tag on their food was far too high, and the after-dinner innuendo gave him indigestion.

Amanda relaxed. They all moved inside, and Max gave Billy detailed directions to the store. Together they shifted the small mountain of luggage the women had brought into the bedroom, and then Billy left with a list she and Amanda had compiled after studying the contents of the fridge and cupboards.

Max felt that perhaps he should have gone with Billy, but Noah had said he might call tonight if he happened to be by a phone and if he happened to find out anything new at all about where Charlie had gone. And the new hobo, the man called Cosmo, had said he'd come by for an interview a little later.

That wasn't going to work too well with Amanda and Billy here. He'd have to set up another time with young Cosmo, but you couldn't exactly phone a hobo and say tonight's not convenient, could you? Hobo jungles didn't come equipped with all mod cons.

Lord, what a mess it was all becoming. Surely by tomorrow he'd come to his senses and realize how impossible it would be to have these women around for any length of time, considering his situation.

In the meantime...well, in the meantime, he had to admit it was pleasant, a lot more pleasant than interviewing hoboes or worrying about Charlie or tactfully avoiding the Matrimonial Brigade. He could relax for once, and just enjoy these few moments alone with the delightful woman called Amanda.

"Where do you keep your large pots, Max?" Amanda called from the kitchen.

"I never use any, but I think there might be some in the bottom cupboard, to the right of the stove."

There were, and he watched with interest as she bent to retrieve them. His body stirred to life, acknowledging the appealing roundness of her buttocks in the thin blue cotton slacks she wore. It had been a while since his body had responded to a woman in that particular way, and Max felt a surge of pleasure and male pride in his aging libido. Everything was still working, and wasn't that fine?

"Amanda," he said, testing out the syllables on his lips as much as drawing her attention. It was a quaint, old-fashioned name, and he liked it. "Tell me, Amanda, how long have you lived in Vancouver?"

She twisted her head around so she could see him over her shoulder. Her face was a little flushed, and the extra color suited her.

"Vancouver? Oh, I've been there most of my life."

Max watched as she focused her attention for another moment on the pots and pans in the cupboard, then straightened and turned so she was looking at him, her eyes bright in the overhead light she'd switched on.

She leaned back against the sink. "I grew up in a little coal-mining town in eastern B.C., and I married John right after high school. He was ten years older than me. He was an accountant. When he got a job with a large Vancouver firm a year after our wedding, we moved to the coast, and I've lived there ever since."

Max wondered about the spaces in her story. What was this man John like, the man she'd married and lived with...how long? How long had she been a widow?

As if reading his mind, she added, "John drowned four years ago—well, it'll be five next April." Her eyes skidded past his, and her voice became careful, even and remote. "Our son, Graham, was with him. A friend offered them the use of his boat, and they went fishing. A storm blew up, and they were both drowned. It was a freak accident. Graham and Billy had been married only two and a half years."

"God, that's rough. I'm sorry, Amanda." His words felt so inadequate.

"Me, too." She looked at him, and her eyes were infinitely sad. "Graham was our only child. I'd always wanted a big family, but it didn't work out. Do you have children, Max?"

"Two daughters, from when I was married to Fran. Actually, Fran is the only woman I've ever been married to. The girls are grown and married themselves now, one in Vermont, one in Saskatchewan. Three grandchildren—two boys and a girl." He almost hated telling her. It seemed such riches after hearing of her losses. But the smile she gave him was genuine, pleased for him.

"Grandchildren. How lucky you are. Do you have pictures?"

He hauled out his wallet and showed her some recent snapshots. She lingered over the one of his three-year-old granddaughter.

"She's adorable. What's her name?"

"Sophia. And she's a hellion. She can swear like a longshoreman already."

"Good for her. If I had it all to do over again, I'd swear more."

Amanda laughed, and he was relieved that the sadness had passed so quickly. He wanted to know more about her. He wanted to know everything about her.

"Do you work, Amanda?"

"Yes, on Dunbar, you know the street?"

He nodded. "I used to live in Shaughnessey—that's nearby."

"Right. Well, Dunbar's near where I live, too. I work at a small secondhand bookstore there, The Book Bin. It's hardly a challenging career, but I've worked there for years and I like it. Reading's always been an addiction with me, and I get plenty of opportunity to indulge myself."

He smiled. "I envy you. I've always had a fantasy about owning my own bookstore when I retire."

"What kind of work do you do, Max?"

He sent her a rueful grin. "I'm just a stodgy old university professor. My field is sociology. I teach at the University of British Columbia—have done for years. But I'm on a year's sabbatical at the moment."

They were silent, both pondering the strange coincidence of living and working within a few miles of each other half a continent away, then meeting here.

"Is a sabbatical like a holiday, or are you working while you're here?"

He'd brought two of the chairs from the dining area into the kitchen, and they sat down on them now.

"Every fifth year profs are eligible for a sabbatical. We get paid half our wage, and it's an opportunity to study or work in our field at something we're interested in. I'm here because I'm writing a book on hoboes."

"Hoboes?" Amanda's expression reflected her surprise, and her interest. "Heavens, are there still hoboes around? I've never given it much thought, but I'd have guessed that there weren't any real hoboes anymore. I mean, I know there are street people, bag ladies, people who are homeless, but I assumed true hoboes were a phenomenon of the Great Depression, men who couldn't find work and rode the rails from place to place, looking."

Max leaned forward and rested his elbows on his knees, delighted to be able to expand on his favorite hobbyhorse. "That was one type of hobo, all right, but there are a whole lot of others out there, although they're a dying species. That's why I want to write this book. True hoboes hate being labeled bums or tramps, and they'll set you straight about the difference. Hoboes are vagabonds by choice. They're averse to panhandling or mooching, and they'll offer to work for handouts when they're broke."

Was he boring her with all this? Fran used to tell him he was a deadly bore, that he put people to sleep when he talked about his work. But one look at Amanda told him she was interested, eager to hear more. Her eyes sparkled and she leaned toward him expectantly.

"You see, there's a lot of confusion and misconception about hoboes. Being a hobo is as much a state of mind as anything, and a lot of young men—and probably women, as well—fantasize about it at some point in their lives. I know I sure did. Not many of us actually follow our inclinations, but a few do—there's still a small group of genuine hoboes in North America. There are a few right here in Kona. I got to know one of them a couple of years ago, a fascinating man called Charlie, Boxcar Charlie. He'd been on the road since he was a boy. He crisscrossed the U.S. many times on the railroad. Like any sensible person, he decided to retire to Hawaii a few years ago, so he stowed away on a freighter headed for the Big Island."

Amanda smiled and shook her head at the story, and Max nodded. "He's every bit as eccentric as he sounds, a rough-cut rebel who never could bring himself to settle down, until he landed here. He calls Kona 'Hobo Heaven.' Talking with him intrigued me, and I started reading everything I could find about the phenomenon of being a wanderer by choice, but there isn't a whole lot in print. That's when I decided to write a book."

"Max, that's—"

Whatever Amanda had been about to say was interrupted by a loud banging and the simultaneous buzz of the doorbell and ringing of the telephone on the counter.

"That's probably Billy back with the groceries—I'll get it." Amanda was already up and heading for the door as Max reached for the telephone.

"Hello?"

"It's me, Doc." Max recognized Noah's hoarse voice, his rambling, hesitant way of talking. "That Elmer guy, the one I figgered might know where Charlie went to? Well, Elmer turned up here tonight, and he says Charlie never said nothin' to him about goin' nowhere. He says Charlie was plannin' on comin' straight back to camp that night. That's what Elmer says."

Max had been hoping against hope that Elmer would know Charlie's whereabouts. Now he knew that following up even that flimsy lead would be futile. He felt his stomach clench with foreboding, and for the first time he was certain he'd been right in going to the police and reporting Charlie missing.

He thought of the other two hoboes, Blackie Caldwell and Slim Evans, Charlie's friends. They'd been found dead, apparently drowned by the tide, and he sent up a quick and fervent prayer that his friend hadn't met a similar fate.

"Thanks for telling me, Noah. If anything else turns up, you call me, all right?" Max was still thinking about Charlie, and his response was automatic when the other man said goodbye and hung up.

It was several moments before he became aware of voices at the door, Amanda's, Billy's and a deeper, male voice.

Damn, Cosmo was early.

The two women came down the hall followed by a tall, darkly bearded young man whose thick, shoulder-length hair was tied at the back of his neck with a shoelace. He was dressed in scruffy blue-jean cutoffs, a tattered gray sleeveless T-shirt with the neck slit open. He had a pair of brown rope sandals on his bare feet. He was carrying two overloaded grocery bags, and he set them down with care on the table, then nodded hello to Max.

"Evenin', Professor. This lady let me in downstairs. We were already outside your door when I found out we were both coming to the same place."

"Good to see you, Cosmo." Max made introductions. "Amanda Reece, Billy...ummm Reece..."

"Overton Reece," Amanda supplied.

"Billy Overton Reece," Max repeated. "And this is my friend, Cosmo." Max had learned not to ask hoboes for last names unless they were offered.

"Cosmo Menzies." His dark, rather somber face relaxed into a smile.

Amanda smiled back and extended her hand. Cosmo's huge hand engulfed hers.

"Pleased to meet you, Mr. Menzies," she said.

"Just 'Cosmo' is great."

Billy wasn't as polite as Amanda. She gave the tall man a cool nod and set about emptying the groceries, maneuvering with difficulty around the other three bodies in the tiny kitchen space, banging doors open and shut and making disgruntled noises until even Max, still preoccupied with thoughts of Charlie, finally realized he was in the way.

"Come on in the other room and sit down, Cosmo. I'll get us all some juice," he suggested. "Or would you like a beer? I think I'll have one."

"Not for me," Billy said. "Amanda and I had better start fixing dinner. It's getting late." She gave Cosmo a glance that more than hinted that he should politely be on his way.

He ignored her. He accepted the frosty can Max offered and followed him into the living room, stretching his long, muscular frame out in one of the cushioned bamboo chairs as though he planned to stay for the evening.

Which, Max realized, was more or less what he'd led the young hobo to believe when he'd invited him over, so there was only one fair thing to do.

"Cosmo, have you eaten? Would you stay and have some supper with us?"

Too late, Max wondered whether Billy had bought enough to feed one extra. Well, he'd just have to split his share if it came down to it.

"Sure, thanks, I'd like that."

Max was sitting so that he could see Billy. She rolled her eyes heavenward in exasperation, but Amanda said cheerfully, "The more the merrier," and wrapped a towel around her waist for an apron as she set to work.

Billy was feeling unreasonably annoyed at Max and at Amanda as well for inviting the man called Cosmo to eat with them. Most of all, she was royally put out with him for accepting.

He'd had her on edge from the first moment she'd laid eyes on him, twenty minutes before. She'd been struggling with the grocery bags and the key to the street door downstairs when he'd crept up behind her.

"Need some help there, ma'am?"

She'd nearly jumped out of her skin. He was large and dark and rather savage-looking, and his abbreviated T-shirt exposed the rock-hard muscles in his arms. There was an anchor tattoo on his right upper bicep, a bicep that convinced her she wouldn't have a hope in hell if he decided to grab her.

Some of what she was feeling must have shown in her face.

"Sorry," he said with a grin that showed amazingly white, even teeth. "I didn't mean to scare you."

Scared, nothing. She was petrified. It was already getting quite dark, even though it wasn't very late, and just as before, there wasn't another soul to be seen around the entire place.

Billy was beginning to suspect that Max was the only inhabitant in the entire Kona Beach apartment complex.

She still couldn't get the darned outside door to open, either, and her heart was hammering against her orange T-shirt. Her hands were shaking. She dropped the key and swore under her breath, wondering if this ill-fated first day in Hawaii was going to culminate with her getting mugged.

"I'll get that for you."

His voice was a deep, baritone rumble, she noted, as he bent and retrieved the key, then inserted it smoothly into the lock and opened the door for her, standing back politely to let her past.

She swept through with as much dignity as the two overflowing grocery bags would allow, her heart still hammering. He'd followed her in. She was pathetically grateful when the elevator opened and two middle-aged ladies got off, smiling at her in a friendly fashion as they came across the lobby.

The mugger was in the elevator before her, again holding the door open. He moved like a cat, quick and light on his feet.

She wasn't going to get on, but another man appeared out of nowhere and waited politely for her to board before him.

She punched the button and stared at the wall all the way up to four. She could feel her would-be assailant's eyes boring into the back of her head.

He followed her off, but the other man stayed on. She was alone with him again. The soft lights along the walkway weren't exactly bright, and Billy's heart started banging even harder as she hurried along the deserted corridor. He was right behind her every step of the way.

"Why not let me take one of those bags for you? They look heavy."

If his arms were full, he wouldn't be able to do much to her, would he? So she lost thirty-seven dollars and eighteen cents' worth of groceries in American funds. It was a small price to pay for her safety.

She turned so fast he almost fell over her. She dumped both bags into his arms before she took off again, heading for Max's door at a trot.

He was still hard on her heels when she reached 410, and she banged on the door and rang the doorbell for good measure before she reached to retrieve her groceries.

He was smiling at her again, his lips defined by the short curly mustache and beard, and the smile made him look a lot less threatening. She noted now that one of the very white teeth in the front had a chip out of it.

His nose was a little crooked, too.

His eyes were dark under well-shaped brows. She couldn't be sure under the artificial light if they were black or just an intensely deep shade of brown. He had all this incredibly thick, curly hair, and dark whorls of chest hair were revealed by the cut-down neck of his shirt.

For a second her initial fear disappeared and she was intensely aware of him, man-woman aware, as if electric vibrations were pulsing between them. She was conscious of how few clothes he had on, of how he towered over her, which was unusual, since she was only a hair under six feet herself. She could almost taste his vibrant maleness.

"Thanks, I'll take those bags now," she managed to say, just as Amanda opened the door behind her.

But he held on.

"Since we seem to still be going in the same direction, I can carry them in for you."

"But you . . . this isn't . . . how do you . . ."

And then Max introduced them.

Billy could only feel ridiculous when Cosmo smiled and gave her a mock bow with his head. He was laughing at her, damn him!

So she'd acted like some kind of up-tight nerd or something. How the heck was she to know he was Max's friend? He looked downright dangerous, and she was a stranger in a strange land. He could have said something, couldn't he, instead of just dogging her heels like that and scaring her half out of her wits?

Embarrassment made her haughty. She didn't return his smile or say anything to him, but she was intensely conscious of his large frame blocking her every move when she tried to unload the groceries, and she was aware, as well, that his dark eyes watched her more than they should have.

She took elaborate care not to touch him, and she was relieved when at last the two men took the hint and moved into the living room.

"Billy, if you peel these potatoes, I'll get started on the hamburger."

It was a relief to turn her thoughts to food. "I got some cheese and some lard, Amanda, and there's flour in that canister, isn't there? I wondered if maybe you could make one of those pies of yours, hamburger in pastry with cheese on the top?" The vivid memory of that particular dish made Billy's mouth water.

Amanda nodded, laughing. "That's an inspiration, under the circumstances. That's called Cheeseburger in Paradise. It also makes a couple of pounds of ground beef go a long way. I wonder if Max has any ketchup or Worcestershire sauce around?"

A rummage through the cupboards yielded both, and Amanda set to work, deftly making pastry and lining the pie plates Billy had unearthed.

She and Amanda chatted as they worked, about the flight over, the difference in the humidity here in Hawaii, the compact efficiency of the small kitchen. They were used to sharing chores in a kitchen, and they didn't get in each other's way or need to discuss what jobs each would do. From long practice, Amanda assumed the more complex cooking tasks, and Billy did the peeling, chopping and washing-up.

Billy found herself trying to overhear what Max and Cosmo were discussing, but apart from an odd word here and there, she couldn't catch very much of their conversation.

Max put a tape on the stereo, and soft music muffled their voices even more. One side of the kitchen was open to the living room, and as she worked, Billy glanced up now and then. Each time, it seemed to her that Cosmo's eyes were on her, and her discomfort and annoyance grew.

Why the heck did Max have to ask this guy to dinner, anyway? But after all, she reminded herself, this was Max's apartment, as they'd unfortunately found out. She and Amanda were here on sufferance, and it would be wise to remember it. Max Caplin had a perfect right to ask anyone he wanted to stay for dinner, even this strange man who looked as if he could use a barber and a visit to a decent men's clothier. To say nothing of a shoe store. Where had he found those outrageous rope sandals?

Just who was this Cosmo character, anyway? He looked like a pirate or a beach bum to her, and he sure wasn't dressed for dinner, but undoubtedly Hawaii's balmy climate made for a more relaxed dress code than cool Vancouver.

If he was a beach bum, he was a well fed and clean one. He made the chair he was lounging in look fragile. He had far more muscles than were absolutely necessary, she decided primly. After all, there was a point at which muscle became ostentatious and insulted her artist's concept of a beautiful male body.

Although he did have a beautiful male body, regardless of muscles, she admitted reluctantly, still sneaking looks whenever she thought she could get away with it.

Why on earth should he be disturbing her like this? For a long time now, she'd been successful at keeping men at arm's length, at not noticing whether their bodies were sexy or not. It was a lot safer that way. it kept her from being hurt all over again.

She wondered sometimes if the bitterness ever wore off. Would she want a man in her life again someday? She was young and healthy, and she had erotic dreams more often than she cared to admit. But the physical part of a relationship was all tied up with the rest of it, the deceit, the crumbling of trust, the loss of respect and, finally, the utter destruction of love itself.

Once burned, twice shy, wasn't that how the old adage went? So what about twice burned?

She tossed a peeled potato into the sink with far more vehemence than was necessary, then swore under her breath when water droplets flew all over her.

Cosmo noticed and grinned.

Billy scowled at him.

Why did he keep looking at her like that? she wondered irritably. He was making her absolutely paranoid.

CHAPTER THREE

COSMO FIGURED she was one of the most attractive women he'd laid eyes on in a while, and that said a lot, considering the parade of half-naked, nubile females who crowded any one of Hawaii's many beaches every single day of the year.

It wasn't that she was beautiful; she was too lean and lanky for real beauty, and her chin was a little too square, despite the cleft in the middle. A face with that much character didn't qualify for picture-book pretty. But there was definitely something about her that set all his wheels in motion, that was for sure.

Narrow hips and long, elegant legs, in close-fitting faded denims. Long-fingered hands, ringless and delicate, somehow, like the bones in her face. Her pale, short hair shifted and resettled each time she moved her head, and the back was cut in a way that showed off the vulnerable nape of her long, slender neck.

He moved a little on the cushions so he could see her better.

"Did you happen to notice the sunset tonight?" Max was asking him. "It was particularly fine. I never get tired of Hawaii's daily spectacles."

"Me, either," Cosmo agreed fervently. He still wasn't used to Hawaii at all, the constant sunshine, the slow pace, especially the good-natured, easygoing ambience of the Honolulu Police Department. Transferring from Seattle to Hawaii had been the fulfillment of a lifelong dream of being able to live and work in a tropical paradise. But dream or not, the move had still resulted in a fair bit of culture shock.

And, of course, he'd gone undercover again within three weeks of the transfer. Lucky thing he'd never cut off the hair and beard he'd grown for the job in Seattle. The boss over in Honolulu figured his mop of hair qualified him for hobo duty, right enough.

Impersonating a hobo wasn't bothering him particularly; he was enjoying it so far. His mother might have said it was type-casting, considering the number of times he'd hiked off on endless camping trips in his teens. When he'd come home she'd always given him what-for over the condition of his clothing.

Clothing was still a big issue with his mom; Amelia Antonelli lectured him about his wardrobe, or lack of it, regularly. Just before he'd moved she complained because he didn't own a decent suit.

He did have a suit, although it was about seven years out of style by now. Well, maybe eight, going on nine. He'd bought it to be best man at his youngest brother's wedding, and it must be nine years since Robert had gotten married. God, the kid was hardly out of diapers! But the Menzies boys all married young.

Except for him.

Nine years ago for sure. Cosmo had been twenty-six at the time, and his thirty-fifth birthday had come and gone last May. Jeans and rugby shirts were still his chosen uniform. And, as he told his mother, a guy could get away with a sports jacket over a pair of Levi's these days, with a clean white T-shirt underneath.

Except for weddings and funerals, of course.

He was pretty much allergic to weddings, after going through them with all four of his brothers, and although death occurred with disturbing regularity as a part of his job on homicide, he didn't usually have to attend the funerals.

He was more concerned with finding out who helped the deceased meet his untimely end, which was precisely why he was a hobo at the moment. His thoughts skittered over the case he was working on, then insisted on homing in on the tall blond woman peeling potatoes a few yards away.

Who the heck was this Billy Reece, anyway, and what was she doing in Max's apartment, with—if he'd figured this out right—her mother-in-law, of all people?

Where were their husbands?

With an effort of will, he dragged his attention away from Billy and tried to focus on Max Caplin. There were things about this professor he needed to know.

Business before pleasure, Cosmo, old son.

"So what sort of questions do I get asked for this interview of yours, Max?"

"Oh, I'm interested in what attracted you to this life-style, how long you've been on the road, whether you think you'll ever drop back into mainstream society," Max said. "You're younger than most of the men I've interviewed, and I'm interested in your viewpoint. But we don't have to get into all that right now. I don't have my tape recorder set up, and judging by those wonderful aromas coming from the kitchen, it seems supper will be ready before long." He gave Cosmo an engaging grin. "I can't concentrate on anything but food when I'm hungry."

It was probably a good thing, Cosmo reflected. He wasn't exactly hitting on all cylinders himself tonight. He couldn't seem to keep his eyes away from the kitchen. Billy was chopping salad greens now, periodically glaring at him.

Cosmo looked straight into her stormy brown eyes, wondering what she'd look like if she ever smiled. She was one cranky lady, but that didn't diminish her sex appeal one little bit.

THE FOOD WAS a huge success, and Amanda couldn't help but feel pleased and gratified by the appreciative remarks with which it was received.

There was an immense bowl of creamy mashed potatoes, two golden cheeseburger pies, a large bowl of mixed salad and some carmelized carrots done her own special way—plus a basket of lightly browned baking-powder biscuits that had risen to immense proportions even by her exacting standards.

Simple enough, but effective. And filling, which was a blessing when she saw how much the three of them could put away. She was used to Billy's appetite, of course, but she hadn't cooked for two hungry men for a long time. When Max, then Cosmo, reached for second and third helpings, she was glad she'd doubled the amount she thought she might need.

Max had produced a bottle of wine, and after the first few ravenous mouthfuls of food, he lifted his glass and inclined his head toward Amanda, his blue eyes twinkling at her in a way that made her feel warm and appreciated.

"My compliments to the cook. This is ambrosia."

Cosmo and Billy lifted their glasses and echoed the toast, and Amanda felt herself flush with pleasure.

"Actually, it's plain old hamburger pie with cheese on top, but I'm glad you like it."

"It's sure got bananas and beans beat all to heck," Cosmo declared.

"Is that what you mostly eat, bananas and beans?" Billy knew her tone of voice was downright sarcastic. And it was the first time all evening she had said anything directly to Cosmo.

Cosmo didn't seem to notice her hostility. He nodded at her. "Yeah, along with fish and fruit. It's pretty easy to live off the land here in Hawaii, as long as you don't mind being a vegetarian."

"So what are you, then, some kind of leftover hippie?" Billy raised her glass without looking at Cosmo, took a long gulp of wine—and promptly choked on it.

Cosmo was sitting at the end of the table, next to her. He reached over and rubbed her back as she coughed into her napkin. His long, slow strokes were more a caress than an effort to keep her from choking to death.

"You okay? You don't need mouth-to-mouth or anything?"

He sounded concerned, but there was an undertone of amusement in his voice and a challenge in his eyes. Billy jerked away from his touch as if she'd been burned. She caught her breath and dabbed at her streaming eyes with her napkin.

There was a moment's silence while she got her breath back, then Cosmo said in a companionable voice, "I'm a hobo, actually."

"Excuse me?" Billy was frowning at him now.

"You asked if I was a leftover hippie. Well, I'm not. I'm a hobo."

"You're putting me on. Nobody makes a career out of being a hobo."

"Some people do, Billy," Max intervened. "I was telling Amanda earlier that I'm writing a book on hoboes. Cosmo is one of the people I'm interviewing."

Billy was staring at Cosmo as if there were something about him that she'd missed earlier.

"What? Have I grown horns all of a sudden?" He smiled at her, but there was a bite to his words.

"I've just never met a hobo before, that's all. It seems a weird sort of occupation. How do you live, anyway? Do you just panhandle, or live on welfare, or what?"

"At the moment, I do some drawing—scenery, mostly—and a friend frames the pictures and sells them to tourists," he answered with quiet dignity. "I also do caricatures now and then, quick funny outlines of people's faces that I sell for five bucks. I make out pretty well, all things considered. Hoboes are a self-respecting lot. We don't usually panhandle and we don't take welfare, either. We earn what we need to get by on. Nowadays we're vagabonds by choice more than necessity."

"I heard Boxcar Charlie say once that hoboes work, tramps can't and bums won't," Max interjected.

"That's as good a description as I've heard," Cosmo agreed, but he kept his eyes focused on Billy. "And now that you know all about me, what about you?" There was a hint of challenge in his tone. "I bet your husband's a businessman and you're some kind of high-powered career woman. Doctor, lawyer, stockbroker?"

"I'm a widow, and I'm a window dresser for several large stores in Vancouver. It pays the rent. The rest of the time I like to draw, just like you."

"You're an artist?"

Billy shrugged. "I don't earn much at it, but it's what I enjoy doing. Maybe someday I'll be able to call myself an artist, but not yet. How about you? How come you don't say you're an artist instead of calling yourself a hobo? You earn a living at it. That makes you an artist, doesn't it?"

Cosmo laughed. "It depends on what you consider a living. It's not what I do all the time. I've had other jobs. I'm doing it here because there seems to be a market for it and it allows me to buy the odd luxury. Like toilet paper and toothpaste—you've heard of them?" All of a sudden he sounded as sarcastic as Billy had earlier.

Max intervened again in an obvious effort to break the tension.

"What sort of art do you do, Billy?"

She shot a quick look at Cosmo to see if he was about to ridicule her, but he was staring down at his plate, not paying attention. "Pen-and-ink drawings, mostly. Some watercolors, some oils. But I like charcoal and pen-and-ink the best."

"Billy's very good," Amanda said with a distinct note of pride. "Several of her sketches of Vancouver scenes were included in an exhibition, and they won top honors."

Billy smiled fondly at her mother-in-law. "Thanks for the vote of confidence, Amanda, but my stuff's not exactly in high demand." She tilted her chin up and gave Cosmo a challenging glance, as if he'd questioned her ability, even though he hadn't said a word. "Not yet, anyway."

"Well, you must visit the galleries here in Kona," Max went on. "Kona's full of artists. There's a group of them exhibiting and selling their work from small booths at the market."

"I'd like that, but I won't have time to do much sight-seeing," Billy said with a rueful shake of her head. "We're probably heading back to Canada tomorrow if the airlines can change our return reservations that fast."

"How long have you been here?" Cosmo asked.

"One day," Amanda supplied when Billy didn't answer. "Well, actually, only one afternoon in Kona. We landed on Oahu this morning and took an afternoon flight over here."

"And you're heading back tomorrow?"

Cosmo looked mystified, so Amanda explained about Billy winning the trip and how there'd been the mix-up with the apartment. She told of Max's kindness in asking them to stay the night, adding that she and Billy couldn't afford to stay their allotted three weeks unless they found someplace extremely reasonable to rent. "You see, we both live on limited incomes," she finished.

"And where do you live, Cosmo?" Billy asked suddenly, slathering butter on one last biscuit and taking a huge bite.

"It's more a question of where I sleep," he said with a wry grin. "I tend to move around a fair bit, but right now I'm in a park a few miles away. There's a sort of hobo jungle there. Four or five of us have a camp. As long as we keep it clean and quiet the bulls leave us pretty much alone." He looked alarmed all of a sudden. "But it's no place for a couple of women, if that's what you're thinking. That's not what you're thinking, right?"

Amanda laughed at that. "Heavens, no. Not a chance. I've only been camping twice in my entire life, and I'd just as soon not do it again. Between the bugs and the hard ground, I didn't enjoy it a whole lot. I'm afraid there's not much pioneer blood in me."

"Well, I'd sure give it a try if I had the stuff to do it with," Billy stated. "But I didn't bring a sleeping bag or towels or anything, just a couple of suitcases full of clothes I'll probably never wear, anyway. And my art supplies, of course."

"What you ought to do is try to sell some of your art over in the market the way I do," Cosmo remarked. "Not that I'm getting rich on it, but there are a lot of tourists around here."

"And make enough to stay on here, you mean? What a hope. As I said before, my stuff's not very successful commercially."

"Sunsets. Try doing sunsets," Cosmo muttered under the cover of Max's voice.

"I'm sure we'll come up with a place for you to stay in the morning," Max was telling Amanda with hearty assurance. "And now, how about a cup of our famous Kona coffee? Making coffee's my one claim to fame in the kitchen."

"I bought ice cream and cookies for dessert—I'll get them," Billy said, rising.

"No, I'll do it," Amanda insisted. "You two go on out on the deck—the lanai, rather. We won't all fit in the kitchen, and it would be nice to have dessert out there under the stars. Max can do the coffee and I'll serve the rest."

Outside the open glass doors, a spill of silver moonlight outlined the palms across the road and glinted on the dark, restless waters of the ocean. Billy went out, and Cosmo followed.

In the kitchen, Amanda scooped ice cream into bowls as Max measured scoops of the rich-smelling coffee Kona was famous for into his coffee machine. Working together in companionable silence, they put the ice cream and mugs on a tray and arranged the macadamia-nut cookies in a napkin-lined basket.

Amanda smothered one yawn and then another as they waited for the coffee to perk, and Max smiled at her. "Jet lag's getting to you, huh?"

"That and my normal boring schedule. I'm afraid I'm in the habit of going to bed early with a good book."

"Me, too," he agreed. He folded his arms across his chest and leaned back against the counter. "It's lonely sometimes, isn't it? I mean, books are great, but I often think it would be nice to have someone to discuss them with."

"Why didn't you remarry after your divorce?" She'd wondered about it earlier but hadn't felt brave enough to ask.

He shook his head. "I was married to Fran for nineteen years. I was forty-five when she left—that's ten years ago now—and I just couldn't seem to get interested in dating, going through the process of getting to know someone all over again. I thought I'd be with Fran the rest of my life, you see, and it was a tremendous shock when she asked for a divorce. I was too shattered at first to want to form a new relationship, and then, as time passed, I guess I got used to being alone."

Amanda knew exactly what he meant. After John's death there'd been months when she'd felt shell-shocked, as if a thick gray blanket separated her from the rest of the world. And later, the few times she'd been lured by well-meaning friends into going places where there were single men her own age, she'd felt absolutely ridiculous. And the men had seemed universally old and boring.

Max didn't strike her as old at all, though, and certainly he wasn't boring.

The rich, mouth-watering aroma of the coffee gradually filled the kitchen.

"Shall we shuffle this out and see what the youngsters are up to? They got along so well at dinner we really shouldn't leave them unchaperoned for too long." Max gave her a lewd wink.

"Heavens, yes. It was love at first sight, wasn't it?" Amanda shook her head and set the coffeepot on the loaded tray. "I thought they were going to stab each other with the dinner forks, for goodness' sake. It wouldn't surprise me to find out they'd shoved each other off the balcony by now."

They were both laughing as they carried the laden trays outside.

BILLY LEANED her elbows on the railing and gazed out at the picture-postcard scene, doing her best to ignore the man standing close beside her...far too close, she thought irritably, edging away from him until there was a good two feet between her arms and his on the waist-high railings.

She could feel him staring at her, and she stubbornly refused to turn and meet his gaze.

"Let me guess."

His deep voice sounded different to Billy in the darkness, more resonant.

"You've got a lifelong vendetta against hoboes, right? Or... hey, I know. You find me personally disgusting. I have body odor and halitosis despite the fact I spend a good portion of every day in the Pacific and scrub my teeth diligently. Maybe you've got a man back home you're committed to." He lowered his voice. "Or is it simply that you feel the same things I'm feeling, and they scare the living daylights out of you?"

She swallowed and tried to sound haughty. "I don't have the foggiest idea what you're talking about, you know."

"C'mon, Billy, let's be honest here. There's more going on between us than this verbal sparring, right? I'm attracted to you—you turn me on. That's no crime. It's still a compliment to a lady when a guy finds her irresistible, isn't it? So I figure it's a shame to waste these couple of short hours we get to spend in each other's company pretending we hate each other. We're just a couple of strangers who find each other attractive. It might be fun to admit it and really talk. Why not loosen up and enjoy a little flirtation with me here? Hoboes have morals, whatever you've heard to the contrary. I'm not going to lock Amanda and Max in the bathroom and try to jump you on the living room rug, cross my heart."

He was outrageous. He was also bone honest, cutting through the defensive wall she'd erected without consciously understanding why. It was difficult to admit even to herself, but his assessment of the situation was absolutely right.

She was attracted to him, just as he'd said. It did scare her spitless. She swallowed hard and turned to look at him, her own innate honesty forcing acknowledgment of what he'd said.

"You don't smell." He did, though. There was a clean, salt odor to him, as well as a hint of his personal male scent, which she found arousing. "Your breath is fine. There's a touch of wine, but it's quite pleasant, actually. And there's nobody in particular back home." She drew in a deep breath. "Nobody at all, as a matter of fact. And, yes, I am attracted to you, although I don't want to be."

He blew his breath out in a relieved sigh. "I figured you might be about to punch me in the ear."

She grinned at him at last. "It crossed my mind. You take some pretty big chances."

Even by moonlight, her smile almost made his heart stop. "Only if I figure the payoff is worth it."

Her defenses went up again. "What sort of payoff are you expecting here?" Her voice was huffy and the smile had disappeared.

"Nothing major or illicit, so don't get in another snit. An hour or two of friendly conversation? A few more of those smiles you dole out once in a while?" His grin came and went. "Maybe breakfast in the morning?"

"Fish and fruit?"

"Oh, I can do better than that. My sketches were quite a hit with the crowd from Japan who arrived on that tour boat out there, so I'm pretty flush at the moment." He pointed to a white shape floating in the harbor, brightly lit and sparkling in the moonlight. Music floated across the water—what sounded like a Strauss waltz. "We could eat at Hugo's, just down the road. He does a great breakfast and the dress code is minimal.''

What the heck, Billy decided. She'd never see the guy after tomorrow. What was the harm, as he had said, in a little flirtation? And she loved breakfast—it was probably her favorite meal. After lunch and dinner.

"Okay. Thanks, I'd like that."

"Seven too early? I'll come by and walk you over."

"Seven's fine."

"Coffee, you two?"

The screen door behind them opened and Max carefully set an oversize tray on a low, round table. Amanda poured for all of them and handed out bowls of ice cream.

The stars were out, their constellations foreign to Billy, their size and brightness another reminder that she was far from home. A warm breeze moved the palm fronds on the trees across the road, and up and down the sidewalk, four stories below, people wandered back and forth, laughing and talking. From the huge hotel complex on a spit of land not far away, soft Hawaiian music floated on the balmy air, and over it all the tropical moon spilled its light, casting palm trees and buildings and people into stark black-and-white silhouettes.

Billy took advantage of the moonlit darkness to openly study Cosmo's profile as he spooned up his ice cream and sipped his coffee. There was an indefinable sensuality about him, the way he moved, the way he slumped casually back in the reclining chair, his large body graceful in repose. On a less masculine man, all that hair could have been a mistake, but on Cosmo it emphasized his maleness.

Cosmo. It was an unusual name. She wondered about it, as she put small dabs of ice cream on her tongue and let them melt into liquid sweetness in her mouth. Greek? Italian?

She'd ask him tomorrow. In fact, there was a whole list of things she intended to ask him tomorrow.

CHAPTER FOUR

BILLY WAS AWAKE the next morning shortly past six. She'd always been an early riser, and she never had to rely on an alarm clock.

Even before she'd opened her eyes, she'd thought of Cosmo Menzies and their breakfast date, and a feeling of delightful anticipation had begun to grow. It was fun meeting a man for breakfast. How long had it been since she'd had breakfast with a man, anyway? She tried to figure it out and couldn't.

Amanda was still asleep in the other bed, and Billy showered and dressed as quietly as she could, pawing through her suitcase and debating over what to wear, liking the irony of worrying over what clothes to wear to breakfast with a hobo.

She finally pulled out a pair of khaki walking shorts that were wide enough to make her legs and hips look good and skinny. Then she tugged on a canary-yellow T-shirt, fastened gigantic matching yellow hoops in her ears and tiptoed out of the room, softly closing the bedroom door behind her, a pair of worn leather sandals dangling from one hand.

Max was already in the kitchen making coffee.

"'Morning," he greeted her as she worked her feet into the sandals. "You're up with the birds. I thought the two of you would probably sleep the morning away. That's what I do after a long flight."

"Amanda might. She's still dead to the world in there."

"We'll try not to disturb her, then. Coffee'll be ready in a minute. I'm off to the showers, then we'll see about breakfast. You can start with cold cereal— there's plenty of milk."

"Actually, Max, I'm...uh, I'm going out for breakfast. With Cosmo."

Now why the heck should that simple statement make her blush?

Max looked surprised, but only for a moment. "That's a fine idea. He's an interesting guy. Well, see you when you get back. There's a spare set of keys to this place hanging by the door. Take them with you." Whistling a soft tune, he went into the bathroom and shut the door.

Billy found her purse and dropped the keys inside as she headed for the elevators. By the time she got downstairs, Cosmo was already in the lobby.

He was wearing a sleeveless white T-shirt and another version of the cutoff blue-jean shorts. Billy figured these must be his best, because they didn't have any rips that she could see. Did he have access to showers, or had he been swimming already? His hair was still damp, neatly combed and tied in a curling clump at the back of his neck.

He smiled at her and took her hand, and she liked the admiration on his face.

"'Mornin', pretty lady."

His skin was rough, his fingers and palms callused and hard against her own. His touch sent a response skidding along her nerve endings.

"'Morning. Wow, it's a glorious day."

"Nearly always is here in paradise."

The walk to Hugo's was only a few blocks. Even at this early hour, the sun was bordering on hot. People dressed for work hurried past on foot and in cars. A few early-rising tourists in what seemed to be a uniform of white shorts and electric Hawaiian shirts ambled by on their way to an early breakfast.

The whole way, Cosmo held firmly to her hand, and Billy didn't object. He pointed out the fishing boats in the harbor, unloading their catch. He told her the names of several of the fishermen. He knew what the flowering bushes were called, and he showed her a magnificent banyan tree overhanging the sidewalk, where hundreds of birds nested every night.

They soon arrived at an unpretentious open-sided building with a sign that said Hugo's, and Cosmo found them a table in a corner where the sun filtered in through palm trees. A scarlet-and-green parrot squawked from a gilded cage hung on a tree limb.

Groups of cheerful people were sitting at wooden tables, wolfing down eggs, pancakes, bacon and toast, and soon Cosmo and Billy were doing the same. They were quiet as they ate their way through lavishly generous platters of food. At last Billy sat back with a sigh, adding a generous dollop of thick cream to an aromatic mug of local Kona coffee.

"I'm stuffed. That was a great breakfast. Thanks for bringing me."

"I figured it was touch and go whether you'd actually come or not."

Billy shrugged. "I don't go back on my word. Besides, what you said last night made sense. About being strangers and getting to know each other a little."

He nodded and smiled at her. "Let's get on with it, then. I get to go first. How long have you been a widow, and how did your husband die?"

He was direct, if nothing else. Most people avoided asking such personal questions right away. But it was his bluntness that intrigued her, and after all, she'd probably never see him after today. It made it easy to be honest.

"I've been a widow nearly five years now. My husband, Graham, drowned in a boating accident. He was with my father-in-law, John. They both drowned."

"Were they commercial fishermen?"

His eyes, which she'd thought black last night, were actually deep mahogany brown, she realized, with fleck of green. They were full of compassion as he waited for her answer.

Billy shook her head. "Nope. My father-in-law was an accountant. Graham was a fireman. A friend offered them his boat for the day, and they went fishing. A sudden storm came up, and they capsized."

She'd done the laundry that Sunday, cleaned out the refrigerator. There was rock music on their second-hand stereo, and she'd just washed her hair, when Amanda appeared at the door with the policemen.

It took a moment now to realize that Cosmo was talking to her.

"How long had you been married?"

She was silent until the waitress refilled their coffee cups and moved away.

"Two and a half years."

"Still newlyweds."

She remembered the bitter fights, the loneliness, the feeling of being trapped—the despair that was so intense it hurt her chest, made it hard to draw in a deep breath at times.

And the awful guilt at having wished herself free and then having it come true.

His gaze slid past Cosmo. "Yes, I suppose so."

"And obviously you've stayed close to your mother-in-law. Amanda's a nice lady."

This time it was easy to smile and agree. "Way beyond nice. Amanda's something special. I liked her the moment I met her. There were never any of the problems you're supposed to have with a mother-in-law. She and I always got along, and after... well, afterward, we stayed friends. We have dinner together at least once a week. When I won this trip for two, she was the only person I wanted to ask along." She frowned and shook her head. "I feel terrible for her, having it turn out the way it has."

"Have you thought of calling the organization that sponsored the draw, this symphony committee or whatever? Seems to me they have a responsibility in all this. Maybe they could find you alternative accommodation."

"I'm going to call later this morning. But I doubt there's much they can do. It's not really their fault."

"Damned right it's their fault! They ought to come through with accommodation—they've got a moral and probably a legal responsibility here."

She looked at him, surprised at the vehemence of his response. "Hey, calm down. I thought hoboes were supposed to be laid-back, easygoing, accepting and philosophical."

His eyes crinkled at the corners. "Whoever told you that?"

Billy lifted one shoulder and let it drop in a characteristic shrug. "Nobody, really. It's just a preconceived notion I had, I guess. But, then, I've never met a hobo before, so how should I know?" It was her turn to ask questions. "How'd you decide to live your life this way, anyhow? Do you have a family? What do they think of it, or do they know?"

He looked at her for a long moment, as if there were something he wanted to say. Then he looked away. "Oh, yeah, they know all right. They just figure I'll come to my senses sooner or later. When I grow up. You know what families are like."

She shook her head. "Actually, I don't. Amanda's about the only family I've got. I was a hellion of a foster kid—I had ten different placements before I was sixteen and able to care for myself." Now what had possessed her to admit that shoddy piece of her history to him? Usually she didn't talk about it much.

His voice was low and gentle and his eyes held hers. "You've had it rough, Billy."

She gave him the defensive, cocky grin she'd perfected long ago. "Yeah, well, I've got a theory. If the first part of your life is nothing but grief, the second part is going to be unbelievably great. I'm twenty-eight. I figure mine's about to change direction any moment now."

He laughed with her, and before he could say anything more, she said, "So tell me about your family. Where did you grow up?"

"Seattle. I've got four brothers and one sister. I'm the second youngest."

"Wow! What did your dad do to support that many kids? Must have cost him the earth for food and all."

There was that strange, calculating expression in his eyes again. Maybe his childhood had been bad. Maybe she ought to shut up. She hated people probing her own early years, and here she was doing it to someone else.

But Cosmo was smiling again. "Dad? Oh, he was a cop. One of Seattle's finest. Which is probably why I'm a 'bo. Rebellion and all that."

She raised her eyebrows at him. "Aren't you a little long in the tooth for that sort of teenage nonsense?"

He laughed. "I'm only thirty-five, and I was always a slow developer. Who knows, maybe I'll outgrow it yet."

The waitress offered more coffee, and Billy shook her head. "It's the best, but I'll be absolutely wired all day if I have any more." When the woman left, she said thoughtfully, "Well, I don't know much about being a hobo, but the way I see it, it's probably got being a policeman or fireman beat all to heck."

His eyebrows went up in surprise. "How so?"

She frowned and said slowly, "Men who are drawn to those jobs are a certain type. I should know—I met enough of them when I was married. They're attracted to danger, they crave excitement in their work and their play, most of them are party animals and a lot of them drink way too much."

She saw the speculative look on his face.

"Is that what your husband was like?"

She felt uncomfortable for the first time all morning, not with him but with herself. "I suppose so. He was young. We both were. I was barely twenty when we married. Graham was only two years older than me. He probably would have changed when he got older. Maybe."

Cosmo shook his head. "That's where you're wrong, believing that. People don't change as they get older—they just get more like themselves."

She gave him a long, considering look. "That's pretty deep philosophy. You sure don't talk like a hobo. Did you go to university?"

"Nope. This is just how hoboes talk. We're a much maligned species." His eyes twinkled. "Did you know Jack London was a 'bo for a time? So were Kerouac and Woody Guthrie and Louis L'Amour. I'm in elite company here—I've got one hell of a lot to live up to."

He was teasing her, and she liked it.

"Elite or not, you still haven't told me much about this weird career choice of yours. Hoboes travel by train, don't they, riding the rails and all that? So how did you ever get to Hawaii across all that water? What other places have you been?"

"I spent a couple of years riding the rails on the mainland. Got down into Mexico once and spent some time there. I liked the hot climate, so I took a job on construction. Like I said last night, we do work whenever we get the chance."

She nodded. This morning she didn't mind him watching her with that peculiar intensity.

"Anyhow, I saved my bread till I had enough for a plane ticket over here. I knocked around Oahu for a while and then offered to crew on a yacht to get over here. I've only been on Kona a couple of weeks."

The restaurant had emptied and filled again while they talked. Billy hadn't noticed until now. She glanced around and then looked at her watch. "Lord, it's after ten already. I've got to get back to the apartment and make some phone calls."

Cosmo walked back with her. "Are you coming up with me?" she asked as they stood once again by the elevators in the Kona Beach Apartments.

Cosmo shook his head. "It's time for me to get busy earning my keep," he told her with a wink. "All that nice tourist money's out there going to waste. I'll head over to the square and do some caricatures for a while."

"Well, it's tough to be a working man." She smiled at him, but there was a catch in her throat. "I guess this is goodbye, then. I probably won't see you again. I think we'll be leaving today. Thanks for... for such a great breakfast. And for setting me straight about hoboes."

He was looking deep into her eyes, and she couldn't seem to look away. There were two steps separating them, and he took them, putting his hands gently on her shoulders.

"My pleasure," he said. "Very much my pleasure."

Billy knew he was going to kiss her, and she didn't mind a bit. She was grateful now for the deserted lobby, the empty office, the swimming pool where no one swam.

His hands slid from her shoulders down around her back, and he drew her into his embrace. His eyes searched her every feature, then he bent his head and placed his mouth tenderly on hers.

The kiss was chaste at first, innocent and light. Even so, her heart began to hammer and blood coursed into every hidden spot in her body.

He tasted clean, like coffee and fresh air. His mustache and beard weren't prickly at all, the way she'd thought they might be. They were soft, caressing her face, tickling just a little. She could feel the bare, smooth skin of her legs touching his, and the contrast between rough and smooth made her shiver.

He was incredibly strong. She could feel muscles tense in his shoulders and arch across his back when she slid her arms around him in a friendly hug. But then his hands tightened, slipping down to her waist, and he drew her even closer, molding her hips and breasts to his wide frame. One hand cupped her behind, almost lifting her off her feet, making her aware of his arousal and conscious of the thin layers of cloth that were all that separated them. He made a sound deep in his throat, and his lips gently parted hers, his tongue seeking reassurance that she was as needy as he.

Without thought, she gave it. Now the kiss became intense and urgent, and she felt a raw and savage fire flare between them. Passion Billy had subdued and ignored for years sprang to life within her, catching her off guard, taking charge for the long timeless moments the kiss lasted.

The elevator sighed to a stop behind them, and in the instant before the doors opened, Cosmo released her, taking her hand. In one smooth motion he turned her body protectively so her back was to the sedate elderly couple who stepped into the lobby.

When the street door closed and the lobby was once again deserted, he turned and looked into her eyes. He was breathing as hard as she, and she could see a pulse beating in his temple, in perfect time to her own racing heartbeat. His voice wasn't quite in control.

"Remember what I said about being a gentleman last night? Well, I take it all back. If there were even a broom closet handy..."

She was trembling and she struggled to control it. She tried for a light, easy tone of voice and failed. "There isn't one, and even if there were, we wouldn't fit. We're both far too big for closets. Besides, I do have to go up now."

His quick smile came and went, and he planted one last quick kiss on her tingling lips. "Aloha, then, beautiful lady."

He pushed the elevator button and the doors opened. She climbed on, and when the doors shut again she slumped against the wall.

What on earth had come over her, letting herself get carried away like that with a man she barely knew? She stared at the panel as the numbers slid slowly past.

With one regrettable exception, she'd been celibate since Graham. At first she hadn't wanted to get close to anyone; she'd needed to fit the shattered pieces of the jigsaw puzzle that was Billy back together again. She'd gone back to art school, made casual new friends, moved from the house she and Graham had rented into a high-ceilinged old apartment near the beach.

And there, fragile self-esteem barely congealed, she'd fallen for the man next door.

Graham had been the kind of man who watched football three times a week and played rugby on the days left over, so any good psychiatrist might have warned Billy she'd be vulnerable to Graham's diametric opposite.

Thomas Pershell worked at the Museum of Anthropology, taught night-school classes in art appreciation, liked poetry. He was charming, gentle, romantic, thoughtful; the perfect lover. He was also a world-class liar, as she'd learned just in time.

Four flashed on the panel, and the elevator stopped.

Billy got out, but instead of going directly to Max's apartment, she stood for a while at the iron railing, looking down at the turquoise swimming pool in the courtyard and thinking over her meeting with Cosmo.

She'd never say it to Amanda, but at this moment she was vastly relieved they were heading back to Vancouver. Wanting Cosmo a continent away was cowardly of her, but she didn't give a damn.

After Thomas, it had been almost easy to stay a good arm's length away from any serious involvement with the opposite sex, but she was afraid Cosmo could change that. There was some powerful chemistry at work between them that made all her good intentions disappear. In his arms, she felt as if she were returning to a place she'd been many times before, a place where she belonged and longed to stay.

A man appeared beside the pool far below and began cleaning the surface with long, leisurely strokes of a net. Billy slapped her palms down on the railings, deliberately breaking the reverie she'd fallen into, and the man looked up, smiled and waved at her casually. She waved back, contemplating her choices in men.

First a jock, then a crooked intellectual and now a self-styled hobo. Her selections left something to be desired, that was certain.

Maybe it was time she seriously considered an analyst.

She rummaged in her bag and found her key, hurrying to Max's door. It was time to get the show on the road. She'd call the airlines and find out about changing their tickets. She rushed into the apartment with an increasing sense of urgency.

Amanda didn't appear to share Billy's concern at all. She was sitting on the lanai dressed in her pale blue cotton skirt and the white shirt whose vee neckline dipped to the top of her breasts. She had her oversize sunglasses on, the ones she and Billy had spent hours buying just for this trip. She looked flushed and voluptuous, and she'd pulled her skirt up over her knees to get some sun on her legs.

She and Max were relaxing on lounge chairs, coffeepot handy on a small table, and they were laughing together.

"Hi, you two," Billy said from the doorway. For a moment, she had the feeling she was interrupting something personal, but they both greeted her with smiles and cheerful hellos.

"Find a cup and join us for coffee," Max suggested.

Billy shook her head. "Thanks, but I figure I should call the airlines and see if—"

Max interrupted her. "No need, no need at all. We've come to an agreement here, haven't we, Amanda?" He was smiling, and appeared inordinately pleased with himself.

Amanda looked up at Billy. She shoved her glasses up on her head. Her green eyes were wide and full of shy excitement. "It's wonderful, Billy. Max has convinced me that it's perfectly all right for us to stay here in the apartment for the rest of the three weeks. He says that if we do the cooking, it'll make up for any inconvenience we cause him."

Max was quick to confirm the invitation. "After that dinner last night, I know I'm getting the best of this deal."

Billy could feel anxiety rising in her. She really wasn't sure she wanted to stay in Hawaii at all now, and she certainly didn't think it was a good idea moving in with Max this way, interrupting his work. She said so, adding, "Besides, you use that bedroom as a study and your computer's in there. It's not fair of us to shove you out. I really think we should—"

"Nonsense, nonsense," Max said, dismissing her objections with a wave of his hand. "There's a perfectly good work area in the living room. There's even a desk for my computer. And as far as my work goes, you'll both be out a fair amount, sight-seeing. At the moment, I'm out myself a great deal of the time, interviewing the hoboes. It'll work out just splendidly. You'll see."

It seemed it was all decided, and apart from making a ridiculous scene, there was nothing Billy could do about it but accept gracefully.

Well, she told herself with grim resolve, for the next three weeks she could and would make absolutely certain she stayed totally, completely and absolutely away from a charming hobo named Cosmo.

SOAKING UP THE SUNSHINE from her reclining chair, Amanda studied her daughter-in-law from behind the glasses she'd slid back down her nose.

Billy's face must have already picked up some color from the sun, because her cheeks were touched with a dusky rose. Her dark brown eyes shone, and there was an air of contained excitement about her that was most attractive. But, then, Billy was always attractive. The difference was, right now she looked almost radiant.

Billy had told her before they'd fallen asleep the night before that she was meeting Cosmo for breakfast this morning. That was a surprise, because Amanda had gotten the impression that Billy and the handsome young hobo didn't get along at all, which was stupid of her.

How could she have forgotten that the sparks young people struck off each other were more often than not sexual, and their arguments a cover-up for intense physical attraction?

Amanda had always enjoyed sex, even though her own experience had been anything but sophisticated or wide ranging. There'd been John, and for a period of three magic months, years and years before, one other lover in her entire life.

She'd never talked about O'Reilly to anyone. He was her secret. He'd loved her body, her breasts, admired her lavishly in a way John never had.

O'Reilly had called her his "little plum—" Now, what had made her remember a silly thing like that at a time like this? After all, O'Reilly was long since gone from her life, and even her husband had been dead almost five years.

The sad truth was, there was no one to care how her body looked anymore. Except herself, of course. And narcissism got boring after a while.

Max's voice called her back to the present.

"Amanda, can I get you anything from the kitchen? A glass of juice, maybe?" he asked.

"No, thanks." She smiled up at him. He was a nice man.

It had been strange, getting up this morning to find herself alone with him in the apartment. At first, she was afraid the easiness that had been between them the night before would be gone in the harsh light of morning, but she'd been wrong.

He'd made her coffee and toast and two poached eggs, which had touched her. She was so used to providing other people with food, it was a rare and precious thing when someone cooked for her, however simple the meal.

They'd brought their plates outside and fallen right into an easy conversation interspersed with comfortable silences.

The ringing of the doorbell had interrupted one of those quiet moments, and Max had gotten up to answer it.

She'd heard him greet someone named Daisy, who had a rather loud, high voice. She must have brought him something, because Amanda could hear Max thanking the woman graciously. A moment later, he'd brought her out and introduced her.

"Daisy Seibert, Amanda Reece."

Daisy looked as though she were close to Amanda's age, late forties or early fifties. She wore white tailored linen pants and a red silk shirt and rather a lot of makeup.

"Pleased to meet you, Daisy." Amanda got up from her reclining chair, smoothing down her skirt and smiling a welcome at the tall woman with the carefully made-up face and perfect hairdo. She was aware that she was being scrutinized from top to toe from behind Daisy's modish red-rimmed glasses. They matched her lipstick and her shirt exactly—a feat that awed Amanda.

"I didn't realize you had company, Max"

The smile Daisy wore looked pasted on, and there was a definite hint of frost in her tone.

"Amanda's a friend of mine from Vancouver," Max replied easily.

Amanda wondered if he realized that sounded as if they'd been friends much longer than they really had.

"Are you here on holiday, Mrs. Reece?" Daisy asked, then added with a hopeful note, "With your husband?"

"Oh, no, I'm a widow. I'm here with my daughter-in-law, actually. But—" Amanda was about to explain the circumstances that would make her visit extremely short when Max interrupted.

"Amanda and Billy will be staying here with me for the rest of their holiday," he said smoothly.

Amanda shot him an astonished look. Then she was taken aback by the venomous glare Daisy leveled at her.

"And how long will that be?" Daisy's high voice had become almost a squeak.

Again, Amanda had just opened her mouth to answer, when Max said hurriedly, "Oh, we haven't decided that yet, have we, Amanda?"

He gave Amanda a long, pleading look that she didn't begin to understand and then turned his charming smile on Daisy.

"They only arrived last evening, so we really haven't had a chance to discuss anything yet. We had a rather late dinner and then Amanda slept a bit late this morning. We've only just had our breakfast. Jet lag, you know."

There was much more going on here than Amanda could fathom, but she certainly understood that Max, without saying a thing that wasn't ultrapolite, was also somehow giving Daisy the impression that he and she were far more than just casual friends. It was the intonation in his voice, the warm, intimate way he pronounced her name.

Daisy sniffed, then sniffed again. "Well. Well, I came down to ask if you would care to join us this afternoon for happy hour, Max, but I can see you're busy." She got stiffly to her feet, her chin in the air. "I'll leave you two alone, then."

There was a rather nasty undercurrent to her words, and it was obvious she didn't intend to invite Amanda anywhere.

Totally befuddled, Amanda got to her feet and smiled apologetically at Daisy, making an effort to clarify the situation. "Actually, Billy, my daughter-in-law, and I will likely be going—"

"Shopping this afternoon," Max supplied firmly. "And I have an appointment I mustn't miss, so unfortunately we'll have to pass on happy hour. Another time, Daisy. Give my best to the others, won't you? And tell Rebecca that Amanda and I will very much enjoy her marmalade. It was kind of her to send it down."

Daisy had swept out with much less exuberance than she'd shown coming in, and Amanda had thought she heard Max give a low, relieved whistle after the door closed. He walked over and sat down beside her again, and the look he finally gave Amanda was both sheepish and triumphant.

"Sorry about that. I should explain."

"Yes. You did give her the wrong impression, you know, Max." Amanda felt like grinning at the abashed look on his face.

"Yes, I did, and it was quite deliberate." He was actually blushing underneath his tan. "You see…" He paused and rubbed a hand over his hair. "Damn it all, Amanda, the truth of the matter is, I've ended up in a tricky situation here. Daisy is one of four single women, all about my age, who live in this building year-round. When I first arrived, they made a point of dropping by and giving me all sorts of valuable information about shopping, doctors, dentists, things like that. Naturally I was grateful. They asked me to dinner and dropped by with casseroles and . . . and things like this jar of marmalade." He raised a hand and rubbed the back of his head, frowning. "Before I even realized what was happening, I was in over my head."

He was scowling now, and Amanda stifled the urge to giggle at his obvious discomfiture.

"They seem to have me pegged as some sort of eligible old bachelor, some prize trophy to be landed, and to be honest, Amanda, they're driving me nuts. I swear to God they're hunting me, as if I were wild game. All hours of the day and night, they're either on the phone or at the door. They have more problems with stuck windows and broken screens than the rest of Hawaii put together. And they've tricked me into the damnedest things—you just wouldn't believe it."

Horror was evident on his face. "Why, I even ended up escorting Rebecca to a funeral last week! I didn't know the deceased, and I finally realized she didn't, either. It was just a convenient way to get me alone for a few hours. They're obsessed with marriage, those four women, and they don't seem to care which of them gets me, as long as it's one of their group." Max swiped at his perspiring forehead and groaned. "I tell you, Amanda, I feel like a piece of meat in a butcher shop at times. I secretly call them the Matrimonial Brigade."

"They sound slightly . . . incestuous." It was all Amanda could do to keep a straight face. Max's discomfiture was genuine, but the situation was hilarious.

"Believe me, they *are* incestuous. I'm running out of excuses with them, too. When Daisy appeared at the door just now, I have to confess that you provided me with the best alibi I've come up with so far. I didn't plan it, honestly, but I couldn't resist, either."

"I rather think Daisy got the impression we were having an affair, Max."

"God, I can only hope so," he said fervently. He lay back and closed his eyes. "Amanda, this brings up something I want to discuss with you."

For one mad instant, she thought he was going to proposition her. Instead he asked in a different voice, "Would you and Billy consider staying on here at the apartment for the rest of your holiday? Please, Amanda. As a great favor to me?"

It wasn't what she'd been expecting at all, and she stared at him for a moment, unable to reply.

His invitation meant that she and Billy could stay on in Hawaii. But there was bound to be a price tag attached, and Amanda could only wonder if the cost was one she could afford.

Max, aware of her reservations, had held up a staying hand.

"Just hear me out, Amanda. Last night you made it clear you're not interested in a romance, and believe me, neither am I. But we do get along. You've got a great sense of humor—I relax around you. And I've got work to do, important work on this book I'm writing, a research project for a periodical. And those damned women are wasting my time. With you here my problem will be solved. You'll be a buffer, they'll lay off me and I can get busy on my book. After you leave, I can let them think I'm being faithful to you. You have no idea how it will ease my predicament, Amanda.''

She had to admit it made a peculiar kind of sense. And the last thing she really wanted to do was fly back to Vancouver this afternoon. Already Hawaii had her in its spell.

"We'll buy all the food and do the cooking," she negotiated.

"Nonsense." Seeing the stubborn set of her chin, he added, "We'll split the bills down the middle and I'll take you out to dinner now and then. Deal?"

She gave him a long, thoughtful look. There was danger here, she knew it. He was attractive, and she was still a woman.

On the other hand... never look a gift horse in the mouth.

She reached out a hand and he took it, giving it a hearty shake.

By the time Billy had returned, the deal had been struck.

CHAPTER FIVE

MOVING WITH DEFT EASE through the ambling tourists later that afternoon, Cosmo made his way through the open-air mall that housed the Kailua Shopping Center. There were specialty shops, restaurants, banks, and in the central area, amid palm trees, umbrella tables were set up where shoppers could relax with takeout food or a cool drink from one of the many eateries.

On the periphery of this open area, small stalls sold everything from live birds to hand-painted Tahitian pareaus.

Cosmo moved purposefully to a booth with an unpretentious hand-lettered sign that red Aloha Art by Ema.

The lovely Hawaiian woman in the booth was smiling a farewell to a middle-aged man and woman dressed in identical oversize turquoise blue Hawaiian shirts and white shorts. The woman was cradling a parcel wrapped in brown paper.

"Hope you enjoy your painting. Come back and see me next time you're in Kona," the woman in the booth crooned in a sweet, lilting voice that spoke of her multiracial heritage. The tiny booth had vivid paintings and drawings of all sizes hanging from cords strung up between the wall posts. There were brightly colored, almost childlike scenes depicting sunsets over the ocean, one or two views of the local fishing fleet sailing in with their catch and some pen-and-ink sketches of the village and surrounding areas.

Cosmo waited until the couple had disappeared in the direction of Drysdale's Pub before he spoke.

"How's it going? Don't tell me you sold another painting."

Ema Weiler nodded and grinned at the consternation on his face.

Ema was also an undercover officer from Honolulu P.D. She was Cosmo's contact on the murder case they were currently working on involving the violent death of the Kona socialite named Liza Franklin.

She flashed her exotic eyes at Cosmo and wrinkled her nose.

"That makes four I've sold in two days, partner. You better make with the paintbrush, Leonardo, or I'm gonna have nothing left to peddle out of here. And if you think turning these pictures out is tough, consider what I'm going through. My entire knowledge of art came from one high-school appreciation class, and I have people asking me questions about my technique, no less. It's getting embarrassing. The regular gallery owners are all stopping by and asking if I wouldn't prefer showing with them. They're more than a little green at the success we're having."

Cosmo groaned. "Who could've figured these damned oil paintings would be hot sellers? Why not the pen-and-ink sketches? At least I can do those openly. It seemed like the perfect cover, making out you were the one working in oils. I could've sworn they'd never sell. If I'd known they'd go like this, I swear I'd have quit the force and become an artist long ago. I never spend more than half an hour on any one of them, and the exorbitant price tags you slap on should mean one sale a year if we're lucky. Instead..."

Ema grinned. "Instead we're moving them like Auntie Pasta's Pizza. Ironic, isn't it? There are at least twenty galleries around Kona going broke trying to peddle local art, and we're making a killing."

"Don't even mention the word."

Ema gave him a sharp look. "Anything on Charlie yet?"

Cosmo shook his head. "I saw the professor last night, but it wasn't a good time to get him talking about Charlie. He had company." Like a videotape running nonstop through his head, he saw Billy, scowling at him while she peeled vegetables, smiling at him across the breakfast table this morning, looking up at him with that dazed look on her face after he'd kissed her a couple of hours ago. What the hell, he still felt pretty dazed himself.

"Who are the visitors?" Ema busied herself straightening pictures.

"Two women from Vancouver. No connection to the hoboes at all." He heard himself telling Ema about Billy winning the trip and bringing her mother-in-law along, then finding out their apartment was already occupied.

"They didn't have the money to stay anywhere else, so they were heading to the mainland this afternoon to get their reservations changed and go back to Vancouver."

"What a shame. Too bad you couldn't have let them share our apartment. Your room is just sitting empty while you camp out," Ema reflected.

"Except for my painting stuff, which is strewn all over the place. I'm gonna have to sneak over there and do a couple more sunsets in a hurry, I guess." Cosmo sighed. Ema's suggestion made him wish he *could* have offered Billy the apartment. Working undercover was a major pain sometimes, with its need for lies and subterfuge. He'd never minded much before, but he'd found it surprisingly tough lying to Billy.

What the hell, Antonelli, you'll never see the lady again, so forget it.

Menzies, *idiot*, Menzies. *Start thinking of yourself by your undercover name or you're gonna slip when it matters.*

"You get anything new at all on Caldwell and Evans?"

Ema was smiling at him, pretending to flirt for the benefit of the other merchants. She and Cosmo had subtly promoted the impression that they were having a romance. The shopping center was a perfect spot to hear all the gossip that made the rounds in Kailua town, which was exactly why the department had chosen the booth as Ema's cover.

Cosmo played along with the flirtation, lounging against the corner of the booth, standing provocatively close to Ema. Both were keeping a wary eye on the crowd, making certain no one was close enough to overhear their conversation.

"The other 'bos aren't talking much, but it's a damn sure thing Blackie Caldwell and Slim Evans didn't just have too much to drink and fall asleep on the beach so a nice convenient wave could come along and drown them. Forensics says they both had high levels of whiskey in their stomachs at the time of death, all right, but hoboes drink wine—they don't have money for whiskey. And even drunk as newts, they've got enough sense not to lie down right where the tide's gonna get them.''

"But nobody's saying anything to you yet that might link their deaths to Liza Franklin?'' Ema put a hand on Cosmo's forearm and smiled up into his eyes.

Cosmo covered her hand with his own. "Nope. The hoboes are scared witless. They're not saying anything to anyone, as far as I can figure. If the department hadn't ordered them to stay put, the whole bunch of them would have disappeared by now, back to the mainland if they could rustle up the bread or hitch a ride on a boat.''

"Do you think that's what Boxcar Charlie did? Headed to the mainland?''

Cosmo shook his head regretfully. "Nope. I'm afraid he's still around here somewhere, either hiding or dead.''

Ema agreed. "Max Caplin apparently told the local cops that Charlie knew something about Liza Franklin's murder, but Max didn't know what it was. That information went over to our boss—he told me about it yesterday. Charlie apparently wouldn't tell Caplin what he knew, except to say that he was scared. Maybe the professor knows something he's not telling, maybe not. But Caldwell and Evans probably knew the same something as Charlie, and it got them murdered.''

"That's my theory, too. I really hope Charlie's not dead, as well. But under the circumstances . . .''

"Cool it. There are two women over there, and one of them is heading straight toward us.'' Ema gave Cosmo one last provocative smile and stepped back.

He turned and felt a physical shock ripple through him.

The women were Billy and Amanda Reece.

BILLY HADN'T seen him at first. She was trying not to stare at an unusual woman with wild yellow hair and monstrous gold hoops in her ears sitting under a palm tree surrounded by live birds, some in cages, some loose. On top of her head squatted a brilliant turquoise parrot, while another, smaller bird rode happily back and forth on one of her earrings, leaning out at intervals to peck at the woman's mouth. The woman was feeding the bird some kind of nuts she held in her teeth.

"Billy, isn't that Cosmo over there?"

Amanda's question made her turn away from the bird woman fast. She saw him right away, smiling down in intimate fashion at an exotically beautiful woman with long black hair in one of the booths. The woman was laughing up at him, her hand on his forearm. Billy's heart seemed to clench with an emotion she didn't want to acknowledge.

She turned away quickly, longing to disappear before he glanced over and saw them, but Amanda was already walking in his direction.

The dark woman said something, and Cosmo turned around.

His smile broadened, and in another moment he was beside them, nodding to Amanda in friendly fashion while taking Billy's hand in his own, even though she tried to pull away.

"You've decided to stay on?" His question was directed at Billy but she was relieved when Amanda answered.

"Max has kindly offered us his spare bedroom for three weeks."

"That's marvelous." Cosmo squeezed Billy's hand, punctuating his words. "Come over here. There's someone I'd like you to meet."

Billy had no choice. He led them over to the art booth.

"Ema Weiler, this is Billy Overton Reece and her mother-in-law, Amanda Reece. Billy's an artist, too, Ema. You two have lots to talk about."

Billy thought she saw a caustic look pass from Ema to Cosmo, but it was gone so quickly she must have imagined it.

Ema took Amanda's hand and shook it, smiling in an engagingly friendly way. "Cosmo mentioned meeting you. I'm glad you're staying on in Hawaii. We love to show off our islands to visitors."

Amanda grinned. "Not half as glad as we are, I can tell you that. Being here still seems like a dream come true to me. It's the most beautiful place I've ever seen. Have you always lived here, Ema?"

"I was born here, but I grew up all over North America and even parts of Europe. My dad was in the army. We finally settled on Oahu when I started college. I haven't been on Kona long."

"Where did you study painting?" Billy was looking closely at the array of pictures in the booth, trying to figure out which might be Cosmo's and which Ema's.

"Actually, I didn't study much at all. I just started painting a short while ago, not long before I opened this booth. Earn as you learn, I guess you'd call it."

"These landscapes are powerful. They have a sort of raw energy about them. I especially like the fishing-boat scenes."

"Thanks." Ema didn't elaborate on the paintings. She changed the subject rather abruptly, asking if the women had seen much of the town yet.

Billy liked her for that; so many artists she'd met would happily go on for twelve hours about themselves and their work, given a chance.

"Would all of you like a cup of coffee? Grab that table that's just come empty, Billy, and I'll go and get us some." Cosmo hurried off.

"I'll come along and help carry." Amanda followed him, leaving Billy alone with Ema.

Billy felt miserably uncomfortable. She'd spent the past few moments agonizing over what the relationship was between Cosmo and this elegant woman. There'd been such an air of intimacy between them when Billy had first seen them.

Could Cosmo be the type of man who romanced every woman he met? Billy wondered. The memory of the kiss they'd shared was foremost in her mind each time she looked at him, and irrational jealousy swirled inside her as she imagined Cosmo kissing Ema the same way.

She was being an idiot. She had only met him last night—what did she really know about him? He had had a life before she'd come along, she reminded herself. He was an attractive man, in an offbeat sort of way.

C'mon, Billy, get real here. He's attractive in any sort of way. He's captivated you, and you barely know him. Why shouldn't he have the same effect on other women, as well?

"If you want to do some shopping while you're here, I can steer you toward the best places to go," Ema was saying. "Not that I buy all that much myself, but listening to the other merchants is an education when it comes to bargains around town."

Billy smiled. There was a warmth about Ema that made her likable. "Amanda and I are here on a shoestring, I'm afraid. We won't be buying much, but just being here is a high for both of us. Neither of us has ever been far from Vancouver before." She described the contest, the elation she'd felt when she'd won, the horrible feeling when they'd walked into the apartment yesterday and found Max already there.

Ema was a good listener; her dark, tip-tilted eyes stayed fixed on Billy's face, and her features reflected interest and empathy.

"The poor man was only wearing a towel when we barged in," Billy elaborated. Ema giggled, and Billy went on, "He'd just had a bath, and I unlocked the door. Do you know Max Caplin?" It was sneaky, but she was waiting for Ema to say Cosmo had already introduced them.

Instead Ema shook her head. "I haven't met him. Actually, I don't know many people over here on Kona. As I said, I've only been here a short while, and I spend most of my time in that booth." Almost as an afterthought, she added quickly, "Or painting."

"I brought my charcoals along, but I can certainly see that oils capture the intensity of the tones here. You work mostly in oils, Ema?"

"Yeah." Ema's thoughts were obviously on things other than art. "You know, Billy, if you and Amanda wanted to do some shopping on a shoestring, you should go to the Kona Gardens Flea Market. It's held

Wednesday, Thursday and Saturday, from eight in the morning till two. It's on Alii Drive across from the Keauhou Beach Hotel, just a couple of miles from here. I've got a bike you could borrow, and we can probably rustle another one up for Amanda. I know you'd enjoy it—there's a ton of bargains. There's this little round man there who sells quartz crystals—are you into that sort of thing? I got this one from him.'' Ema touched the sparkling crystal she wore on a gold chain at her throat.

"I don't have one, but lots of people back in Vancouver are really interested in New Age stuff—crystals and astrology and all that. Amanda reads a lot of books about it.''

They were deep in a discussion about metaphysics when Cosmo and Amanda arrived, laden with mugs of Kona coffee and a bag stuffed with fat cookies. Cosmo took the chair next to Billy, and Amanda sat by Ema. For a few moments they sipped their coffee and devoured the cookies in companionable silence.

"Billy tells me you're interested in metaphysics,'' Ema remarked to Amanda, and soon the two of them were involved in an animated conversation.

Billy was intensely aware of the man at her side. His arm brushed against hers now and then, and she imagined she could feel the warmth of him, close beside her. She concentrated on her coffee, hoping he wasn't aware that her hands were actually trembling as she cradled her coffee. The effect his presence had on her was nothing short of ridiculous, she lectured herself impatiently.

"I'm really glad you're staying on in Hawaii, Billy,'' he said in a quiet voice, under the cover of the dialogue across the table. "I'd like to show you around a little. How about coming for a swim with me later today? I always go just before sundown.''

She wanted to ask if Ema would be there. She desperately wanted to know what the relationship was between the two of them. Would he have the audacity to invite her out this way, with Ema right across the table, if he and Ema were involved? It didn't seem likely.

She relaxed a little. Going swimming in the Pacific for the first time here in Hawaii was bound to be an event. And going with Cosmo made it special, indeed, she admitted to herself.

She remembered her intentions about staying away from him. Exercising her female prerogative, she changed her mind about that.

''I'd like to come.''

He smiled, his teeth a gleaming white against the darkness of his beard and mustache.

''Good. I'll come by the apartment about five.''

SHE WAS WAITING for him in the open lobby. She'd put on her faded blue bikini and then pulled an oversize red cotton shirt and her white shorts over it. Her towel, sun lotion and wallet were stuffed into a terry drawstring bag.

She saw him coming along the sidewalk before he spotted her, and for a moment she was free to admire the animal grace of his tall, muscular frame. His walk was unique, the smooth, swinging gait of a natural athlete. He was wearing what she was beginning to suspect was his uniform: cutoff jeans, abbreviated T-shirt and rope sandals. He had a plastic grocery bag in one hand, with the corner of a striped towel sticking out the top. He smiled when he saw her, a wide, delighted grin that sent warmth shooting through her body and made her smile back.

"All set? Let's go." He grabbed her hand, then hustled them outside and across the street. Then he turned to face the oncoming traffic and stuck his thumb out boldly.

Billy had hitchhiked several times in her life, but not since she was a teen. It hadn't crossed her mind that this was the way they'd get to the beach, and she felt horribly self-conscious, standing beside him while he begged a ride.

"Cosmo, I've got bus fare, can't we—"

Before the sentence was finished, a battered brown Jeep with an open top and stuffed with what seemed far too many teenage boys had pulled to a halt beside them. There were several surfboards lashed to the back, and all the occupants wore bathing trunks.

"Hop in." Then the young, bare-chested driver waved a thank-you to the cars behind who'd had to stop when he had.

Cosmo and Billy piled in. Young brown bodies seemed to be stacked every which way. Everyone good-naturedly scrunched together until there was almost enough room for one person on the back seat. Cosmo sat and pulled Billy down on his lap, and the driver put the Jeep in gear and stepped on the gas.

"Where you headed, man?" The balmy wind tossed the words back to them.

"Out to Magic Sands," Cosmo called.

"Us, too. Surf's up."

Crammed amid the cheerful, laughing group, Billy was far more conscious of Cosmo's hard thighs beneath her than she was of the spectacular scenery speeding past. She could feel the roughness of the hair on his legs against the back of her thighs. His arms were looped around her, holding her loosely against his chest as the Jeep stopped and started at lights and wound up and down hills. He felt solid and tremendously strong, all hard muscle and sinew. Her fingers touched his arm; she could feel his warm breath on her back, and she was agonizingly conscious of her scantily clad body in close contact with intimate parts of him. Despite the cooling effect of the wind rushing by, her body seemed to radiate heat. She wondered if Cosmo could feel it.

She was enormously relieved when they finally turned into a parking lot near a sandy beach right on the ocean. The boys clambered out, retrieving the surfboards and calling to one another exuberantly.

"Thanks for the ride," Cosmo said to the driver.

"We'll be heading back into town after it gets dark. You're welcome to ride back with us."

"We'd appreciate that."

The crowd of young men took off at a gallop for the water, leaving Cosmo and Billy to make their way among the relatively few people stretched out on the rough sand.

Cosmo led the way to an area some distance from the main beach. On a strip of deserted sand he spread a worn beach towel from his bag, carefully weighting the corners down with stones so it wouldn't blow away in the brisk breeze. Then he doffed his shirt and pulled off his shorts, revealing an abbreviated black suit.

He was tanned the same rich nut brown shade all over. His shoulders were square and wide, and his body narrowed in a perfect vee, broad chest, narrow waist and hips, strong thighs.

Far too conscious of the beauty of his nearly naked, hair-dusted shape close beside her, Billy sank
down on the towel and made a show of studying the
wide green waters of the Pacific, shading her eyes with
her hand.

"C'mon, let's go get you wet in the ocean."

She turned to look up at him, and he was smiling
down at her, waiting.

A fit of shyness came over her now that the time had
come for her to strip off her own shorts and top. Her
bikini was perfectly decent, but she was suddenly
aware of her body in a way she'd seldom been in her
life.

Cosmo, and indeed everyone else she could see on
the wide beach, was tanned from the powerful Hawaiian sun, beautiful dark natives who looked as if
they belonged to this tropical landscape. She knew
she'd look mushroom pale beside them, bleached and
faded.

But Cosmo was waiting for her.

She swallowed and slowly began to unbutton her
shirt. She let it slip off her shoulders, and without
looking at Cosmo, she wriggled out of her shorts, as
well. The slight breeze cooled her bare skin, and the
tropical heat of the sun felt like a caress.

"We'll go for a swim, then we'd better get some of
that suntan lotion on you or you'll burn."

Cosmo's voice was matter-of-fact, and Billy realized how silly it was to be self-conscious about her bikini here. She could see at least a dozen other women
along the beach wearing skimpier ones than hers.

He grabbed her hand in his and they walked to the
edge of the sand. Waves broke with rhythmic force
around their legs.

"You used to swimming where there are waves, Billy?" Cosmo had to raise his voice a bit over the pounding of the surf. "This beach isn't protected, and they can get pretty big."

"I'm a good swimmer. I had a couple of years of swimming lessons," she boasted. Her pale skin tagged her as enough of a greenhorn without admitting that she usually swam in pools.

She let go of his hand and in one shallow dive was in the water. Then she turned and looked back at him, laughing. "C'mon in, the water's fine." It was delicious, cool enough to be refreshing, but nothing like the icy Pacific around Vancouver. This cool blue water was playful, sensual in its motion and warmth.

In a moment he was beside her. He was a powerful swimmer, and they swam out a short way, side by side. The waves were a bit intimidating, but Billy was sure she'd get the hang of them soon. At least, she hoped so. The truth was, there was no comparison between these powerful breakers and the small waves she'd experienced on Vancouver's beaches. Here, the turquoise water went on and on until it touched the horizon, with nothing to interfere with the breakers. Back home, there were miles of inlets and islands and barriers before the open sea, so there was never a sense of the ocean's unbridled power the way there was here in Hawaii.

She tried to copy the way Cosmo slipped like a seal in and out of the breakers. He teased her, catching her playfully at the crest of a wave and holding her for a moment before he let her go again.

She didn't even see the approaching wave until an instant before it broke over her. She was laughing at

Cosmo, teasing him. Suddenly he made a lunge toward her, his expression filled with concern.

"Here's a big one. Dive, Billy, dive..."

She looked behind her, at the ocean, and saw the wave.

"Dive, dive..."

It was like a wall of water, obliterating the sky. It came roaring toward her, and she was frozen, petrified with fear.

Then the world exploded with a force she'd never experienced before. Water covered her, pulled at her, sucked her under, and she had no control over what was happening. She could feel sand grinding into her body, water filled her ears and nose and mouth as she tumbled into a green underworld, and she knew this was how it felt to drown.

CHAPTER SIX

BILLY STRUGGLED in an agony of terror, fighting with all her strength against the murderous power of the wave, conscious that it was a fruitless struggle, that she was about to die because she couldn't get her breath or stop tumbling helplessly, over and over, held under by the monstrous weight of water surrounding her.

Time was no longer measurable. She'd been fighting for hours or seconds, she couldn't tell, when strong arms closed around her, and an eternity later, she was lying on wet sand, out of reach of the waves.

Still terrified, she tried to struggle to her feet, and made it as far as her knees.

Choking, she began to retch, aware that Cosmo was holding her against his body. Her eyes, ears, mouth, throat all felt full of sand and seawater. Her bikini top was askew, exposing one of her breasts. With shaking fingers she tugged it into place, but under the blue fabric, she could feel sand grating into other, more intimate parts of her body.

She felt more helpless than she had ever felt in her life, battered and soaked and sore. There was a long scrape on her right thigh, and another on her arm.

She began to sob as Cosmo rubbed her back and cradled her in his arms. "I want...want to go...go home," she choked out.

"Easy, honey, easy. It was just a big wave. It happens to all of us. Damn it to hell, I should have been more careful with you. I thought you knew..."

Cosmo held her tight in his arms, brushing her drenched hair back from her forehead, gently trying to comfort her.

"I need...need a tissue," she finally gulped. "My...my bag..."

He helped her to her feet. Her knees were trembling, and he slid an arm around her and supported her over to where they'd left their towels.

"There's a shower house just down the beach a ways. Do you want to try to get some of the sand off?" He'd draped her towel around her shoulders and was rubbing her arms with the corners.

Billy groped through her bag and found a tissue. She blew her nose and nodded.

Cosmo gathered up their belongings in one hand and walked beside her, holding her tight against his side with the other arm all along the beach. Billy was certain everyone was staring at her, and she felt humiliated and bedraggled, but when she dared to glance around, no one was paying any attention.

"I'll wait right here. Take your time." He sat down close to the entrance.

Inside the cement building, she stripped off her suit. It fell to the floor with a thunk. It looked as if it had a sand lining. She looked into the mirror. Her hair was glued flat to her skull, sand grated in her scalp, her eyes were red and bloodshot from the saltwater and there was an angry scrape across one cheek. She stared at herself, aghast.

This was a holiday?

Fifteen minutes later, as repaired as she could manage, she came out wearing her shorts and shirt.

Cosmo was waiting. He got up and came over to her. "Where's your swimsuit?"

"In here." She held out her bag. "I'm not going back in the water today. You go ahead and swim if you want. I'll just sit up here on the sand."

Cosmo looked at her with narrowed eyes. "Go back in there and put your suit on, Billy," he ordered in a soft, determined voice.

Billy shook her wet head, annoyed. "I told you, I don't want..."

"You're going back in the ocean, suit or no suit," he said calmly. "You know what they say about horses—if you get thrown, you climb right back on. Well, this is the same thing. I made a bad mistake, thinking you knew what you were doing in the waves. Now I'm going to teach you what I should have in the first place."

Billy looked down at her toes and gulped. "Cosmo, please, I really don't want to. The truth is, I'm scared. I'm really scared of those waves. I had no idea what they could do...."

Cosmo's voice was rough and gentle. "I know that, honey, and I blame myself for not being more cautious with you. But if you wait, the fear will only get worse. So go and put on that great-looking blue bikini, and I'll teach you what you need to know so you never have to be scared of the ocean again."

Wishing fervently that she were back in Vancouver in her own bathtub, Billy went back to the change room and struggled into her clammy suit.

"YOU'RE A good teacher, Cosmo." They were seated in a McDonald's, wolfing down hamburgers and fries and thick shakes.

Outside, darkness had come down with the abrupt shift from day to dark Billy was beginning to recognize as typical of the tropics.

Cosmo smiled at her, and once again she was aware of how his mustache and beard defined his mouth and his white teeth.

"You're not scared of the waves anymore, huh?" he asked.

She shook her head. "I've got a healthy respect for them, I'll tell you that. I never realized how dangerous the surf could be."

He nodded. "The ocean takes its share of lives because people don't respect it enough."

"How did you learn to swim so well?"

"My older brothers taught me. But one of the other hoboes here showed me a lot of the stuff I passed on to you today."

"What's his name?" Billy found herself more and more intrigued by Cosmo's choice of life-style and his companions.

"Kalani. He's Hawaiian. He used to be a world-class body surfer, but he drank too much."

"Do most of the hoboes drink a lot?"

Cosmo shrugged. "Some of them, but not the majority. We all share a couple of bottles of wine now and then, when we can afford it."

His dark eyes crinkled at the corners as he laughed at her, Billy saw, gently teasing.

"Just like ordinary folks," he added.

Billy chewed and swallowed the last bite of her second hamburger. She'd worried about the money he'd spent on their meal, offering to pay her own way, but he'd brushed aside her offer.

"By hobo standards, I'm well-to-do," he'd remarked. "I told you my paintings sell, and when you live the way I do there's not much to spend money on. No car, no house insurance, no rent, no income tax, no fancy clothes. Not even a lot of food expenses. There's a plentiful supply of free food here if you know where to look."

"But I eat an awful lot, Cosmo. And after swimming, I'm worse than usual." Better to be up-front than starve, she'd decided philosophically.

He'd just smiled and ordered doubles of everything.

Being with him the past few hours had emphasized for Billy how attracted she was to him. The disaster with the waves had shown her a tender, nurturing side of Cosmo, a deeply gentle and protective quality in his nature that didn't show ordinarily. He was tough, too; he wouldn't take no for an answer when she'd wanted to quit, but once he'd coaxed her back into the surf, he'd held her until she felt secure again, protecting her with his muscular arms and body, talking to her constantly in a reassuring way.

She'd felt a touch of regret at eventually being able to swim off on her own under the huge waves.

"Cosmo." There was something she had to know before this went any further between them, and it was difficult to put into words, but it had been bothering her all afternoon.

"Cosmo, are you and Ema...is she your...I mean, are you involved with her? Because I like her, and I wouldn't want her to think..." She looked directly into his eyes, bracing herself for the answer she dreaded. "I'd just like to know," she said.

"Ema and I are friends, and that's all. There's nothing between us in a man-woman sense, Billy."

He looked directly into her eyes as he spoke, and she couldn't doubt the honesty and directness there. He was telling her the truth, and she felt as if a weight had been lifted from her heart.

"Oh. Well, then." She sucked up the last drops of her second shake, fighting the urge to grin at him like a total idiot. "I'm glad. I mean, don't get me wrong— I'm not suggesting that, well, anything, really. I just..."

"You just have a lot of the same feelings I do, right?" Cosmo's voice was low and thick, rough with emotion. "Holding you in the water today almost drove me nuts. I wanted to tear off those silly blue scraps, drag you to shore and make love to you on the sand."

Billy swallowed hard. He had a way of putting into words what she was doing her best to avoid admitting. "But I only met you yesterday."

His smoldering eyes caught and held hers for an instant, and the intensity there made her look away.

"Right. And that's why we're sitting here eating instead of lying under a palm in some deserted place in the dark while I strip off your clothes and worship every part of you."

His words sent ripples of indescribable sensation shooting through her, warm and arousing.

He reached across and deliberately cupped her chin, forcing her to look at him. His voice had dropped to a whisper. "I want you, Billy. And I intend to make love to you before many more days go by."

Each word seemed to caress her, bring alive parts of her body that had been dormant for a long time. She fought the feelings, striving for a light, dismissive tone. "Are you always this up-front when you proposition a woman?"

Anger, cold and hard, flashed across his features, and for an instant she was almost frightened, glimpsing a man totally different from the easygoing, almost gentle person she'd thought she was getting to know.

"This isn't a game I'm playing with you, Billy. I'm being totally honest about how I feel. I'm not a subtle kind of guy when it comes to this. You're an adult— you can choose to go on with me or not—but don't reduce it to some silly male-female banter."

The harshness of his words took her aback and then made her angry. "Look, mister, don't mistake me for some frustrated bimbo looking for a holiday thrill, that's all."

He surprised her by laughing.

"So what's funny about that?" She was getting really mad now.

"The idea that you could think of yourself that way. My God, Billy, you'd need more than a couple of hours of lessons to learn how to be a frustrated bimbo. I've met a number of women like that even in the short time I've been here, and believe me, they don't act anything like you do."

"So how do they act?" She wasn't sure whether to be insulted or complimented.

"Seductive. Aggressive. Hungry. Like barracudas with their teeth filed down. They have a certain way of looking at you, brushing against you, making it plain they're available."

She wasn't sure she wanted to hear this, either, but she couldn't stop herself from asking. "So do you ever..."

"Take them up on it?" he gave her a steady look. "I'm still old-fashioned enough to want to think I'm the aggressor in my relationships."

"Aha, a chauvinist." She gave him a tiny smile so he'd know she was joking.

"Nope. Just a man, Billy."

There wasn't the slightest doubt about that.

THE CONVERSATION lingered in Cosmo's mind after he'd escorted Billy to the apartment building and kissed her good-night.

He'd kissed her thoroughly, and it took almost the entire long walk back to the hobo jungle before the physical consequence of those kisses wore off a little.

She was having the damnedest effect on him. He had to be cautious, on guard with her, because the urge to spill out the truth about who he was and what he was doing became almost irresistible at times.

He hated having to lie to her. He'd come within a hairbreadth tonight of telling Billy that Ema was a police officer, his partner, and the impression they gave of being sexually involved was just a big act, part of their cover.

Sure, Dumbo. Smart move. One careless word on Billy's part and the whole elaborate structure the Honolulu department had put into place could tumble down around their ears. It wasn't fair, telling her anything. It put too much responsibility on her, and anyway, he couldn't.

Lives were at stake here; this was a vicious murder investigation, not a traffic offense.

He slouched along, as inconspicuous as he could make himself among the evening crowds heading from one night spot to the other. He'd spent a lot of time learning not to walk like a cop, not to carry himself with authority, not to look people straight in the face and challenge them with his eyes. Even now, he constantly studied the speech patterns and the body language of the hoboes he lived among, picking up hints for his own performance.

Being undercover was like deliberately splitting himself into two separate personalities. The ideal was to become totally the person he pretended to be, to live, breathe, eat, sleep, think and dream like a hobo.

On his last job, infiltrating a group who brought illegal aliens into the country, he's managed to assume the persona so thoroughly he'd had trouble finding Cosmo Antonelli again when the job was done. He'd actually become Mario, the smart-mouthed Italian hood he'd impersonated.

He'd been doing great this time, as well, until the other night. When he'd met Billy Reece. Something about her had sliced straight through to the core of him, to where Cosmo Antonelli really lived.

Which was exactly why, before now, he'd dropped whatever casual romance he was involved in when a job like this came along. A week after going undercover, he'd barely remember the name of whoever it was he'd been seeing.

So what the hell are you doing this time, hotshot?

He prided himself on being bone-honest with any ladies in his life, letting them know right in the beginning that he wasn't husband material. For now, at least, he had no desire to see half a dozen little Cosmos running around. He was strictly a here-today, gone-tomorrow sort of dude, take it or leave it. Not that a short-term affair wouldn't be fun; he had hot-blooded Italian ancestors, after all.

He just didn't fancy marriage and all that went with it.

Anyhow, his brothers had made certain the Antonelli name was in no danger of disappearing. Was it eleven or twelve nieces and nephews he had now? Robert had four, Ken three...

He was avoiding the issue here, and the issue was Billy.

If he had a grain of sense, he'd go out of his way to avoid her for the whole three weeks she'd be in Hawaii. He had a gut feeling this thing with her wasn't going to be the same as other times.

It's been a blast, honey. Great to know you. See you again sometime. 'Bye....

He ought to get out now, right in the beginning. Trouble was, he'd already said he's see her tomorrow. He'd show her around a little; they'd do a bit of sketching together.

The morning was going to be busy. He had to get up at dawn and sneak back to the apartment so he could spend a couple of hours turning out the oil paintings Ema supposedly did.

He was starting to despise sunsets. And what the hell, seeing Billy gave him something to look forward to.

Every hobo needed something to look forward to, didn't he?

AMANDA HAD BEEN horrified when Max had told her about the murders.

She'd made a casserole for dinner that evening, using the fresh seafood she and Billy had bought at the market in the afternoon and a bag of noodles from the cupboard.

Billy had said she was going swimming and that she'd probably be either late for dinner or else she'd have something with Cosmo, so Amanda had gone ahead and made a salad and some fresh rolls for Max and herself. They'd had a glass of wine as they'd watched the sunset, then moved inside to eat. They'd chatted in the companionable way that seemed natural between them, about the parts of the village Amanda had explored that afternoon with Billy and the meeting with Ema, whom Max didn't know, although he said he'd noticed her booth at the market.

When dinner was over, they'd taken their coffee outside again. The air was balmy, and a huge moon was rising.

They were laughing together about some joking remark Amanda had just made, when the phone rang.

Max had gotten up to answer. When he'd come back, Amanda could sense a change in his mood. Instead of sitting down again, he stood at the railing, and she could see the grim, tight line of his mouth.

"Is anything wrong, Max? The phone call wasn't bad news, was it?"

"No. Well, at least not in the sense of a family problem or anything like that." He sighed and flopped back down beside her. "It's a bad situation I've somehow become involved with. That was the police. They wanted to check with me again over this hobo thing, see if I'd heard anything from Charlie." His voice was tense and it was obvious he was worried.

Amanda didn't have the faintest idea what he was talking about. "What hobo thing, Max?"

He sighed and rubbed his forehead with his hand. "It's a nasty business. You see, two hoboes were found drowned on the beach a short time ago. It looked like an accident, as if they'd had too much to drink, passed out on the beach and then been drowned by the incoming tide. That's what the news reports claimed, and I think that's what the police thought, as well, at first. But one of the men I was interviewing, my old friend Boxcar Charlie, suddenly blurted out to me that the two of them, friends of his, had been murdered because of something they knew. He wouldn't tell me what it was, but he was frightened enough to convince me he was telling the truth. Then, the day after our conversation, Charlie disappeared. Nobody's seen him, from that day to this, and in light of what he confided to me, I was...I am...terribly worried about him. I waited a day, and when there was no trace of him I contacted the police and told them what he'd told me."

"Max, that's dreadful. Has he...he still hasn't been found...?"

Max shook his head. "No one's seen him at all. It seems I was the last one to talk to him."

Amanda shuddered. She knew it was naive, but she'd somehow felt that this tiny Hawaiian village would be immune to things like murder. it seemed a dreamland to her, a place where bad things couldn't happen because of the beauty of nature and the friendliness of the inhabitants. Max's story was a reminder that Kailua was unfortunately very much part of the modern world for all its seeming tranquillity. She tried to make sense of what he'd told her. "Max, why on earth would anyone murder two harmless hoboes?''

Max blew out a long breath in frustration. "The police figure it has to do with another murder, the death of a woman named Liza Franklin. Six weeks ago, her body was found on a deserted beach a short distance up-island. She'd been beaten to death and robbed. There was a lot of publicity about it because she had inherited one of the large Kona coffee plantations, and her husband's a bigwig here on Kona and around the other islands. His name's Harrison Franklin. He's a real-estate developer, a real mover and shaker in Hawaii. There's talk that he plans to enter local politics in the next elections."

Amanda shivered again. "The poor man. Why, it must have been terrible for him, losing his wife that way. How did it happen?"

"It was pretty common knowledge that Liza Franklin was in the habit of drinking too much and then going for walks along the beach in an area that was part of her late father's estate. Apparently, that's what happened that night. She was beaten and robbed. Her car, jewelry and handbag were all missing when she was found."

Amanda shook her head. "It's hard to believe things like that could happen here."

Max agreed. "This sort of thing has happened on the other islands, occasionally to tourists, but mainly on Oahu. Till now, there really hasn't been much violent crime on Kona at all. Liza Franklin's death got huge coverage in the media, and because all the Hawaiian Islands rely heavily on tourism, it's very bad PR. Everyone wants the responsible persons caught. Harrison Franklin has a lot of clout, and he's offering a substantial reward for any information about his wife's murder.''

"But I still don't understand what the hoboes had to with all this, Max."

He sighed and picked up his coffee cup, draining the cold liquid before he answered her. "Unfortunately the hoboes have an encampment right on the edge of the park where Liza Franklin's body was found. And, of course, at first they were the prime suspects."

"I see." Amanda was silent for a moment, thinking about all that he'd told her. "You don't think it might have been them, do you?" she asked. Apprehension began to grow in her, because at that very moment, Billy was out somewhere with Cosmo. Amanda had liked him from the moment she'd met him, but realistically, what did any of them really know about Cosmo?

And Max spent long periods of time alone with the hoboes, too. The idea that he and Billy might both be in danger sent cold shivers up her spine.

Max was reassuring. "I'm absolutely certain the hoboes had nothing to do with it. I'd bet my life on it. I told the police exactly that in no uncertain terms. Liza Franklin's murder was violent, according to all the reports in the papers, and from what little the police revealed to me when I talked with them, it would have taken a particular kind of person to commit a crime like that. I told them that in my opinion, not one of the hoboes I've met here would be capable of that sort of thing, and I've always considered myself a good judge of human nature. I know from what Charlie told me that the investigating officers tore the hoboes' camp apart for evidence and questioned every one of them extensively, but they didn't find a thing.

All the hoboes were warned not to leave the area, and except for Charlie, none of them have."

A long moment passed before he added, in a less assured manner, "However, I think some of them might know more than they're telling about what did happen. Charlie certainly hinted he did, and from what he said, the two hoboes who died must have known something, as well."

"But he didn't say what it was?"

Max shook his head. "No. I tried my best to make him tell me, but he clammed up. He was obviously terrified. And I have the feeling now when I talk to the others that most of them are frightened, as well."

"Do you think this Charlie is dead, Max?" Amanda's voice trembled. "I mean, if someone murdered the other two hoboes..."

Max reached across and took her hand in his own and gave it a squeeze. "I hope not. God, I hope not," he said fervently. "But of course it's crossed my mind. I'm trying everything I can think of to locate Charlie, and now the police are, too, but with no more success. Not one of the hoboes has any idea where he might be, which is unusual. You'd think he'd have talked to someone, been seen somewhere by now. The police have checked the other towns on the island, but he hasn't turned up." Max sighed again, a frustrated, tired sound in the darkness. "Anyway, Amanda, I shouldn't burden you with all this on your vacation." His voice was full of remorse. "I apologize."

"Don't be silly. I'm sure I'd have heard about it, anyway—there must be articles in the papers and on television. I'd much rather get it all straight from you, so I really understand what's going on."

She liked the feeling of his hand holding hers, perhaps too much. She gave his fingers a friendly squeeze and then drew away. "Shall we go inside and put another pot of coffee on to drip?"

Max reached out and helped her up from the low recliner, but as soon as she was on her feet, he let her go again. They made their way to the kitchen, set the coffee machine in action and went to sit in the living room.

Each was lost in private thoughts for a time and then Amanda broke the silence.

"Max, it's probably silly of me, but hearing all this has made me a bit anxious about Billy. More than a bit, to be truthful. You know she's with Cosmo right now. Max, how well do you know him? Was he one of the hoboes the police investigated?"

"No, he wasn't on the scene at all. Cosmo didn't appear until after the hoboes drowned. But I must admit, I was suspicious, anyway. He's different from the others, younger and... well, I can't put my finger on it, but there's something about him that sets him apart, something besides his age. Nothing bad, mind you. Just an air he has about him. So when I talked with the police, I asked them right out if they'd considered him as a suspect, and they said they had, but they'd done a check on him and he was... 'clean' was the word they used."

The coffee maker gave one final gurgle and stopped. Max got up and brought Amanda a mug of the fresh coffee, taking his own back to the rattan easy chair where he'd been sitting.

"When I went to the police, I hadn't talked much with Cosmo myself. The first chance I really had to get to know him was last night, when he turned up here just after you'd arrived. I paid close attention, and I wouldn't waste any time worrying about him, Amanda. I got the impression that he's intelligent and honest, even if he's not ambitious in the usual sense.''

Amanda felt herself relax. "I liked him, too," she admitted. "And I was so pleased when Billy decided to go out with him. She's led such a lonely life since Graham died. It's good for her to be with someone her own age, having fun. It's just that I love her very much and I worry about her.''

"You're a warm and loving woman, Amanda Reece.''

There was open admiration in Max's tone, and he lifted his coffee cup to her in a courtly salute.

Amanda was touched, but she hid it by giving him a mischievous grin. "I haven't a doubt that Daisy Seibert told the other ladies exactly that about me this morning, Max Caplin. I'll bet she said that I was a warm and loving woman." She gave the words a more suggestive, sarcastic intonation.

The somberness of the past half-hour fled. Max threw his white head back and laughed, a hearty, cheerful guffaw.

"I'm quite sure she used those exact words, Amanda.''

AFTER COSMO LEFT HER just inside the door, Billy sauntered in a languid fashion through the softly lit apartment lobby toward the elevators.

Her lips still burned from his kisses. Her body was tingling, from the embrace at the door and also from the hours spent in the sun and surf, and she felt pleasantly weary and slightly lightheaded as she waited for the elevator.

As usual, the lobby seemed deserted, but the elevator was extraordinarily slow tonight. She pushed the button, and when several minutes passed, she pushed it again, shifting her bag from one hand to the other and finally dropping it at her feet as she waited, her thoughts entirely on the eventful hours she'd spent with Cosmo.

It took her a while to figure out that the elevator must be detained, perhaps with someone moving in or out on one of the upper floors.

Well, it wouldn't kill her to take the stairs.

She bent to retrieve her bag, and as she straightened, she caught sight of a figure standing in a shadowy corner near the doorway to the pool area. He startled her, because she'd thought herself entirely alone.

He looked young, maybe thirty. He wore khaki shorts and a dark T-shirt, not a tall man, but stocky, his blond hair cut in military fashion close to his head. He stood as still as a mannequin, and the thing that caught her attention was the dark wraparound glasses he wore, even though it was dark outside and the lights in the lobby were muted.

The tiny hairs on Billy's neck stood up as she looked at him, and a tingle of uneasiness ran down her spine, because she was certain that from behind the dark lenses he was staring directly at her. He gave no sign of recognition, though. He simply stood unmoving, his hands at his sides, his feet planted solidly on the carpet, the dark glasses hiding his eyes.

It was eerie and somehow ominous.

She turned hastily away and punched the elevator button one last time, but there was still no response. Forcing herself not to look over her shoulder at the figure in the corner, she walked quickly to the stairwell. Tugging the heavy door open and hurrying through, she was certain she could feel his eyes on her back.

She was around the first turn before the door sighed shut behind her. The stairwell echoed with the sound of her sandals slapping against the concrete.

Her heart was beating unnaturally fast. The man had unnerved her, and she found herself listening intently for footsteps behind her. She began taking the steps two at a time, and she forced herself to slow down.

Idiot. You're paranoid. The poor guy was probably blind. He was waiting for a cab, he was... She took a deep breath and stopped abruptly. *Get hold of yourself, Billy.*

And then she heard the sound of someone climbing not far behind her, heavy shoes deliberately striking each stair. Her heart gave an enormous thump, and she began to race upward, the muscles in her legs beginning to ache with the effort. She strained to hear, and it seemed to her the footsteps behind her increased their tempo now, coming closer.

She rounded another corner, and there were two pay telephones and a reinforced glass door that said three. She could race out in the hallway and scream. Surely someone...

She burst through the door. Two women and an elderly man were just getting on the elevator, and they turned and stared as she raced down the hallway toward them.

The man held the door, detaining the elevator until she could rush inside.

She ducked in. No one else arrived, and after what seemed an eternity the doors began to close. She was trembling, and she could feel cold sweat trickling down her shoulder blades.

"You okay, miss?" They were all looking at her, curious.

One of the women pushed four and they began to rise slowly.

Suddenly Billy felt ridiculous. What, really, had happened? Nothing at all.

"I...waited downstairs, and the elevator didn't come, so I took the stairs and..." She shuddered. "I got nervous, I guess. Silly of me."

"Not at all." The white-haired woman patted her arm. "I know just what you mean, dear. I'm always sure someone's behind me when I have to climb the stairs. I don't know what's wrong with this elevator tonight. We must have waited a good five minutes ourselves, right, Blanche? You'd think..."

The elevator slid to a halt at four, and the women, still chattering, got off with Billy. They turned the opposite way, and she hurried toward Max's door, glad that she didn't have to pass the stairwell on her way. She turned the key in the lock and then, with her hand on the knob, she stared at the entrance to the stairwell down the hall, her heart thumping hard in her chest.

The sound of the women's voices faded as they entered an apartment on the far side, and although Billy lingered for what seemed a long time, the hallway and stairwell remained deserted.

You're turning into a neurotic, Billy. What made you think the guy was after you? It might not even have been him.

She opened Max's door at last and went inside, and the sound of Max and Amanda sharing a joke of some kind banished the last traces of terror.

CHAPTER SEVEN

SEVERAL HOURS LATER, when she and Billy were in bed, Amanda quietly told her daughter-in-law about the murders and the suspicion that had fallen on the hoboes. "Naturally, the first thing I thought of was you, Billy."

"You were concerned about me being with Cosmo?"

The lamp was on beside Amanda's bed, and the soft glow illuminated her curly hair, the curve of her shoulders and breasts in her cotton nightgown. She was wearing a pair of reading glasses, half lenses that perched cheekily halfway down her nose. She looked over the top of them at Billy, a few feet away in the other bed.

They were both propped on pillows, with books in front of them, although neither was reading.

Amanda nodded. "Max has done some checking, and he reassured me that Cosmo wasn't even around at the time of the murders. All the same, dear..."

"You want me to know, and to be careful." Billy's tone was flat. She thought about the scare she'd had in the stairwell earlier that evening. She'd felt embarrassed about it and hadn't said anything to Max and Amanda. Now she wondered if she should have mentioned it, after all.

"Yes, I do. Want you to be careful. I hate sounding like a nervous Nellie—you know I'm not like that. I want you to enjoy this holiday to the fullest, but you're very dear to me, Billy. I don't want you hurt—in any way."

"Well, you can stop worrying about Cosmo being a crazed murderer. I nearly drowned all on my own in that damned ocean, and he hauled me out and then insisted on making me wave-proof. Not exactly typical behavior for a murderer, right?" She described the scene for Amanda, making it sound much more humorous than it had been at the time. "Tomorrow he's going to show me around the village and we're going to do some sketching." She grinned across at her mother-in-law. "I don't know him all that well yet, but I do know he's no murderer. So relax, okay?"

She reached across and gripped Amanda's hand. Her voice was uncharacteristically shy. "Don't get me wrong here. I never had a mother to worry about me, and it's kinda nice having you wringing your hands and stewing over who I'm out with, even if I am getting a little long in the tooth for it."

Amanda looked at her over her glasses, her eyes soft and caring. "No matter how old children get, Billy, a mother goes right on worrying about them. And I think of you as my daughter as well as my friend."

Billy had to swallow hard before she could answer. "Thanks, Amanda."

BILLY WAS SITTING cross-legged on the grass beside Cosmo the next afternoon, her sketchbook resting on her knees, her pencil lying idle on the ground beside her.

They were under a banyan tree in a park not far from the apartment building. It was hot. She could feel sweat trickling down her back, under her T-shirt and into the waistband of her shorts.

Cosmo seemed comfortable and cool. He wore clean cutoffs and a wrinkled blue sleeveless cotton shirt. He must have a thing about sleeves, Billy thought drowsily. Well, anyone with arms like his *should* wear sleeveless shirts. She loved the smooth muscles of his arms; they were pleasing to look at. She even loved the anchor tattoo on his bicep.

The heat was making her sleepy, and she listened in a pleasant daze to what Cosmo was saying. They'd been talking about drawing, about the techniques they each used to capture the images in their mind's eye and reproduce them on paper.

"I was a little kid when I first found out that if I couldn't draw something the way I wanted it to look, it helped sometimes to try to draw it upside down, like so..."

Cosmo's long, nimble fingers sketched a few quick lines, and there was an image of her, standing on her head like a yogi. He'd made her slightly cross-eyed as well as more voluptuous than she really was.

"Idiot." She gave him a friendly shove. She liked touching him.

He laughed with her, teasing, but she couldn't help but be impressed by his ability. He had an ease and a natural talent that she might have envied if she didn't have some of it herself. As it was, it formed a bond between them, this mutual delight in recreating visual images to suit themselves.

"Did you ever go to art school, Cosmo?"

He shook his head. "I had an aunt, a real eccentric, who taught me the basics when I was a little kid. And I never really had a burning desire to be a starving artist."

"You'd rather be a well-fed hobo, right?" Billy still had problems with that. Despite the fact that her own childhood had been anything but typical, she'd realized since meeting him that she had a set of middle-class values that made it difficult to accept his chosen way of life. It seemed aimless to her, unfocused.

"Yeah, something like that." He wasn't at all perturbed by her pointed remark.

"Cosmo, did you know the two hoboes who died a little while ago?"

He stopped what he was doing and looked at her, a long, level look. "Not personally, no. I've heard the other hoboes mention them, though."

"Do you think they were murdered?"

He set his paper and pencil down on the grass and gave her his full attention. "Some of the guys think they might have been. Did Max tell you about them?"

"Amanda did. Max told her. He seems to think their deaths were linked with that other murder, that poor woman who was robbed and beaten?"

He nodded, bending his head and picking up the paper again, doodling circles and intricate lines. "I heard about that, too. What exactly did Max say about it all?"

She shrugged. "Amanda says he thinks the hoboes knew something. About what happened to her. That Liza Franklin."

"Hmmm. Did he say what?"

"He doesn't know. He's just going by what this hobo friend of his told him. But now the friend's disappeared. His name was Charlie."

"Yeah, I heard about that, but I didn't know Charlie firsthand, either."

"Max is really worried about him."

"And Amanda's worried about you being with me, right?" He squinted up at her, his fingers still moving across the pad.

Billy grinned at him. "Right. How'd you guess? It's so weird, having her fuss about me. I've been on my own since I was fifteen. I can take care of myself."

He tore the sheet off and crumpled it, tossing it to the ground before he answered. "It's natural she'd be concerned, Billy. You and I may feel as if we know each other by now, but Amanda's really only met me once."

"Well, I reassured her. I told her you're after my body all right, but not the way she figures."

He shot her a look and then gave her a slow grin when he saw she was joking with him.

"Actually, Max checked up on you. Apparently he talked to the police about Charlie's disappearance and asked them about you while he was there."

"And they gave me a clean bill of health?" The words were serious, but his dark eyes were filled with humor.

"Yeah, as a matter of fact they did."

"Well, that's nice to know. Does Amanda keep tabs on who you're seeing when you're back in Vancouver, too?"

Billy's legs were starting to ache. She moved them, stretching them straight out and leaning back on her elbows in the cool, rough grass. "Absolutely not. We see each other once a week and talk on the phone in between, but this is the first time I've ever known her to be concerned about who I was seeing or anything. We respect each other's privacy."

He waited for a while before he spoke again. "You said there wasn't anybody back in Vancouver that you're serious about."

"Nope. I'd have told you if there was."

"You've been alone a long time." He was regarding her closely. "Haven't you thought about marrying again?"

The sun was coming down through the branches and spilling its heat over her body. She tipped her sunglasses down over her eyes and flopped flat on the ground. "I've had one...romantic episode—" her voice was filled with sarcasm "—since Graham died. His name was Tom—Thomas Pershell. Or so I thought. He worked at the university, in the Museum of Anthropology. He taught art appreciation at night school. He read Emily Dickinson and Yeats, and he was involved in Save the Whales and Greenpeace."

"Sounds like a real winner to me."

Billy couldn't tell if he was being serious, but she thought not.

"He was. He was also a liar. He lived in the same apartment building I did, and about five months after we'd started seeing each other, a private investigator came to my door. He worked for a woman's support group, and he'd been trying to track Tom down for more than three years. Thomas wasn't Thomas at all, you see. His real name was Douglas Evans. He had a destitute wife and two little kids back in a small town in Ontario. He'd walked out on them when he found out the baby was retarded. Tom certainly cured me of any romantic notions for a long, long time."

Cosmo sat comfortably cross-legged and listened while she talked, his expression impossible for Billy to read.

"So he lied to you."

"Did he ever. I was vulnerable and far too trusting at that point in my life." There was disgust in her voice when she added, "Any drugstore shrink could have told me I'd go straight from a jock like Graham to a gentle, sensitive con artist like Tom. Anyway, since that I've steered clear of serious involvement. There are a few guys I see now and then, but it's strictly on a friendship basis."

Cosmo was studying her with a strange, closed look on his face that made her uncomfortable.

"Do they know that—that it's only friendship?"

She shoved her glasses up and frowned at him. "For heaven's sake, Cosmo, of course they do. Usually all they want to talk about is some fight they've had with their girlfriends, anyway."

"I can't imagine any red-blooded male being around you for more than five seconds and still wanting to be just friends." His voice was almost a growl, and there was no longer a hint of laughter in his tone.

Billy felt herself flush at the intensity of his words. She closed her eyes again and listened to the timbre of his voice.

"If it's any reassurance to you, I've never been married, Billy. As far as I know, and I think my information's pretty accurate, I don't have any kids needing my support, either."

He sounded serious, and she opened her eyes and slanted a look up at his face from between half-closed lids.

"I've been pretty footloose and fancy-free, as Frisco Joe would say, but I also believe in being responsible."

"And you're honest," she added, surprising herself. "Having someone lie to you is the worst thing. It makes you doubt everything about them afterward. About yourself, too."

"I suppose it does."

There was a bleak note to his voice, but she missed it.

"Have you ever come close to marrying anyone, Cosmo?"

"Not really. Last proposal I made was to my first-grade teacher, Miss Mortimor. She was one good-looking woman. And smart, too. Why, she even knew how to read."

Billy giggled. It pleased her that Cosmo didn't have an ex-wife or two, like so many men nowadays. Although why it should matter was beyond her. She'd be flying home in three weeks and probably never see him again. The thought of leaving Hawaii and going back to her everyday life depressed her, so she shoved it out of her mind. She still had most of her holiday to enjoy, after all.

There was silence between them for a while, a comfortable, restful silence. Then Cosmo whispered, "Have you ever seen a mongoose, Billy? Sit up slowly and look over to the right."

She did. A small agile brown animal that looked a little like the weasel she'd once seen in the Stanley Park Zoo was playing at the base of a nearby tree. It had short legs and a long body, and when it turned to look at them, its eyes glowed a bright red.

"The mongooses were brought here to Kona in the early days to control the snakes. They eat rodents and snakes, and because they don't have any natural enemies in these parts, there are a lot of them around by now. They sure did their job with the snakes, though."

"Do they bite?" Aware of her bare legs and arms sprawled in the grass, she scrambled hastily to her feet.

The mongoose ran off, and Cosmo laughed.

"They're quite friendly. You don't need to be afraid of them. You'll see a fair number of them around Kona." He got to his feet beside her, picking up the paper and pencils they'd scattered around and stowing them in the backpack he'd brought along. "Let's go over to the square near the market and see if I can find anyone who wants their picture done."

For the next hour, Billy sat on a bench in the square and watched him as he talked and laughed with tourists, doing clever caricatures of them and selling his work with ease.

There was an art to this type of selling, and Cosmo had mastered it. It didn't hurt that he looked slightly Latin and extremely attractive with his dark eyes and shining hair caught back in its leather thong. In fact, he looked criminally handsome, and it wasn't surprising to Billy that a lot of the buyers were women.

First, he'd make eye contact with someone and smile at them, commenting on the sunshine. They'd stop for a moment, and he'd ask where they were from, always remarking on how beautiful he'd heard their homeland to be and usually mentioning some specific quality about it, as well. All the while, his fingers were swiftly sketching the person's face, capturing the dominant features and turning the whole into an intimate, amusing portrait. He'd hold it up when it was done.

"You just draw that? Hey, it even looks like me."

They'd examine it and invariably hand over five dollars.

Within a short time he had a crowd gathered around, waiting for caricatures.

When at least the crowd thinned and then disappeared, he got to his feet and stretched. "Now let's go get a cool drink. We've earned it. Besides, we're rich." He shouldered his backpack and tugged at her hand.

There was a juice bar in the shopping center, and he ordered them large pineapple drinks thick with fruit and ice and chunks of fresh coconut. They sat at one of the tables, sipping the delicious concoction.

After a few minutes, Billy excused herself to use the nearby bathrooms. When she returned a short while later, Ema Weiler was sitting beside Cosmo. Billy noticed again how exotically pretty Ema was. Today she wore a soft cotton skirt and matching blouse in a crimson shade that set off her dark good looks. Her silky hair was drawn up in a high chignon.

She was deep in conversation with Cosmo, but they broke off abruptly when Billy neared the table.

It made her feel bad. She hated suddenly feeling uncertain about, and if she was honest, even a little jealous of, the obvious intimacy between Cosmo and Ema. Billy told herself it was dumb of her to doubt Cosmo's assurance that he and Ema were just friends.

To counteract the feelings she couldn't control, she tried to give Ema an extrawide smile and a friendly hello, but it seemed to Billy that she sounded odd.

Ema didn't seem to notice. She greeted Billy with the same friendly openness she'd shown the previous day. "I've located a second bicycle," Ema said enthusiastically. "If you and your mother-in-law want to borrow them at any time you're most welcome. One's a man's bike, but I didn't figure you'd mind."

"Not at all. That's really kind of you."

"Uh-oh, I'd better get back to my booth. Looks like there are a couple of interested ladies over there. Duty calls. See you later."

Ema hurried off. Billy glanced at her watch and swallowed the last of her drink. "I'd better be going, too. I told Amanda I'd go grocery shopping for her this afternoon and it's getting late."

"Mind if I tag along? I like grocery shopping, and there are some things I have to pick up myself."

"Sure, come if you like. Although, how anyone can actually like grocery shopping is beyond me. I only do it because it's not quite as bad as cooking."

They strolled back toward the apartment. Billy was gradually beginning to adjust to the leisurely pace of life here in Hawaii. Walking slower, she took time to appreciate the smells of exotic flowers and trees and to notice the lavish beauty all around. The village was charming, and she'd enjoyed Cosmo's unorthodox tour earlier. In the light of day, she was certain she had overreacted to the incident in the stairwell the night before.

Cosmo took her hand in his, and Billy didn't object. The misgivings she'd felt when they were around Ema totally disappeared when she was alone with him again.

"How did you happen to grow up without a family of your own, Billy?"

They were walking close together on the narrow sidewalk, and he'd been quietly thoughtful for some time.

"Did your parents die?"

She'd been asked the same question so many times over the years that it didn't bother her much anymore. "No, my mother wasn't married. She was only sixteen when I was born, and whoever my father was, he didn't want any part of a family. She kept me a year, but I guess things got too tough, so she put me in foster care. The first foster home kept me three years, and during that time she just disappeared. She'd never signed adoption papers for me, so from then on I just went from one foster home to another." She wrinkled her nose in distaste. "I was a weird little kid. I wet the bed, had nightmares, didn't talk much. I was skinny and too tall for my age, all knees and elbows. I guess I wasn't very appealing, and there was the complication of my mother's disappearance, so I stayed a ward. None of the homes was terrible, but none of them was very wonderful, either. I know there are great foster homes out there—I've talked to other kids who got lucky—but the kind I was in, I never really belonged. I was always there on sufferance, one of a crowd of natural and foster kids. As soon as there was a problem, the foster kids were the first to go."

"Jesus. That was a hell of a way to grow up, Billy."

Cosmo's voice was thick with emotion, and she shot him a surprised glance. There was tenderness and compassion on his face, and he had her hand squeezed so tight in his own it was almost painful.

She was touched, but she was also long past feeling sorry for herself, and it amazed her that he'd be affected by the rather sordid tale of her childhood. She

forced a cheerful note into her voice. "I did get lucky
in my teens. I had a social worker who seemed to care
about me—she got me into art classes and practically
forced me to join a little theater group. I could never
bring myself to get up on a stage and act, but I loved
designing sets. I still do it for a couple of little theater
groups in Vancouver." She swung his hand back and
forth, trying to lighten the atmosphere. "And I
stopped wetting the bed somewhere along the line—
that has to be a big plus."

Cosmo didn't smile, though. They'd reached the
Kona Beach Apartments, and Billy let them in. She
couldn't help glancing over her shoulder several times
at the corner of the lobby where the blond man had
been the night before.

Of course there was no one there.

"Who are you looking for?" Cosmo was watching
Billy closely.

"Nobody. Well, nobody I know. Last night...well,
it was stupid of me, but I got nervous about a guy I
saw in the lobby. Then I thought he'd chased me up
the stairs. The elevator was stuck or something, and
there was this sort of weird-looking man over there in
the corner. I started up the stairs and...I don't
know...for some reason I got it in my head he was
chasing me. I could hear footsteps behind me and I
panicked and ran. It probably wasn't him at all."

Cosmo's voice was casual, but there was a hard note
in it. "What'd he look like?"

She described the man as well as she could, and
Cosmo didn't say anything more. When they reached
the fourth floor, they could hear voices floating up
from the swimming pool in the courtyard, and she
recognized Amanda's laughter.

Leaning over the railing, she and Cosmo yelled down a greeting. Amanda and Max were sitting close together on the edge of the pool, and they'd obviously been swimming. They waved cheerfully.

"I left a list on the table for groceries, Billy, but use your own imagination, as well," Amanda called, wrapping a towel around her shoulders. "Do you want to take potluck with us tonight, Cosmo?"

Cosmo shook his head. "Thanks, but I'm busy tonight. I'll take a rain check, though."

Billy was disappointed at his refusal. She shot him a dubious glance. Was he feeling peeved because she'd told him Max had checked him out with the police? What did a hobo have to do that was so important it forced him to turn down a dinner invitation, anyhow? But she bit back her annoyance, and within minutes they'd retrieved the shopping list and were on their way to the nearby food market.

Shopping with Cosmo was an experience.

He took a basket of his own, and at the produce counter, he smiled a greeting at the clerk. "Anything today, George?"

"Got a whole bag of cuttings for you. Drop by the back door when you leave."

At the meat counter, Billy picked out the hamburger and chops Amanda had on the list, while Cosmo politely asked the butcher if he had any meat scraps. He ended up with a huge bagful of bones with plenty of meat still on them for the ridiculous price of fifty cents.

Billy bought milk and was about to buy a loaf of packaged bread, when Cosmo stopped her.

"We'll be hitting the bakery next. They have the best bread in town."

He picked up half a dozen dented cans of spaghetti sauce, a marked-down economy-size package of pasta and a large bagful of bulk dried beans. He also bought hand soap and laundry detergent, both on sale, and a large tube of toothpaste.

When it came time to check out, his tab was nine dollars and forty-three cents, and his purchases barely fit in his roomy backpack. Billy's groceries came to thirty-nine sixty-five, and they fit into two plastic bags with room to spare.

Outside, Cosmo knocked on a door by a loading bin, and his friend George handed him out a cardboard carton stuffed with lettuce leaves, overripe tomatoes, cabbages that had begun to wilt and lots of broken-off celery stems. There were also some onions and potatoes.

"What on earth are you going to do with all that stuff?" Billy's curiosity finally got the better of her.

"Make supper, of course. I told the other 'boes I'd do them up a mulligan stew tonight. Once or twice a week we each take turns fixing a big meal for everybody." He adjusted the box so it fit under his arm. "Now to the bakery."

"I didn't know you could cook."

He raised his eyebrows at her comically. "Madam, I have lots of hidden talents that'll delight and amaze you."

"I don't doubt it."

The bakery was only a block away, and it was closing for the day when they arrived. Billy bought two loaves of heavy peasant bread, then couldn't resist a bag of dinner rolls and four pieces of wonderful-looking carrot cake.

The plump Hawaiian woman who served her obviously knew Cosmo. She greeted him warmly and went into the back, returning with an overflowing bagful of bread. "I burned a batch of rye bread on the bottom—you want it as well as the day-old?"

"Sure do, Auntie Pari. Thanks."

The woman smiled at him and threw in two dozen giant oatmeal cookies that she said were starting to go stale.

Billy paid six-eighty and Cosmo a dollar fifty.

They left the store and made their way down the street. Cosmo's arms and pack were overflowing with food, and Billy was more and more intrigued by the way he lived.

"I wish I could ask you to come and have supper with me tonight, Billy," Cosmo said suddenly. "I'd like to, but I can't. A hobo jungle's no place for a woman."

It was almost as if he'd been reading her mind. She'd been wondering, hoping, that maybe he'd invite her along, and she was let down by his words. She really wanted to go with him. She was curious about the other hoboes; she wanted to see for herself how Cosmo really lived, but she had to admit the main reason was she simply enjoyed being with him and hated to have the day end. She was having more fun with him than she'd had in years.

Maybe ever.

"It's no problem, I didn't expect you to invite me," she lied. "Besides, I'd feel sort of guilty abandoning Amanda again tonight." Then she looked up and caught his eye, and the truth came tumbling out. "I'd love to come with you if it were possible, though," she admitted ruefully.

"Look, there's time for a quick swim before I go, anyway. Why don't we take that stuff up to the apartment and you can put your suit on? We can use the little beach right across the street. It's rough lava rock, but if you wear some thongs or something it won't wreck your feet."

Max and Amanda were still by the pool, and they volunteered to help carry groceries up. Cosmo said he'd wait for Billy in the tiny park by the water. "Saves packing all this junk of mine up and then down again," he explained.

The truth was he needed some time to think.

There was a makeshift picnic table, and he slipped off his backpack, put his bundles on the table and sat down. The afternoon was waning, and the sun wasn't far from the horizon. The reflection on the water was almost blinding, and he squinted out at the ocean without really seeing anything, worrying over the man who'd frightened Billy.

Was there a connection to the murders? In his job, it was all too easy to mistake accident for menace. But what if someone was watching Max's apartment? What if Billy was in danger just by being there?

His fists clenched and a cold knot formed in his stomach, despite the heat of the tropical sun. What possible reason could anyone have for harming Billy? He struggled to be objective, to try to figure out how close they were to solving this thing.

Ema had told him that afternoon that the police investigation into Liza Franklin's death was leading to some surreptitious digging into Harrison Franklin's affairs. It seemed that Franklin was overextended financially. His wife's death and his consequent inheritance of her sizable estate would save his neck.

Convenient timing, Ema had remarked. A real co-incidence.

It turned out Franklin also had a mistress tucked away in an apartment in Waikiki. The "business" trips he made there several times a week were only a blind for romantic trysts, according to the detective who'd been tailing him.

But there was still nothing concrete to link Franklin to the murder of his wife, or to the drowning deaths of the hoboes.

There was plenty missing, such as an eyewitness or someone who could put Franklin at the scene of the crime.

If only old Boxcar Charlie would come forward with whatever it was he knew—if he was still alive. It might be enough to nail Franklin, then this whole charade that Cosmo was involved in would come to an abrupt end.

But Charlie was nowhere to be found, and try as he might, Cosmo couldn't crack the code of silence the other hoboes had drawn around whatever it was they knew. He was going to try again tonight, with the help of several bottles of wine he planned to pick up on his way back to camp. He was impatient with the whole damn thing, and he knew it was a bad way to be on an investigation.

If this case was solved, he could tell Billy the truth about himself. The burden of his real identity was becoming heavier to bear all the time, especially after the conversation they'd had about the creep she'd fallen for back in Vancouver. Cosmo's hand curled into a fist. He'd give a lot for a short session alone with the dude Billy'd known as Thomas Pershell.

Don't be so sanctimonious, hotshot. Pershell isn't the only one who's lied to Billy.

Cosmo wearily rubbed a hand over his beard. How different, really, was what he was doing to her right now? She thought he was one thing, when he was quite another. The way she tried to accept him in his role as a hobo touched him deeply. Most of the women he'd ever known would have run a mile after finding out he didn't have a car, or much spare cash, or prospects for some kind of future.

Damn it all, he couldn't even take her out to a good restaurant without looking suspicious. He couldn't take her back to his apartment, and he sure as hell couldn't take her to the hobo jungle, although he'd come awfully close to inviting her there tonight.

Romancing a lady became a real battle of wits when you were impersonating a hobo.

A grin came and went as he remembered what Ema had suggested. It was a small thing, but at least Billy would be making use of his bicycle. She wouldn't know it was his, of course.

When Ema had asked him if she could offer it to the two Vancouver women along with her own, Cosmo had been sorry he hadn't thought of it himself. It was an expensive trail bike he'd bought just before he left Seattle, and it was sitting doing nothing in the storage room at the apartment.

Hoboes didn't own things like bikes, and it made life downright inconvenient. He cast a disparaging glance at the heavy load of groceries beside him and decided he'd resort to hitching again tonight. He didn't relish the idea of walking all the way to the hobo jungle with this stuff, that was certain.

He looked over at the apartment and saw Billy come out the door, her silvery blond curls gleaming like a halo in the light. She waved at him and started across the street, pausing for traffic.

He studied her, the graceful way her lean body moved as she walked, the long, clean lines of her shapely bare legs. She was smiling at him, that captivating, wide-mouthed smile that gave her features a kind of rare beauty.

He thought of the offhand way she'd described her nightmare of a childhood, and something inside him contracted in pain. He'd wanted to fold her into his arms at that moment, assure her that nothing would hurt her ever again, because he wouldn't let it.

You're going soft, Antonelli. Nobody in their right mind would put you in charge of anyone's happy-ever-after.

"I brought us a couple of towels," Billy said as she joined him. She stripped off her oversize shirt and her shorts, revealing the blue bikini. "Do you have your swimming suit on, Cosmo?"

He watched her, loving the vulnerable shape of her near-naked body, the way her bikini clung to her breasts and hips.

"No suit, but these cutoffs are the ultimate in multipurpose beachwear." He took his shirt off and caught her hand in his, leading the way over the rough lava rock to the water. "We'll have to dive right in— the bottom drops off steeply and these rocks are treacherous."

In a moment, they were in the water. It felt cool and refreshing after the day's heat. Cosmo kept a careful eye on Billy, but she managed the waves like a pro.

When the sun was dipping close to the horizon and they'd had enough, he helped her clamber back up on the beach. He draped one of the towels over her shoulders and smoothed her dripping hair back with his fingers.

"I have to go now. I should get back to the camp before it's dark. What are your plans for tomorrow? I have some things to do during the day, but maybe we could have a dinner picnic on the beach tomorrow evening."

She was shivering a little, and he wondered if she was cold, or if it was the same reaction he experienced each time her body was close to his.

"That sounds great. I thought Amanda and I might borrow the bikes Ema offered us and ride to the swap meet in the morning."

"Good idea." He took hold of the ends of her towel and drew her into his arms. Her cool body came in contact with his own, both of them dripping wet, and he was amazed there wasn't a sizzle as heat flashed through him.

"'Night, Billy." He lowered his head and found her mouth. She tasted of salt, and he angled his lips closer, teasing until hers parted and allowed him access. His arms went around her, and he felt her small breasts pressing against his naked chest, with only the scraps of her bikini as a barrier.

He kissed her recklessly, oblivious to the traffic speeding past on the nearby highway, oblivious, as well, to the enclosed balconies along the entire front of the Kona Beach apartments and the residents gathered there at this time of day to watch the sunset.

At last, with great reluctance, he released her.

"To be continued," he whispered, and to his delight, she nodded. "Too bad this place is so public," he added as he put his shirt on and shouldered his pack, tucking the box of bread under his arm.

"Is it a long walk back to your camp, Cosmo?"

Billy's eyes were still soft and her lips swollen from his kisses. He reached out and ran a thumb over them, savoring their softness. "I'm not walking, woman. What do you take me for? I've ordered a limo, and it should be here any minute."

He winked at her, stepped to the side of the road and stuck out his thumb.

CHAPTER EIGHT

MAX AND AMANDA witnessed the passionate kiss from the lanai. They were sipping long, cold drinks Max had mixed and watching the sunset, when they caught sight of the two figures half-hidden by a palm.

Neither of them said a word. They watched as the two broke apart reluctantly and Cosmo moved out to the road to hitch a ride.

A car stopped for him almost at once, and with a final wave to Billy, Cosmo climbed in and the car drove off.

Billy stood for a while, gazing out at the sunset, then she slowly made her way back across the street.

In unspoken agreement, Amanda and Max both got up and went inside, pretending to be busy in the kitchen when she arrived.

THE HOBO JUNGLE was situated to the north of the village in an overgrown area that had been set aside as parkland but wasn't as yet developed.

Cosmo had his first ride let him off in town, where he could buy two gallons of wine. The second ride he hitched took him past the industrial park, and Cosmo asked to be dropped off near some playing fields.

He slid off the tailgate of the decrepit old truck and thanked the farmer who'd picked him up. Then he shouldered his bundles and walked along an old road

for a distance, past several parking lots, until the road
ended abruptly. There weren't many tall trees here;
instead, there were low-growing shrubs buffeted by a
constant stiff breeze off the nearby Pacific.

He made his way across the undulating sand to a
natural hollow surrounded by a growth of shoulder-
high shrubs. The hollow was about the size of a base-
ment excavation. At the lowest point, the hoboes had
built a shelter against the weather, a roomy three-sided
palm-thatched structure that held their bedrolls and
meager cooking supplies, but that was invisible to
anyone walking the nearby beach.

The ocean crashed against the shore only a few
hundred yards away, but in the hobo jungle, there was
a sense of coziness and privacy.

There were four men already there when Cosmo arrived. They were sitting around a small fire. Cosmo
called a greeting to them. Their names were Duke, Elmer, Frisco Joe and Noah. Two others, Kalani and
China Ben, had gone for a swim. Elmer assured
Cosmo they'd be back before dinner.

Duke and Elmer looked to be in their late forties,
but it was hard to tell for sure. Their faces were griz-
zled and lined from living outdoors. Frisco Joe was
younger, probably about Cosmo's age, and Noah was
much older, in his seventies. He had thinning white
hair cut short around his ears, and his shaggy beard
was also white. He was robustly healthy, with a face as
wrinkled as a walnut. He'd been a 'bo most of his life,
and Cosmo loved the stories he told around the fire at
night.

They all wore jeans, either cut off or in various
stages of disrepair, and with the exception of Noah,
their hair was long. Frisco Joe wore a braided head-

band. Most of them had the same sort of cutoff T-shirts Cosmo favored, and they wore beat-up runners or rubber sandals on their feet.

Cosmo unloaded his backpack and the box of groceries in the shelter. "You guys build up the fire," he called to the others. "I've got the makings for mulligan stew here."

Before long the fire was blazing. Cosmo cut up the meat and bacon scraps he'd scrounged and tossed them into a large bucket, along with onion, and set them to brown. Then he cleaned vegetables and added them to the pot, throwing in fresh garlic and adding the contents of several of the dented tins of tomato sauce he'd bought.

"Need some of my spices there, young feller?" Noah produced small tins of spices and carefully measured in dill weed, cayenne and a chili pepper. "Found out long ago a little spice makes a big difference to the way food tastes," he explained for the hundredth time, stowing his tins away again in his pack. Noah was proud of his spice cache and guarded it zealously.

China Ben and Kalani, native Hawaiians, soon hurried into camp. "We could smell that stew a mile away," Kalani boomed. His wide brown face was split by a characteristic grin, and his several layers of stomach overlapped his low-slung shorts.

He and China Ben weren't exactly hoboes in the wandering sense; they'd been born on the Big Island and had never left it, but they were definitely free spirits. Cosmo categorized them as latter-day hippies. They'd been invaluable to the 'boes, freely sharing their knowledge of where to fish and find wild fruit, as well as knowing who was friendly and who wasn't.

China Ben had an extensive knowledge of local folk remedies, and if any of the 'boes got sick, they turned to him for help.

Cosmo chatted with the others as he worked, giving them a rundown on the successful sale of his caricatures.

"Saw you doing them in the square today. You had a pretty gal with you," Duke remarked. "Haven't seen her around before. She live on the islands or is she just visiting?"

Cosmo explained how Billy had won a three-week holiday and had arrived to find the apartment she'd been promised already occupied. The men were sympathetic, especially when Cosmo added that Billy and Amanda didn't have money enough to stay in hotels.

"It ain't too hard for a man to make out without money over here, but it's derned tough fer a couple of ladies," Noah remarked.

"Used to be anyone could camp out safely on our beaches, but it's not like that anymore," Kalani remarked.

Cosmo told them how Max had offered to let the women share his apartment.

"He's a good dude, the professor," Duke said. "He used to come out here sometimes. Last time I spoke to him, he was real concerned about Charlie."

"Ain't we all." Noah and Duke exchanged a long, telling look.

"Anybody seen or heard from Charlie yet?" Cosmo asked casually, stirring the stew.

But everyone shook their heads, and the glances they exchanged were fearful.

"How about a little wine while we're waiting for this to cook?" Cosmo unscrewed the top of one bottle and shared it out in an effort to lighten the mood that mention of Charlie had produced.

"Boy, you musta really had a good day, buyin' wine and all."

Elmer gave Cosmo a narrow-eyed, suspicious look. He was the one hobo who hadn't entirely accepted Cosmo into the group.

"All for one and one for all, right, Elmer?" Cosmo smiled at him coolly and held up his tin cup in a mock toast.

"If you say so." Elmer downed his wine without further comment and accepted a refill.

The stew bubbled away over the fire as darkness fell, and the mouth-watering aroma wafted over the campsite.

Cosmo set a large can of coffee to boil beside the stew pot. When the food was ready, he served it out along with thick slices of bread.

"Never had but one bad stew," Noah commented. "That was back on the mainland. Some crazy 'bo from New Orleans cooked up a whole calf head, eyes and all."

Noah always dredged up his worst stories for mealtime, but they never seemed to dampen anyone's appetite. The stew, the coffee, the cookies and then the rest of the wine disappeared.

Cosmo did his best to steer the conversation to the issues he wanted to hear about, but the hoboes were reluctant to talk about the murders. What little he'd learned had been pieced together from many such conversations.

"Too much been said already. Idle talk makes trouble," Noah declared when Cosmo asked him point-blank what he figured had happened to Blackie and Slim. "What's done is done. No sense cryin' over spilt milk."

As the tropical night deepened, Noah told tales of his days on the road, and Frisco Joe hauled out his harmonica and played one haunting tune after another. The fire died down, and when the last drop of wine was gone, the men found their bedrolls and stretched out under the stars.

Cosmo lay awake a long time, staring up at the constellations, pondering the murders that had taken place within three miles of where he lay. He was no closer to solving them tonight than he'd been the day he'd arrived in the hobo camp. It was a depressing fact.

Gradually his body relaxed, and his thoughts turned to Billy. Was she sleeping by now, safe in her bed? Somehow he'd have to find a way to keep watch over her, to make sure she didn't come to any harm.

He imagined her, soft and vulnerable, her arms and legs folded, her silvery cap of hair against the pillow.

He fell asleep imagining how it would feel to crawl in beside her, curl himself around her, wake her ever so gently with his mouth and his hands...

BILLY WAS UP early the next morning. She left the apartment just after eight, went for a long walk along the waterfront and at ten made her way to the market to find Ema to see if she could arrange to borrow the bikes.

The morning was brilliant, hot and filled with birdsong and the smells of ocean and flowers and freshly brewed coffee. Everyone Billy passed smiled and spoke, commenting on the weather or just wishing her a fine morning. Good-natured friendliness and Hawaii seemed to go hand-in-hand.

The shops in the market were just opening when Billy got there. Ema had recently arrived and was busy hanging some new paintings in her stall. She greeted Billy and then asked for help with the pictures.

"Here, do you think? Or should I put this one here?" She held two small canvases for Billy to compare.

"Why not one here—" Billy indicated a different spot "—and the other right in the middle of those two? It makes for good contrast—the colors complement each other."

Ema sighed with relief and agreed. "You've got a good eye."

Billy was examining the paintings. "So have you. These are your latest?" They were vivid portrayals of sunrise over the ocean. "There's a primitive quality to your work that's strong and very unusual, Ema."

Ema looked uncomfortable. "Thank you." She reached into her cash drawer and took out some money. "Billy, you stay here and sell as many of these as you possibly can in the next five minutes. I'm going to get us coffee and pastries. I got up too late for breakfast."

She hurried off. Billy spent the time looking at the other paintings, admiring the dashes of pure color, the confident brush strokes used to depict trees and shoreline. There was a striking boldness not unlike the technique she'd admired in Cosmo's sketches. Ema was a supremely confident painter, and trained or not, she had a most distinctive style.

Ema was back in a short while with a tray overflowing with toast, fruit, muffins and pastries, as well as coffee. "I'm starving. Let's go sit over there and eat." She led the way to one of the tables. "You're not on a diet, are you? I didn't even ask if you'd had breakfast already."

Billy had eaten breakfast much earlier by herself; Amanda and Max had sat up very late the night before, watching an old movie on television, and they were still asleep when she'd left the apartment.

"I've never been on a diet in my life, and I can always eat a second breakfast," she assured Ema, accepting one of the muffins and a cup of coffee.

"My ex-husband used to say it was cheaper to clothe me than to feed me." Ema smeared jam on a piece of toast and rolled her eyes. "He had a whole inventory of stock phrases like that to suit any occasion. It was like listening to a tape play over and over. I married him four weeks after I met him, and I didn't realize I'd be listening to the same old jargon year after year." She grinned ruefully. "Actually, it turned out okay, because he met somebody who was a much better listener and dumped me two years later. What the heck does a girl know at eighteen about choosing a husband, anyhow? No wonder I screwed up."

"I know what you mean. I was nineteen when I got married, and not smart at all."

"You're a widow, right? You ever thought of getting married again?" Ema waved at several other business people and went on eating.

"Nope. Being single suits me. How about you?"

Ema shook her head as she poured cream into her coffee. "There's a guy I'm fond of, but my job's a big problem between us."

Billy's insides contracted as she immediately thought of Cosmo, but what objection would he have to what Ema did? They were both artists, after all.

Puzzled, she frowned across at the other woman. "You mean he doesn't want you to be an artist?"

Ema's glance was startled. "No. I mean, yeah. That is, he'd...he'd like me to have a more traditional job. See, he's in banking, and he has this sort of image thing."

Billy felt like reaching across and hugging Ema. Despite Cosmo's assurances, she'd still wondered about their association, but if there was some staid banker in the picture... A weight inside her lifted, leaving her feeling light and airy and elated.

"Ema, you're going to be rich and famous before long. That'll convince him an artist has the right image."

Billy smiled widely at the other woman, and Ema agreed. Then she made a suggestion that caught Billy off guard.

"You brought your art stuff over with you, didn't you, Billy?"

Billy said she had—she just hadn't seemed to have much of a chance to do anything with it yet.

"Well, get busy, do a few things, charcoal sketches or scenery or whatever turns you on, and bring them to the market. I'll show them, and if they sell, it'll mean some extra dollars in your jeans."

The idea excited Billy. "But won't you be hurting your own sales by including my work?"

Ema waved a hand dismissively. "It'll be good for business to have some variety for a change."

"Well, I'd insist on you taking commission if anything did sell."

"We'll worry about that when the time comes. Just bring me some stuff soon, and we'll see how it goes."

The conversation veered to clothes, and what it was like to live in Vancouver, and what books they liked to read. There weren't too many shoppers yet, and Ema was able to sit for the better part of an hour. By the time she returned to her booth, Ema and Billy had agreed to meet for lunch early the following week.

Hesitantly Billy asked about the bikes, and Ema promptly made a phone call to a friend with a truck, who promised to drop the bicycles off at Max's apartment within an hour.

Billy left the market feeling she'd made a good friend. Hurrying back to the apartment, she looked at the Kona street scenes with an artist's eye, framing in her mind the wonderful face of the old Oriental woman on the corner, the multiracial mix among the children being led along the street by their Hawaiian teacher, the gnarled hands and lined faces of the fishermen gossiping at the wharf. Her fingers itched for paper and charcoal.

THE BIKE RIDE OUT to the flea market was strenuous, partly because of the heat, to which Amanda and Billy were still not entirely accustomed. For Amanda, there was also the fact that she hadn't been on a bike in twenty years. The old adage was true; you never forgot how to ride one. You simply forgot how much it hurt.

Fifteen minutes into the ordeal, Amanda wasn't at all sure she was going to make it, at least not alive. Her leg muscles were cramping, her shoulders ached and her throat was parched. There was a small shopping area coming up on her left, and she called to Billy to stop.

"There must be somewhere here where we can get a cool drink. It's either that or an ambulance for me."

Billy laughed and pointed at a sign: Momi's Coffee Shop. Hot and Cold Drinks. They leaned their bikes against a rack in front of the building. There were a number of signs in the dusty window: Business for Sale the first one read. Help Wanted read the second. No Reasonable Offer Refused said the third.

"Sounds like they're getting desperate," Billy remarked. She pulled open the door and they went inside the small café.

It held four tables and a long counter, with a kitchen visible in the back. It was rundown and dingy but clean, and the round little woman behind the counter had a sweet smile and a friendly greeting for them. They ordered water and large glasses of juice, and Amanda collapsed at a counter stool to drink hers, gulping the water down first in one long draft.

"I may never get back on the infernal machine again," she groaned, savoring the sweet coolness of the mango juice.

Two workmen from a nearby construction project came in and asked for lunch. "Momi got any of that soup she usually makes?" one of them asked. "I'll have that."

"There's just ready-made sandwiches today, cheese and cold cuts over there in the cooler," the woman apologized. "I'm no cook. I'm just filling in for Momi this morning. She's not well."

The men left without buying anything, and soon Amanda and Billy were finished, as well. Amanda was sorry to leave the air-conditioned interior, but there really was no choice except to call a cab and be taken home again in disgrace. With a wistful glance back at Momi's, she got back on the bike and did her best.

By the time they'd puffed their way up the last little hill, both women were sweaty and ready for another long, cold drink and welcomed the chance to walk instead of pedal. They locked the bikes to a stand and bought more icy fruit drinks at a booth, then began to wander among the aisles of the open-air bazaar, admiring the variety of goods offered for sale.

Eelskin handbags and shoes, batik-patterned dresses, pottery, plants, flowers, jewelry, handicrafts and food of all kinds were for sale in thatch-roofed open-sided booths scattered under the shade of wide-spreading trees. There was a carnival atmosphere, with much laughter and calling back and forth from booth to booth.

The sound of music and drums echoed in the air. On a large platform under a palm-thatched roof, Hawaiian women in grass skirts and floral leis were demonstrating graceful native dances. Tourists in their uniforms of white shorts and gaily patterned shirts mingled with locals from the surrounding area.

Billy bought an assortment of shell earrings for two dollars, and Amanda found a scarlet sundress made of a silky fabric for less than ten.

"Look, Billy. There's the man Ema told us about."

At the far end of the row of booths was a table with hundreds of quartz crystals for sale, presided over by an incredibly large Hawaiian man. He was at least six foot six and must have weighed more than three hundred pounds. He wore a blue T-shirt with Aloha printed on the front, and around his neck was a huge crystal that caught and reflected the sunlight in rainbows of color. His hair was a graying mass of electrified curls. A hand-lettered sign read Futures by Tutu Kane, $5.00.

Neither Billy nor Amanda could resist. They paid, and Billy insisted Amanda go first.

Tutu Kane gave them a dimpled smile quite at odds with his homely, wrinkled face and chatted in a matter-of-fact baritone as if predicting futures was the most ordinary thing in the world.

"Ahh, Auntie, you've come from far away where sunshine is rare," he told Amanda, taking one of her hands in his gigantic paw and staring into her face.

Amanda looked a bit like a fairy godmother being held captive by a troll. Her green eyes were wide and her soft mouth open a little as she gazed up at the oracle in awe.

Billy had a hard time not breaking into giggles. That opener would do for three-quarters of the people at the bazaar today, and Amanda's sunburned nose and pale throat were a dead giveaway to the fact that she wasn't a native Hawaiian.

"But," Tutu Kane went on, "I sense that your destiny is here, Auntie, here in Hawaii, if you only have the courage to seize it. There will come a moment of choice, of decision, and this will mark a turning point in your life, a time of transition and much satisfaction. Hard work, also, but much happiness." He took Amanda's other hand and passed it over a tray of small crystals. "One will call out to you. Wear it, keep it near you, and it will help you find the way."

Amanda's fingers closed over a small, irregularly shaped stone.

Tutu Kane strung it on a chain and fastened it around her throat. "Soak it overnight in saltwater from the ocean to clear the residue of others' energy, and it will be yours as long as you need it. Then you must give it away—you will know when the time comes."

Amanda thanked him and paid for the crystal, then it was Billy's turn. Billy almost changed her mind, but she'd already paid, and it would be embarrassing to ask for her money back now. But what a racket, she thought cynically. Pay five bucks for a few sentences that made no sense at all, and get conned into paying another ten for a crystal.

Tutu Kane took Billy's hand in his. His flesh was warm, his hand smooth, and he looked into her eyes for several moments before he spoke.

Billy blinked and had to force herself not to look away. Tutu Kane had intent obsidian eyes that seemed to see into dark places in her soul. He made her feel uncomfortable and edgy, and she wished again she'd never done this.

"You, wahine."

His voice had taken on a stern tone that hadn't been there when he'd dealt with Amanda, Billy noted.

"For you, there is a man."

Billy felt irrationally disappointed. Tutu Kane had such power in his eyes, yet he resorted to the same old fortune-teller garbage. Now he'd add tall, dark and handsome, and happily every after....

"He will find that which he searches for. You will help him without knowing it, but there is much danger. Not for you, but for him. He is a warrior, and death is all around him."

Tutu Kane's voice had dropped in pitch, and the words seemed to penetrate her very pores. They were suddenly ominous to Billy, frightening. She shivered in the hot sunlight.

"Trust in your heart. Listen to the still, small voice that speaks truth. Pride and anger can cause you much harm, and him, also. If you follow your heart, there will be happiness." Almost as an afterthought, he added, "And many *keikis*—I guarantee it."

He gently released her hand and nodded, as if he were pleased with himself. When the physical contact ended, Billy felt irritated all over again.

"What the heck are *keikis?*"

He gave her a benevolent smile, ignoring her bad temper.

"Children. Many, many children."

"That'll be the day." She used to dream of having a dozen kids, but the dream had frayed and worn thin and finally died.

Amanda thanked him politely and they moved away.

Billy was still annoyed. "Well, Amanda, we just wasted ten dollars. Twenty." She'd almost forgotten Amanda's ten-dollar crystal.

"What a crook. He must have slipped up there at the end—he didn't con me into buying a crystal."

Amanda fingered the stone at her throat. "I didn't feel any pressure to buy this at all," she said softly. "At least, no pressure from him. I actually felt as if a magnet were drawing my hand toward the right one. And on some level, what he told me seemed true, strange as that sounds. I've had this curious feeling ever since we came to Hawaii that something's going to change in our lives."

"Yeah, we're both going to get heatstroke riding those damned bikes back to the apartment." Billy glanced at her watch. "Wow, we'd better get going, too. Cosmo invited me on a picnic tonight—I should have told you sooner. You didn't make any elaborate plans for dinner, did you?"

Amanda shook her head. "I rather thought you'd be going somewhere with him, so when Max invited me out to dinner, I accepted."

Billy glanced at her mother-in-law. Amanda looked exceptionally pretty, her cheeks a little sunburned and her eyes bright and rather shy. "So you and Max are dating," she teased. "That old Tutu Kane got things backward. I'll bet you're the one who's gonna end up with a man in your life, not me."

"We're *not* dating. Max and I are simply becoming good friends."

Billy smiled with understanding and squeezed Amanda's hand. "I know exactly what you mean. That's just the way I feel about Cosmo, too—that we're just good friends. Now c'mon, we're both gonna need cool showers before we can go anywhere, and it's a long ride home. I got sunburned on the ride out here today and so did you."

Amanda wondered if Billy really believed what she was saying about Cosmo. The passionate kiss she and Max had inadvertently witnessed certainly didn't seem the sort of thing good friends did together.

She and Max didn't exchange kisses like that.

Her thoughts went to Tutu Kane and his prediction about a man for Billy and many children. Somehow she put more faith in his assessment of the situation than in Billy's.

Although surely he wasn't right about the danger part.

CHAPTER NINE

THE RESTAURANT Max chose was called the Spindrifter, and it was only a short walk from the apartment. The dining room was elegant, all white linen and gleaming silver, and the building, built on pilings, seemed to hang out over the ocean. There was a long balcony, roofed but open on three sides, in the style of so many buildings in Hawaii.

Max had whistled, a long, rude, wonderful wolf whistle when Amanda had emerged from the bedroom wearing the silky bright red sundress she'd bought at the flea market. It tied around her neck, bared her arms and exposed an indecent amount of cleavage. She was getting tanned, and she knew she looked as good as she could possibly look.

Maybe a trifle better, even. She fingered the small crystal that hung at her throat, loving the cool hardness against her skin.

Excitement and pleasure filled her with delicious anticipation as the maître d' seated them right beside the window.

Well, Amanda corrected, where the window would be if there was any window. The waves were softly rolling in directly beneath her, and there was nothing but water and sky between her and the Orient, out there somewhere beyond the horizon.

The sun had just set with its usual glorious fanfare, and the ocean's colors mingled with the hot orange and red of the sunset.

"I still can't get it through my head that it's like this here every single day, even while it's pouring rain in Vancouver."

Max had his reading glasses on and was studying the menu. He smiled across at her over the top of them. "That's exactly why I prefer to be here at this time of year. In the summer, of course, it gets steamy hot and uncomfortable, then Vancouver is much the more pleasant place to be."

"The best of both worlds."

"Why not? It dawned on me rather late in life that I could have both."

Max took his glasses off and folded them, absentmindedly slipping them back into the pocket of his shirt. "Too often, we set our expectations of what life has to offer much too low. We forget how to dream, how to dare. We stay in a place because we've always lived there or because we haven't explored what else is available to us. That's something the hoboes understand, Amanda—that we don't need to anchor ourselves to any one place. We can be vagabonds if we choose."

He seemed to be thinking aloud now, and he settled back in his chair. "You see, before my marriage broke up, I was the epitome of a stodgy-old-stick-in-the-mud. Being dumped by Fran at least shook me out of my safe little world, and I began to realize there were all sorts of ways I could live my life, all sorts of places I could choose, here or back in Vancouver or anywhere else in the world that took my fancy. That's probably why I find the hoboes fascinating, because they seem to be born knowing what it took me years and a painful divorce to learn.''

The waiter arrived, and Amanda absently ordered the fresh fish he suggested. While Max inquired about wine, she pondered what he'd just said. His words made her more than a little uncomfortable, because she had to admit she was guilty of exactly what he'd described. She'd allowed her world to be defined in narrow terms.

The waiter left, and she told Max what she was thinking.

"You know, I've never given any thought even to moving out of the house John and I lived in all those years," she mused aloud. "There's absolutely no reason why I couldn't. I just never thought of it as a possibility. We'd always lived there, so I just went on. I've become a creature of habit, simply because John was.''

"You've never told me much about your husband, Amanda. What did he do? What kind of man was he?''

Amanda's eyes skidded away from Max and she looked out over the water. "John was an accountant, a big, quiet, easygoing man on the surface, but underneath, he was quite ... controlling, I guess you'd say. He spoiled our son, which I thought was wrong, but he refused to listen much to what I thought. He didn't want me to work—at least, not in the sense of having a career. The job at The Book Bin was only part-time at first, but he wasn't happy about it at all.''

Max nodded sympathetically. "A lot of guys in my age group are like that. Fran had some money of her own and never really wanted a career, so it wasn't an issue with us. And if she had, it really wouldn't have bothered me. My mother was a doctor—she worked in an age when it wasn't the thing for a woman to do at all."

The waiter came and poured the wine, and when he left again Max said, "Did you ever want a career, Amanda? What sort of work would you have chosen?"

She sipped her wine, a little shy now at revealing something she'd never discussed with anyone. "It's silly, I know, but I always dreamed of owning a little restaurant, a cozy sort of place where I'd serve home-cooked meals with nice soup and fresh bread and apple pie."

"Sounds like every bachelor's dream café. Did you ever talk to John about it, really try to attain it?"

"Oh, I mentioned it once or twice, when Graham was a teenager. But John insisted there wasn't enough money to take a gamble on something like that." Her voice was scornful, and she couldn't help it. "He was quite willing to gamble on other things, however, as I found out after he'd died. For all his ability with numbers, John wasn't good at managing our money. He made one bad investment after another, most of which I didn't know about. At the time of his death, even our house had a mortgage on it. I didn't know the full extent of it all until after he died and then I was horrified at the amount of money we owed. Angry, too. Insurance covered some, but it's taken me five years of scrimping to pay the rest off."

A vibrant young Hawaiian girl came by with a huge tray of intriguing hors d'oeuvres. "Aloha, folks. Care for *pupus?* They come with the meal."

"What a good idea. Thank you."

Amanda chose several tiny pieces of fruit, papaya and mango, cut into squares and threaded on skewers. Max had oysters arranged on shells with bits of lemon.

"Were you ever able to forgive him?" Max asked when the girl left.

Amanda thought about it. "The money, yes," she said slowly. "The mistakes he made weren't deliberate, even though he should have discussed what he was doing with me. But our son..." Anguish still seeped through her when she thought of Graham. "John encouraged Graham to be selfish. He gave him far too much and didn't teach him responsibility. It's hard to forgive John for that—or myself, either. I should have fought harder for the things I believed were important. It hurts to admit it, but my son was a selfish, thoughtless young man."

Max leaned across the table and took her hand for a moment. "What's done is done. The hardest thing to do is to forgive ourselves for our own mistakes, but it's also the most important thing. We have to learn to move on without tripping over all that old rubbish."

Amanda blinked away the tears that had clouded her eyes. "You're a wise man, Max."

He gave her a broad wink. "Age and hindsight are a deadly combination. They make wise men out of total fools."

THEY STROLLED along the waterfront an hour later, feeling pleasantly full after the delicious meal.

The town seemed to come alive after dark. All the shops stayed open late, and tourists and locals alike crowded the streets, enjoying the relative coolness of the evening.

In a church hall, a group of people were singing traditional Hawaiian songs, and their voices floated out and mingled with the drumbeats and dramatic rhythm resounding from the nightly hula show at Kimo's Restaurant, barely a block away.

Darkness seemed to intensify the scent of jasmine and hibiscus, and the sounds of laughter and conversation floated on the sultry air, mingling with the ever-present muted roar of the surf. They'd been strolling rather aimlessly, not talking much, when suddenly Max made a grab for Amanda's hand, capturing it in his own and drawing her closer to his side.

"Oh, God," he groaned. "We're for it now—the Brigade's on the prowl."

Coming toward them were four women, walking two by two. As they drew nearer, Amanda recognized Daisy Seibert.

"Well, Max, good evening," Daisy called. With much less enthusiasm, she added, "Hello again, Amelia."

"Amanda," Max corrected with an easy smile. He made the introductions. "Amanda Reece, this is Rebecca Monk, Susie Laudon and Sheila Evenbough."

Rebecca was dark and heavy. Susie was tall and thin and rather anemic looking, but Sheila was beautiful. She had the slender body and perfect features of a beauty queen, albeit an aging one, and it was obvious she devoted a great deal of time to taking care of herself. Her hair was expertly cut, and her dress was both classically simple and expensive.

Amanda felt herself being taken apart and put together again as the women appraised her clothing, makeup, hairdo, shoes and jewelry, and for all she knew, searched for signs of cosmetic surgery in the bargain.

"Just out for a stroll, are you, Max?" Daisy batted her eyes and smiled at him.

Amanda was amused by the lipstick smudges on the woman's front teeth. Everything about her was matched as perfectly as it had been the first time Amanda met her, except that tonight Daisy was wearing navy blue instead of red. Her earrings, hose and shoes were the exact shade of her trouser suit.

"Care to join us for coffee and dessert? We're being naughty—we're going to Gelato Tropico for some of their home-made ice cream."

"Actually, we just finished dinner a short while ago," Max explained. "We couldn't eat another thing."

"Where'd you go?"

Rebecca's voice didn't match her girth. It was girlish and thin, almost a child's voice, Amanda decided.

"The Spindrifter." Max slid an arm around Amanda's waist. "It was a pleasant meal, wasn't it, darling?"

Darling? Amanda almost choked on her reply. "It was very...romantic," she managed. She felt Max's arm on her waist tighten almost imperceptibly, signaling his approval of her choice of words.

Daisy's chin lifted several inches, and she sniffed in disdain. "Well, I've heard the service there had deteriorated recently."

"Not that we noticed. We were favorably impressed, weren't we, Amanda?"

Amanda smiled up at Max, wondering if she could possibly manage a simper or two without breaking into gales of laughter. "Very impressed. It was delightful."

"Well," Max said briskly. "We mustn't keep you, ladies. Enjoy your ice cream."

"Max—" Sheila laid a slender, beringed hand on his arm and gazed up into his eyes "—you haven't forgotten happy hour is at my apartment tomorrow afternoon, have you?"

Sheila's voice was soft and breathy, and Amanda could smell her perfume. It was potent and expensive.

"Damn!" Max snapped his fingers and looked apologetic. "As a matter of fact it slipped my mind, and now I've made plans to drive Amanda and Billy out to the Nut Factory for the free tour they offer. We won't make it back in time, I'm afraid. I apologize, Sheila. Maybe another time?"

There was ominous silence behind them when Max and Amanda walked away, which was followed by indecipherable angry buzzing as the distance between them and the Matrimonial Brigade widened.

Max shook out a snowy handkerchief and wiped his brow. "Whew. Now you know what I'm up against, Amanda."

"The Nut Factory? Max, did you make that up?"

He tucked his handkerchief back in his pocket and released his hold on her waist. "Absolutely not. The Macadamia Nut Factory is alive and well and living in Honokaa. It's only a short drive from here. We could actually go if you wanted."

"I've never really longed to visit a nut factory. You're off the hook, you sweet-talker you."

They walked on in silence until Amanda said, "That Sheila Evenbough is a gorgeous-looking woman. Are you quite sure you'd rather not stop running and just let her catch you?"

He shot her an appalled look. "Sheila? Amanda, Sheila is the worst of the whole lot. She's been married three times that I know of. God knows what became of the poor guys. All she talks about is how wealthy they were and how much they loved dear little her and how all alone she is in this great big mean old world. She's a little too cute for my blood, I'll tell you. I actually heard her ask a waiter for the 'tinkle room' when I got roped into taking her out one day. I was utterly humiliated. The 'tinkle room,' for heaven's sake. Amanda, if a woman her age can't ask for the bathroom in everyday plain English, what hope is there for mankind?" His face was a study in outrage.

She couldn't help it. She started laughing and couldn't stop. She laughed so hard she had to lean on the seawall to hold herself up. Max looked puzzled at first, but then he gave a hearty guffaw, and soon he was laughing as hard as she. Passersby stared at them and smiled and went on.

"Max." Amanda finally managed to control herself enough to speak. "Max, I hate to tell you this, but unless you get me to a 'tinkle room' in the very immediate future, I won't answer for the consequences."

He grabbed her arm and hurried her off.

THE FIRE COSMO BUILT glowed red and golden against the sand. The breeze that had been blowing earlier had died away, and stillness blanketed the isolated cove.

The thick foliage surrounding the small inlet had been alive with bird sounds an hour before, but now only an occasional burst of song came from some sleepy bird settling in for the night. The only other noise was the constant rolling in and washing away of the tide.

They'd finished eating and were sitting close together on the blanket Billy had thought to bring, staring out at the dark Pacific. Cosmo's arm was around her shoulders, and Billy was digging her bare toes into the cool sand. She was full of delicious food, aware of Cosmo's arm and totally happy.

It was early, but the tropical darkness had already descended over the deserted little beach. No moon or stars had yet appeared, and there was a feeling of total isolation to the scene.

"I feel a little like Robinson Crusoe," Billy said with a contented sigh.

"Does that make me your man Friday?"

Cosmo's voice had been a pleasant rumble, inches from her ear. "I'm not sure Friday was as good a cook as you are," she answered. "Where'd you learn to make fish like that?"

He'd filleted some kind of small local fish and skewered them to pieces of wood set upright in the sand close to the fire. He'd wrapped potatoes, onions and carrots in foil and set them to roast in the coals, then he'd taken Billy swimming in the surf. When they'd come out, their dinner was waiting, the fish smoked and succulent, everything tasting twice as good for being cooked over an open fire.

"It's a method I learned from the Native American Indians who live around Seattle."

"Did you hang around with them when you were growing up?"

"I had a friend who was Indian. He's a great guy. He taught me a lot about survival skills, and I taught him to draw."

"Upside down, doubtless."

"Absolutely."

"Do you still keep in touch with him?"

"Yeah, I do. He's a fisherman. We exchange post-cards once in a while."

"It must be lonely, living the way you do, moving from place to place all the time and leaving all the people you meet behind."

"It comes with the territory. I guess if it bothered me, I wouldn't be a hobo. I'm not often lonely. What about you, Billy? Are you lonely?"

She thought about it for a while. "Not anymore—or at least, not often anymore. I was really lonely as a kid, but the very worst was when I was married, isn't that weird?" She stared down at her toes for a moment. "I guess I always figured marriage was insur-ance—you had a built-in best friend, you always had somebody to talk with, you weren't ever alone any-more. It didn't turn out that way for me. I realized I really didn't have that much in common with Gra-ham, and he wasn't around very often, either." She knew she sounded bitter, but she couldn't help it.

"Even when he was there, we did more arguing than talking. It was a big shock to find out you could be way more lonely living with someone than you ever were by yourself."

Cosmo tightened his arm around her. "I've noticed that, too, with some people. Tell me, Billy, are you lonely when you're with me?"

She turned to look at him. "With you? Never. There's always something to argue over or discuss. But maybe that's just because this is a strange country and I'm on holiday and we haven't known each other long. Of course our backgrounds are different. And then there's the fact that—"

"Hush." He put a finger on her lips, silencing her. "Don't complicate it when it's really simple. There's just this great thing between us. I told you the night we met that I felt it. I was attracted to you, I wanted to know you better, and you admitted you felt the same. For me, all those feelings have gotten stronger."

Her voice was almost a whisper. "For me, too."

His voice was rough, urgent. "You know I want you, Billy. I want to make love with you. I've wanted that from the beginning."

His forthright words were an invitation, a question.

She swallowed hard. She'd known this time was coming; she'd fantasized and wondered about it. Now that it was a reality, she was uncertain and shy.

"It's only been a few days..."

"We only have a few days. Let's not waste them, okay?"

What he'd said was true. The limited hours of her time here in Hawaii were rushing past. Soon there'd be only two weeks left, then one, then...

This is your dream holiday, a voice inside urged. *Dream holidays include romance. This is once in a lifetime, Billy.*

If only it were that simple. But the emotions Cosmo stirred in her weren't simple at all.

He turned her deftly, so that she was lying across his chest, cradled in his arms. His lips found hers, but the kiss was gentle, tentative. His hand skimmed down her arm, touched her breast, as light as the breeze off the ocean.

"You're trembling. You're not scared of me, Billy?"

"No." She was scared of herself, scared of the way he made her feel.

"You want me to back off?"

She could feel the roughness of his chest hair against her cheek, the way his heart was pounding.

The same way hers was.

"No." Her lips tingled from his kiss; her body felt warm and fluid with his nearness. She didn't want him to stop. She didn't know exactly what she wanted.

"We'll go slow. If you want me to stop, just say so."

He touched her with his lips again, and this time the kiss was deep and long. His tongue met hers, and her heart bumped with recognition.

About a quarter of the way through that kiss, Billy forgot to be nervous and slid her hands away from Cosmo's waist and let them glide up and down his chest, relishing the texture of him, the way his hard muscles quivered at her touch. She'd wanted to touch him like this, to explore the breadth of his shoulders, his jawline, his ears.

She buried her fingers in his long hair. It was springy and rough from the saltwater, but his beard was soft, caressing her face. He smelled like the ocean and also a little like woodsmoke, from the fire, but there was also a personal, clean masculine scent to his skin, and she drew it into her lungs.

Neither of them was wearing much clothing. She had her bikini on under a short cotton T-shirt dress, and he wore only cutoffs. His hands glided down her body, lingering on the bare skin of her thighs, moving back up to outline her hips and waist. Everywhere he touched tingled and glowed.

"You're so smooth and soft," he murmured, trailing kisses down her throat and along the neckline of her dress, his beard tickling tender flesh. "My hands are rough. I'm sorry."

She wanted to tell him she loved the feeling of those hard, callused hands on her body, but he was kissing her again, long, drugging kisses that left her restless, aching for more.

He eased her down on the blanket, angling his strong body half over hers.

She gazed at the sky. The moon was up, and the stars were bright. She could see the outline of a palm tree against the heavens, and suddenly it felt right, absolutely right, to be here with him in this way.

Their kisses were greedy now, a sensual exploration of lips and tongue that sought more, sought deeper. Her nipples peaked, and her body yearned for his touch. He slid a hand under the hem of her dress, letting his fingers glide over her thigh, explore the tender skin of her flat belly, find the indentation of her waist. Then one gentle hand closed over her small breast, still covered by the flimsy bikini top. He drew circles with his palm, slow and sensuous, rubbing the cotton against her nipple, rubbing until she surged up to meet his hand and vivid tongues of desire shot through her from breast to abdomen.

"You feel so good, so very good."

His voice was a warm sigh in between kisses, feverish kisses, hot and sucking and wet kisses she returned with nothing held in reserve.

His hand traced a path down her body, finding the spot where bikini bottom pressed against damp, feminine need, and she raised herself to meet his touch, aware of her own flaming desire and of his tumescence, sheathed inside his cutoffs but straining hard against her side.

She could feel his heart, pounding like a drumbeat, sounding a rhythm that echoed the chaos inside of her. He looped his fingers under the top edge of her bikini bottoms and slowly tugged them down her legs. She kicked the scrap of fabric free, glad to be rid of its constraint. The air was cool against her bare skin, and the moon shimmered silver light over them.

"Your turn."

She sat up and fumbled for the button at the waist of his cutoffs, found it and released it. He drew in a deep, shaky breath, but he didn't offer to help. She located the zipper tab and began to tug the denim down, but it stuck at his hips. Impatient, his hands covered hers, and together they worked the garment down and off his long, muscular legs.

He was like a pagan god in the moonlight, dark and tall and well made, infinitely strong, his swollen body unashamedly yearning for hers. He was her vagabond lover, the figure in all her imaginings, the faceless hero of every erotic dream.

"Now you." He took the hem of her dress and drew it smoothly up and over her head. His fingers found and undid the clasp of her bikini bra, and now she was as naked as he.

He reached out and touched her breast with his hands, wonderfully tender, reverent, his dark eyes unfathomable in the moonlight, his body taut with need but controlled, conscious of her desires,

"I knew you'd look like this, fragile, incredibly beautiful."

"Skinny and flat chested," she denied in a shaky voice.

"Slender and perfect," he corrected in a growl.

Then he dipped his head and caught her nipples in his teeth, first one and then the other, teasing, laving each with his tongue. She gasped and made a pleading sound in her throat as delightful sensation shot through her. He eased her down on the blanket, kissing her eyelids, her mouth, murmuring his need in a deep, intense whisper as his lips sought out her ears, her throat. Then his mouth traveled down, to her breasts, her navel, and still down, lingering at her center until she hovered on the edge of rapture.

"Cosmo, please..." Her fingers tangled deep in his hair, entreating him to join her.

"Patience, sweetheart..." He drew away for a moment, fumbling in the pocket of his cutoffs, finding the small packet that would protect her.

"Let me," she whispered, amazed at her own boldness even as passion dictated her actions.

She longed to touch him, and he trembled when her hand came in contact with his flesh. A moan rose from the back of his throat as her fingers closed around him.

"Billy, my sweet, beautiful Billy."

The ocean seemed louder, the incoming tide sweeping the sand and retreating under the spill of liquid silver from the moon. The pale light cast shadows on the sand as he placed the length of his body on hers, and the delight of having all of him against her, naked skin to naked skin, made her shudder.

"That feels so good..."

"I'll make it even better. Hold on to me, Billy."

Her arms slid up around his neck, and her legs encircled his hips.

His head blotted out the moon. He slid inside her, and it seemed as if the ocean waves caught her fast in their rhythm, their endless surge and withdrawal becoming all that she knew or cared to know. There was a wild abandon in his loving now, and that sense of rightness that she'd felt at the start intensified, clarified.

Just as he'd claimed, there was something, some magic, between them, some old and ancient attraction that made it right, this coming together. She was finally where she longed to be, in a space where she belonged with the man some part of her had waited for all these years.

She wanted to tell him, but he thrust deep, and the cry of release that poured from her throat caught her unawares.

It was joined a moment later by his deep growl of triumphant ecstasy.

COSMO LAY WITH HER in his arms, aware that he'd taken another step along a path he'd never walked before. Sex had always been one of the greatest parts of being an adult, a marvelous game two people played together, giving and receiving all the pleasure bodies could inspire and fertile imaginations could devise. But that was all it was: a delightful game, necessary, consuming while it lasted, soon forgotten when it was done.

He hadn't known this other place existed, this... plateau ... where souls communicated, where it was inconceivable to think of holding anyone but this one person again. There was a name for the feeling he had for Billy, but he wasn't ready to mouth it, even to himself. He'd denied its existence for so long, he couldn't now adjust to the fact that it had happened to him.

And happened now, of all times, when he wasn't even free to be himself. More than ever before, he wanted trust and honesty and integrity to be the guideposts for his actions, for his relationship with her.

What could he say to her that was truly honest?

Trust me, Billy, I'm lying to you about who I am and what I do, but it's for a good cause?

Surprise, Billy, I've got a respectable bank account and a car on the mainland and the use of an apartment here in Kona with a perfectly good bed where we could be right now, instead of out here getting sand in every orifice of our bodies?

Except I have to pretend that none of it exists, and therefore you have to pretend with me.

He wrapped her closer, shielding her with his body from the breeze that had started to blow off the water.

All he could do for her right now was protect her from the truth about himself. All he could give her was the pleasure his body afforded, the small amusements his wits could provide.

It would have to be enough until some later time.

He'd make it up to her. It would probably take a lifetime, but that was starting to sound feasible.

"COSMO?"

She'd been floating in and out of sleep, lost in a glorious place filled with peace and tranquillity. She was curled like a spoon in his embrace, his arms locking her tight to his body, but a cool wind dictated the need to move, to pull on clothing again.

"Is there any coffee left, do you think?"

His mouth was close to her ear, and his voice rumbled pleasantly. "At least two cups. Want some? I'll build up the fire and heat it up." He ran his hand in a last lingering caress down her side, and she felt him press a kiss into the nape of her neck.

Reluctantly they sat up, pulled on clothing, added driftwood to the embers of the fire. Cosmo filled two cups with the remnants of the coffee and handed her one, pulling her against him so her back rested on his chest.

"Is it late?" She hadn't worn her watch, content to let the hours pass unmarked.

"About eleven, I'd say."

"Can you tell by the moon?"

"Pretty much. And the tide. It was coming in when we were eating—it's full now."

The waves were rolling in, heavy and slow, crashing on the sand. To the west the moon disclosed an endless, eerie expanse of ocean that blurred and blended into pewter sky.

"I suppose I should be getting back pretty soon." She didn't want to. She wanted to curl up again on the blanket, sleep under the stars in Cosmo's arms, wake with him at dawn and watch the sun come up.

"Billy."

His arm tightened around her, and her heart gave a jolt at the seriousness of his voice. But all he finally said was "No regrets?"

She tilted her head so her lips brushed his cheek, just above his beard. "Absolutely no regrets." She forced a light, teasing tone into her voice. "Every woman dreams of making love on a deserted beach under a tropical moon, with a handsome, mysterious stranger. Don't you know that?''

"Am I? A stranger to you still?"

He was serious, and she dropped the teasing tone. "In some ways, yes. In others, I feel you never were."

He sighed. "We'll have to change that—the stranger part."

They gathered up their things in silence and doused the fire. When they were leaving, Billy stood for a moment, looking back at the little cove. Did places retain the energy of the people who'd inhabited them? If so, this cove would always hold the essence of her and Cosmo.

They walked back to the highway. It was a long walk, but Cosmo had a flashlight, and he shone it so Billy could see the path. There was a service station a few hundred feet down the road. When they reached it, Cosmo phoned for a cab, and when it arrived, he put Billy in, paid the driver and gave him her address. He'd explained earlier that the hobo jungle wasn't far from where they were, so parting this way made the most sense.

He kissed her through the open window, a soft, reluctant leave-taking. "I have things to do all morning tomorrow, but I'll see you in the afternoon if you're going to be around."

"Amanda wants to explore the old churches in town, then we're going to try the beach near the King Kamehameha Hotel. She hasn't been swimming anywhere but in the pool, and that beach is protected from the breakers."

"Fine. I'll look for you there."

She waved as the cab pulled away. Cosmo was a solitary figure under the lights of the filling station. He returned her wave and then shouldered his backpack.

The cab rounded a curve, and she didn't see him head for the lit phone booth, pick up the receiver and dial.

THE JOY THAT HAD FILLED Billy a moment before seemed to ebb away, leaving depression and emptiness in its place as the cab sped along the highway.

Making love with Cosmo had been a mistake—she could see that now. Before, she'd been able to rationalize the feelings he stirred in her. Some part of her had believed she could view him as a holiday romance, separate from the rest of her life.

After all, he chose to be a hobo. Being with him was an artistic bohemian adventure, wasn't it? It wasn't real; it wasn't part of her everyday, ordinary life. This was Hawaii, a place so separate and foreign to her experience that anything could happen...on a short-term basis. Anything more than that was unthinkable.

When it came to a real relationship, she needed far more stability in a man than Cosmo offered...or so she tried to convince herself.

There was also something she hated to admit. Somewhere inside her, a snobbish little voice whispered that she could always feel a tiny bit superior to Cosmo, because of what he was.

A hobo, after all.

Self-disgust overwhelmed her. How could she be so condescending, pretending to a sophistication she'd never possessed—never wanted to possess? Well, her snobbishness had backfired on her now. She was shaken, badly off balance, because in the past few hours her feelings for Cosmo had become crystal-clear.

Cosmo was the sort of man she'd dreamed of meeting, back when she'd allowed dreams to seem possible. She could see that whatever Cosmo did with his life, who he chose to be, was unimportant. It was the man who mattered to her, the warm, caring, wonderfully loving person underneath the hobo persona, the strong, confident man who made her feel cherished and beautiful, protected and nurtured. And he had taught her also how to have fun, how to play like a child in a way she'd never been child enough to do before.

Making love with him had stripped away the illusions, the barriers she'd created. The problem now was the reality.

She was in grave danger of falling in love with Cosmo, and if she allowed that to happen, she was going to get hurt.

Destroyed, maybe.

She'd promised herself she wouldn't let that happen ever again. After Graham's death, and then again after Thomas, she'd tumbled into a black abyss. Like Humpty-Dumpty, how many times could she put herself back together again after these emotional falls?

The cab stopped in front of the apartment, and she responded automatically to the driver's cheerful goodnight.

She used her key and let herself in. There were three people waiting for the elevator, and she felt a vague sense of relief as she joined them. She glanced around the lobby, and of course there was no one there. The elevator came, and she got on with the others, her thoughts again on Cosmo.

She'd spent almost all day, every day with him since she'd arrived in Hawaii. Being with him was potent, a heady, habit-forming drug that made her feel incomplete and empty when she was alone. She was beginning to rely on him far too much. She was going to have to distance herself from him, learn to fill her days apart from him. She'd been neglecting Amanda, selfishly spending every moment she could steal with Cosmo.

Well, that was over now. As of tomorrow, she'd begin painting with a vengeance. She'd take Ema up on her generous offer to show some of her work. Besides that, she'd plan excursions with Amanda, trips and tours that they could make together. That would fill the days until it was time to go home.

The resolve made her feel desolate.

CHAPTER TEN

BILLY WAS HOPING Amanda and Max would have gone to their respective beds before she got home, but she could hear them having an animated discussion interspersed with bouts of laughter when she unlocked the door of the apartment.

Those two seemed to laugh more than any people she'd been around.

Except for her and Cosmo.

She tried to paste a nonchalant, happy expression on her face as she entered the living room, where they were sitting.

They both glanced up at her and smiled a greeting, and she noticed how pretty and happy Amanda looked. She ought to wear red more often.

"Hi, Billy. How was your picnic?"

Billy described the food Cosmo had prepared, the lovely place he'd chosen, the way he'd smoked the fish beside the campfire. It exhausted her, having to sound lighthearted and enthusiastic, having to leave out the really earthshaking events of the evening.

Amanda listened the way she always did, as if there were nothing she wanted to hear more than what Billy was relating.

"How about you two? How was your dinner?" Billy asked in turn.

Max and Amanda looked at each other and laughed.

"It was delicious—the whole evening was delicious," Amanda declared. "And, Billy, guess what?" Amanda had bright spots of color in her cheeks, and her eyes were bright with excitement.

Billy shook her head and held her hands up. "I give up. What?"

"Max has to do some research for a paper he's working on, and he's invited me to come with him on a trip around the entire island. We'll be gone for four days—we'll leave tomorrow afternoon. I know you and I had planned to go to the beach, but I was sure you wouldn't mind if we skipped it."

"Would you like to come with us, Billy?"

Max's invitation was impeccably polite, but Billy instinctively knew he was hoping against hope that she would refuse. It was evident in the way he talked to Amanda, the way his glance lingered on her when he spoke.

It suddenly dawned on Billy that there was something happening between those two that she'd failed to recognize till now, caught up as she was in her own romance.

There was an awareness, a compatibility, a sharing of humor and an air of closeness that she recognized all too well. It hurt to see it, to recognize in them what she herself would lose when she had to leave Cosmo.

"Thanks, Max, but I'd much rather stay here, if you don't mind. I've..." Billy swallowed and managed the lie with nonchalant ease as she gave up the mental plans she'd made for spending the remaining days of her holiday with Amanda. "I've made plans with Cosmo for the next few days, and...and Ema and

I are going to have lunch, and . . . she's asked me to do some paintings to show in her booth."

"That's a great idea. I'm glad she offered. I'll bet your work will be a big hit. We'll miss you, but as long as you're busy . . ."

Max managed not to sound relieved, even though Billy knew he was.

"We figured you'd probably have a full schedule of things you'd rather do than tag along with a couple of old fogies like us. Stay here by all means. Make yourself totally at home. Ask your friends up to the apartment anytime you like."

"Thanks, Max. Thanks a lot. You're really kind. Now—" she stretched ostentatiously and faked a huge yawn "—if you'll excuse me, I think I'll head for bed."

"There's an old Garbo movie coming on, and we're going to watch it for a while. Good night, Billy," Amanda called as Billy headed for their room.

"'Night." She closed the bedroom door and let the smile fade from her lips. She went into the bathroom, dropping her clothes in a heap on the floor. The hot sting of the shower poured over her, and she realized she was trembling.

Tears began to leak slowly from her eyes, and the sound of the water muffled the sobbing breaths she took.

The intimacy she sensed between Max and Amanda, the decision she'd made about avoiding Cosmo, combined in a welling up of old, confused pain. She was alone again. She'd always been alone, standing outside other people's happiness and looking in wistfully.

As a child, she'd always been an outsider, a temporary visitor in the homes in which she was placed. She'd longed desperately for someone to love her, someone who'd put her first in their heart. She'd thought these past few years that she'd outgrown that childish need, but tonight it was there again.

Those exquisite moments of lovemaking tonight with Cosmo had tricked her, made her believe for just a little while that she wasn't alone, that there really was another half to the jagged edges of her lonely soul.

But of course it was illusion. When would she ever learn that for her, love and happily-ever-after were just not part of her destiny?

SHE WAVED GOODBYE cheerfully from the lanai the following afternoon as Max and Amanda drove off in Max's jaunty red Jeep.

What was she going to do with herself for the rest of the day? For the rest of the four days until they came back, for that matter? The apartment suddenly seemed desolate, empty and uninviting.

She could go to the beach, the way she and Amanda had planned. But Cosmo would be looking for her there, and difficult as it was, she was determined to stick to her resolve, to stay away from him as much as possible from now on.

The bikes Ema had loaned them were downstairs, locked in Max's storage area, and suddenly Billy felt the need for physical action. Perhaps exhaustion would take away the despair growing inside her.

She grabbed an apple and several bananas, tossing them into a paper bag along with a sandwich and a can of juice.

She'd ride the damned bike until physical exertion brought some measure of peace.

COSMO'S EYES swept across the clusters of people basking in the intense heat of the afternoon sun near the King Kamehameha Hotel.

There was no sign of Billy and Amanda, and this was the third time he'd checked. He'd walked through the open corridors of the hotel itself, thinking that perhaps they were exploring the dozens of boutiques inside the massive structure, but they were nowhere to be found.

He hung around for a while, waiting and watching the people drifting along the seawall walk, but there was still no sign of them, and an hour had passed since he'd arrived. He walked through the village to the shopping center and made his way to Ema's booth.

As usual, there were people looking at the pictures he'd painted, and he passed the time by wandering through the center, keeping an eye out for Billy and Amanda. By the time he'd returned to Ema's, she was alone.

"What's new?" he queried, lounging nonchalantly on the post at the side of her stall.

"The department's taking bets that you'll retire from the force and become a street artist when this is over. You're earning far more than your wages on these damned paintings."

"I'm giving it serious consideration." He thought of himself and Billy on the sand the evening before. "At least that way I could sleep in a bed again and have the luxury of a bathroom with running water and even a shower."

"Aha, I detect a note of dissatisfaction here. This back-to-nature stuff's finally getting you down, huh? I knew all this romantic talk about the carefree life of a hobo was a load of propaganda."

"What's getting me down is not having a break in this case. I spent all morning on a wild-goose chase, tracking down an old coot up in the hills above town that somebody thought might be Charlie. Needless to say, he wasn't. And the temperature out there must be setting records. I felt like I was getting parboiled in that sun."

"It's record heat, all right. I heard on the radio. So who was this guy?"

Cosmo frowned. "Some poor soul who's fried his brains on drugs and alcohol. He lives up there in a shack. He figures he's a paratrooper, and he jumped out at me from behind a tree, carrying a loaded shotgun. Scared the living hell out of me, and then, when he decided I wasn't the enemy, he took a liking to me, which was another calamity. He insisted on sharing his pot and God knows what else. I had to convince him I was a religious fanatic to keep him from forcing drugs down my throat."

Ema was heartless enough to laugh. "You could've just told him you were a cop and let him put you out of your misery."

"Don't think I didn't consider it. Speaking of misery, what's shaking with this Franklin thing, anyhow?"

"Lots. Our guys have dug up a load of garbage on Harrison Franklin like you wouldn't believe," Ema confided. "He has some interesting ties with a few of the local Mafia types, and now they figure he was pressuring his wife for the deed to the parkland that adjoins the estate her father left her. He had all the plans drawn up to build high-rise apartments there, but according to one of his secretaries—whom he had an affair with, by the way, and who's talking to us because Franklin dumped her—Liza wasn't happy about his plans for development. She'd always given in before—most of the land her father left her is now part of Franklin Developments—but this park meant a lot to her. It's next to the estate where she grew up, and her father wanted it left as a park for everyone to enjoy. According to some of the household help and this secretary, Franklin and Liza had some pretty vicious fights over it."

"But nobody's come forward and actually said they saw him kill her, right? Does the boss feel we've got anything concrete enough to make an arrest yet?"

Ema shook her head. "Unfortunately, no. It's all still conjecture. Without an eyewitness, we haven't got a case. The orders are still for us to find Boxcar Charlie and pray he knows something."

Cosmo groaned and muttered, "Charlie, where the hell are you, you slippery old reprobate?"

Ema grimaced. "I wish I knew, because I'm heartily sick of peddling sunsets. One of these days, somebody's going to ask me something I can't weasel out of, and the game will be up. Billy almost caught me out the other day. She studied both the oils and the drawings closely, and she's astute enough about art to figure out sooner or later that you're doing both."

"By the time that happens, maybe we won't need a cover anymore. She mentioned that she talked with you. She was grateful for the bikes and the offer you made about showing some of her work here." Cosmo made his request sound as casual as he could. "You haven't seen her around this afternoon, by any chance?"

Ema shook her head. "Nope. I haven't seen her since last night. I hustled over to Caplin's apartment building, just as you asked. I kept an eagle eye on her from the instant she left the cab. Do you really figure somebody's got Caplin's apartment staked out? I checked the stairwell, the lobby and the fourth-floor corridors, but I didn't see anybody I'd remotely connect to the case."

Cosmo shrugged. "At this point I'm not sure of anything, but I figure we're better off taking precautions. It makes sense that we're not the only ones anxious to get hold of Boxcar Charlie, and maybe they figure Caplin knows more than he's letting on. Maybe they want the women out of the way so they can get to him. Who knows? Anyhow, thanks, Ema. I appreciate it."

"Anytime, partner. Want me to give Billy a message if I do see her?"

"No, thanks. I'll find her myself."

Ema grinned at him. "Good luck, son. With your track record on old Charlie, I'm fast losing faith in your bloodhound abilities."

Cosmo grunted and gave her a sheepish grin. "You and me both."

A group of people were approaching the booth, and Cosmo pretended to study one of his paintings, a twinkle of mischief in his eyes. He waited until the shoppers were right beside him to torment his partner. "Tell me, Ema, what did you use to get this asparagus-green shade here? Viridian, for sure, but what proportion black did you mix with it? And what size brush did you use to get this unusual effect with the palm trees?''

"We artists have to have some secrets, don't you think, sir?" Ema's tone was playful and her smile wide, but with her eyes she told Cosmo she'd kill him if he kept it up.

With an easy wave and a teasing grin, he moved away.

BILLY WAS SHIVERING with cold, which seemed bizarre because part of her realized the sun was still beating down with terrible force on the road she was doggedly following back to the village and the haven of the apartment.

The problem was, the road kept moving, undulating before her, making her stomach feel quite sick.

Maybe she shouldn't have ridden quite so far or so hard. She'd pushed her body to the limit, making herself pedal up hills, going faster and farther, trying to escape from the emotions that tied her stomach in knots and the overwhelming desire to turn the bike around and head for the beach, where she knew Cosmo would be waiting.

By the time her body rebelled, it was half past one and she was miles away from the village, not at all certain where she really was. Wheeling off the road, she sank down under a tree, too hot and weary to eat the lunch she'd packed. She was thirsty, though, and the single can of juice was gone in one long draft. She had the beginnings of a headache and began to wish she'd brought a hat instead of the flimsy headband that circled her forehead and kept the sweat out of her eyes.

Funny, she wasn't sweating all that much anymore.

Wishing there were somewhere she could swim, she turned the bike around and tried to retrace her path. But she'd ridden away from the ocean, on winding secondary roads that she now had trouble recalling.

Stopping at a small store, she bought three more cans of juice. Then, standing outside in the shimmering heat, she pressed each of them against her burning cheeks before she drank it. She'd forgotten to use sun block, and she had a hunch she was getting a bit sunburned.

The juice helped for a while. She stopped and asked an old man for directions, but he must have been as confused as she, because after half an hour of riding, she realized she was heading away from the village again.

This time, she pulled into a service station, and the young man at the pumps drew her a map on the back of a paper towel.

She went into the washroom and splashed lukewarm water on her face, shocked at how red she was. When she took off her sunglasses she looked like a raccoon, and her eyes were all bloodshot. She bought a small tube of cream and smeared it on, but by the way her face and shoulders felt, it was probably too little too late.

By four in the afternoon, she was alternately riding the bike and pushing it. It seemed a geographical impossibility, but the entire route back to Kailua-Kona was uphill, even though it had seemed to be uphill the other way, as well.

The afternoon sun grew monstrous in the sky, and her head seemed to swell. It felt as if it were about to split like a ripe mango. The bike grew steadily heavier and harder to pedal, so she got off again and walked. Each step became an effort of will.

At last she reached the outskirts of the village, and she climbed back on the bike. It was all she could do to hold the handlebars steady, and the feeling of intense heat in her body had given way to icy shudders, but she was almost home. It was a very good thing, because she was pretty sure she was going to be sick to her stomach before long.

Really, really sick.

COSMO SAW HER COMING, weaving dangerously in and out of the late-afternoon traffic on Alii Drive. He'd taken up a vigil in the little park across the street after checking the beach and the village again for the two women.

He was worried sick about them.

Don't get paranoid here, fella. They're bound to be around.

But it was all he could to stay calm. He'd followed several people in through the door of the building and tore up the stairs to Max's apartment, ringing the bell repeatedly. Short of breaking in, there was little more he could do. There was a hard knot of anxiety in his gut about Billy, no matter how hard he tried to reason with himself.

She'd probably gone off on some excursion with Max and Amanda. After all, there wasn't any way to leave him a message if there'd been a change of plans, was there?

To hell with it. In another six minutes, he was going to B-and-E Max's apartment.

And then, there she was on his trail bike. He realized right away that she was in trouble, and he used his old traffic-control training to stop the flow of cars so he could lope across the street and get her.

"Cosmo?"

Her voice was thin and reedy, as if it were coming over a bad telephone connection. "You okay, honey?" he asked quickly, yet he could tell she wasn't, and he maneuvered her and the bike up on the sidewalk. "You've ridden too far in this heat. Just hang on to me. Where are Amanda and Max, anyhow?"

She was trembling. "They're gone. They won't be back for four days. They left this morning on a tour of the island. I went for a bike ride. I...I got lost, and it was awfully hot."

"Damned right it was hot. Today set records even for Hawaii. Did you take in lots of liquids?"

She tried to shake her head again and couldn't. "Ouch. Only some cans of juice. Oh, Cosmo, my head hurts, and I'm so dizzy."

He swore under his breath. "You've got yourself a dandy case of heatstroke, by the sound of it. And you're sunburned." He had his arm around her, and he could feel the heat radiating from her body. She staggered and would have fallen without his support. He leaned the bike against the building and took her weight in both arms, cradling her against him.

"Just hold on. We'll have you upstairs in no time. But I need the keys, honey. We need the keys to get in. Where are they?"

She dug in the pocket of her shorts, tried the other side, came up empty-handed and started to cry.

Four well-dressed elderly ladies arrived just then and opened the street door, staring with open curiosity at Cosmo and Billy.

He gave them his most engaging smile. "She's been out bike riding and she's not feeling very well. Could you give me a hand here, do you think?"

"Aren't you one of the women staying in Max Caplin's apartment?" The woman with the red-rimmed glasses had a loud, high voice, and she looked Billy up and down and frowned disapprovingly.

"We met Amelia the other night, didn't we, girls?" the dark, heavy woman with the girlish voice commented. "Are you her daughter?"

"'Amanda.' Her name's Amanda. This is Billy Reece, and Amanda's her mother-in-law. And yes, they're visiting Max," Cosmo supplied. They were blocking the door, and Billy was still crying silently, tears running down her fiery cheeks. Cosmo began to feel a little desperate. Were these women going to stand here all day, peering at Billy as if she were a specimen of some kind, asking dumb questions?

He tried again. "Max and Amanda are off on a trip, and Billy's misplaced her keys. Could you just hold the door..."

Billy slumped against him, and finally they moved aside enough for him to half carry her inside.

"Rebecca, you bring that bicycle in. No point in leaving it out there—it'll get stolen." Red Glasses had taken charge. "Susie, go and push the button for the elevator—you know how slow the silly thing can be."

"Thanks, Mrs.... Ms...."

"Daisy Seibert. And you are...?"

"Cosmo Menzies."

"Is Max expected back tonight?" Daisy sailed along at the head of the procession, leading the way across the lobby.

"Nope, I think Max said he and Amanda would be gone several days."

Daisy gave a disparaging sniff and raised her eyebrows at Rebecca. In a disorderly unit, they all moved toward the elevators, and somehow the six of them plus the bike squeezed inside.

Billy was limp in his arms, still crying but not bothering to wipe the tears away, slumped against his side with her head on his shoulder. She felt fiery hot to his touch.

"Here's a tissue, dear. Blow your nose." Daisy handed it to Billy. "Well, it's obvious that she's gone and overdone it. Is she training for the triathlon?" Daisy seemed to be the group's spokesperson.

"Yeah." It was easier to agree than not. "Would one of you mind helping me to the apartment with the bike?"

They all erupted from the elevator and escorted Billy and Cosmo to Max's door, pushing the bike. Then they stood expectantly, waiting for him to open the door.

"We'll be delighted to come in with you, Mr. Menzies, and help get her settled."

There was more than a touch of avid curiosity on their well-made-up faces, Cosmo noted. "No," he said quickly. He couldn't think of anything worse than having these four around for Lord knows how long. "No, thanks a lot. We'll be fine now. Just lean the bike against the wall there—that's great."

"Get plenty of liquids in her and get her into a cool bath, then give her aspirin every four hours," said the tall, thin woman called Susie. "I used to be a nurse. I've seen this sort of thing plenty of times. She'll be better in a day or two."

"Give Max our regards when he finally gets back, won't you, Mr. Menzies?"

Cosmo agreed and thanked them profusely, then waited until they reluctantly moved off down the corridor before he lifted Billy through the door and kicked it shut with his foot. It didn't dawn on him until he was inside that the door should have been locked.

"Easy does it, love. We're—"

The rest of the sentence died on his lips. The apartment had been vandalized.

"God almighty!"

A chair lay upside down in the hall, and two pillows and an empty drawer blocked the door to the bathroom. From where he stood, Cosmo could see a confusion of items scattered all over the living-room rug. It looked as if every tape Max owned had been ripped apart and dumped in a heap on the carpet.

Cosmo eased Billy to the floor. "Stay here. Don't move." He was back in less than a minute after quickly checking each room to see if the intruder might still be around. But whoever had been here was gone.

They'd wreaked havoc on Max's belongings. The place looked as if it had been stirred with an eggbeater.

Billy was slumped exactly where he'd left her. She looked up at him with a helpless expression, her sunburned face scarlet, her dark brown eyes tear-streaked and swollen. He opened the door and examined the lock. Whoever had opened it had been an expert; it hadn't been damaged at all.

"Cosmo, what's wrong?"

"Somebody's broken in here while you were out. They left a hell of a mess, and there's no way for me to tell whether they stole anything or not." Had they been ransacking the place while he was sitting across the street in the park? He hadn't seen anyone suspicious come or go, but there was an alley out behind the building. They had probably used that.

Billy's eyes grew wide and fearful. "Oh, my God. I locked the door when I left, I know I locked the door."

"I'm sure you did. Locks don't do much good if somebody wants to get in. Look, Billy, this isn't your fault. Things like this just happen once in a while."

He didn't believe that for a moment. This was no random break-in—he'd bet his right arm on that. Somebody was looking for something in particular, and he figured it must have to do with Max's relationship with the hoboes. He thought of the man Billy had seen, and felt cold. Thank God she'd been out today.

Her bloodshot eyes were full of apprehension. "Will we have to call the police?"

"Yeah, we will." It was something he wasn't looking forward to at all. Except for the chief of the local police, who was heading the murder investigation, no one knew who he was or what he was doing in Kona. Undercover investigations like this one were on a strict need-to-know basis, and his job was to preserve his cover at all costs.

In his role as hobo there were going to be awkward questions to answer about who he was and exactly what he was doing here. "Do you feel up to it right now, honey?"

She shook her head. "I think I'm going to be sick," she confided.

He got her into the bathroom just in time.

"BILLY, DO YOU want me to call a doctor for you?" Cosmo had filled the tub with cool water and tenderly helped her out of her shirt and shorts.

Too sick and weak to be self-conscious, she'd tugged her pink panties off and gripped his arm as she'd stepped into the tub, shuddering as the cool water touched her tender skin.

"I can't afford a doctor. My medical insurance won't cover me over here. Anyhow, all I need is to rest. Cosmo, I'm freezing—this is too cold," she moaned, clutching her chest as the water slid up her thighs and back.

"I know it feels cold, love, but you can't take a hot bath with this sunburn. Trust me."

She looked up at him and tried to grin, but it didn't quite come off. "I must or I wouldn't be sitting here without a stitch of clothing on."

He sponged her off, loving the way her long body looked and felt, but resolutely keeping his ministrations as impersonal as he could manage.

Leaving her to soak in the tub, he had to wrestle her mattress back on its frame in the bedroom, locate the sheets and remake the bed, which wasn't going to endear him to the cops when they arrived. Tampering with evidence and all that.

Whoever had ransacked the apartment still believed people hid things under mattresses, which as far as he knew had gone out of style some time ago. The bedroom was littered with lacy underwear and bits and pieces of other clothing.

He glanced into the smaller bedroom, which Max was obviously using. There were papers and books tossed on the floor, and the twin beds were torn apart the same way the others had been.

But Max's expensive computer was still on the small desk in the living room, and he'd noted that in the women's bedroom, a jewelry case also had been ignored. The television was still there, and the microwave oven was in the kitchen.

It confirmed his first assumption: that the motive for this break-in wasn't simple robbery.

They were looking for something specific. Like information?

The professor had been interviewing hoboes. Cosmo would bet somebody had their shirt in a knot over what the professor actually knew. Maybe they figured Charlie had confided whatever it was he'd seen, and Max, being a writer, had either recorded it or written it down.

Had he done that? Only Max knew, and right at the moment, there didn't seem any way of asking him.

Cosmo went in and rescued Billy from the tub, wrapping her in a huge bathsheet, trying not to feel lecherous at the sight of her naked body.

Chivalry was one hell of a tough way to go. No wonder knighthood went out of fashion.

She was shivering and sweating at the same time. "I've never felt so awful in my whole life," she said piteously.

He smoothed the bathsheet down over her hips and drew her against him for a comforting hug. "I know, sweetheart. I had heatstroke once when I was a kid. I still remember how miserable I felt."

She snuggled into his chest. "Cosmo, I'm so glad you're here."

"I'm staying right here, too, so nobody's going to bother you. Let's just get you to bed now."

Having her almost naked, pressed against him like this, was altogether too much of a good thing. "I don't suppose Max and Amanda gave you any idea of their itinerary, or a phone number where they could be reached?"

She shook her head.

In the bedroom, he helped her tug on a long cotton T-shirt, and she winced as it touched her scarlet shoulders. He settled her in bed under a sheet. Then he had to get out of the bedroom before the temptation to crawl in beside her overcame his better judgment.

"I'm going to get you something to drink and some aspirin. You're probably dehydrated." There was plenty of juice in the fridge, and he diluted it with water and insisted she drink several glasses along with the pain reliever he'd found in the bathroom medicine chest.

She curled on her side and closed her eyes. Wisps of blond hair stuck to her cheek, and he reached down and brushed them back, aware of the texture of her skin.

"I'm going to have to call the police soon, Billy, but I'm going to put it off for an hour or so while you rest. They're going to want to talk with you."

"Can't. Can't now." She mumbled something unintelligible and fell asleep.

CHAPTER ELEVEN

"YOU SAY YOU ARRIVED here at what time this evening?"

Billy sank back in the chair and rolled her eyes in exasperation. "For heaven's sake, we've told you fifteen times already. Do we have to go over this again? We didn't ransack the place ourselves and then phone you. Surely you understand that."

Portly Detective Fellerman didn't react to Billy's diatribe. He'd puffed his way into the apartment an hour after the uniformed boys who'd responded to Cosmo's call, and he'd taken charge with a pompous air of self-importance.

Billy, bleary-eyed and obviously feeling miserable, had pulled a pair of cotton drawstring pants over her sleep shirt and was doing her best to answer questions, but she was none too coherent and inclined to be more than a little grumpy when Fellerman insisted on going over and over their report.

Cosmo felt sorry for her, but he could see the humor of the situation from both sides of the fence. Locked as he was in his hobo persona, which required a basic distrust of all policemen, he couldn't help either Billy or the fat detective.

Not that he was all that eager to do anything for Fellerman. The detective was just as suspicious of him as Cosmo had thought he'd be. He questioned him at length, and Cosmo reluctantly admitted to having no fixed address and no bank account, which Fellerman seemed to assume meant he had no legitimate reason for being at the apartment, either. After a few of his barbed comments, Cosmo was beginning to appreciate his hobo friends' negative attitudes toward the law. Fellerman was being a royal pain in the butt, and a bully in the bargain.

"Look, I've told you Cosmo's my friend, I'm sick and he's helping me. I invited him here, so stop badgering him, all right?"

Billy glared at the detective, but Fellerman wasn't at all daunted. He made it plain he suspected Billy's story about Max and Amanda going off without leaving information about where they could be contacted. He was openly skeptical about Billy's recounting of the incident in the stairwell. His expression plainly said he very much doubted the existence of any blond man in glasses who might or might not be involved in the break-in.

"You say Professor Caplin invited you and your mother-in-law to stay here with him during your stay in Hawaii. Do you have anything in writing to confirm that?"

"No, unfortunately I don't. I'm not in the habit of asking friends for written invitations just in case the police need them." Billy was disgusted.

"Professor Caplin is assisting the police in a murder investigation—did you know that? He was given explicit instructions about not leaving the island without notifying us."

"He hasn't left the blessed island! He's on a research trip for four days, driving around. Ohhh, ouch." Raising her voice obviously made her head hurt. She closed her eyes and pressed a hand to the back of her neck.

"We seem to have only your word on that, ma'am."

"That's right. And what exactly makes you think I'm not being honest with you?"

Cosmo saw the deadly glare she gave the detective and fervently hoped he'd never be the recipient of one like it.

"My word's going to have to be enough, because I'm going back to bed right now. I can't sit here one minute longer. I told you an hour ago I was sick, and I feel much worse now. When Amanda calls, if she does, I'll get Max to phone you." Billy got to her feet, then had to sit down again as dizziness overcame her.

Cosmo helped her into the bedroom and back into bed. When he returned to the living room, Fellerman hadn't moved.

"You know the other vagrants around Kona, Menzies?"

Cosmo said he did.

"You're camping out with them at the hobo jungle beyond the industrial park, aren't you?"

Cosmo said that he was.

"Then you're aware that two hoboes drowned out there a couple of weeks ago. Tell me how it happens that we didn't question you about that? Where exactly were you at that point, Menzies?"

"I arrived on Kona the following week."

"That's handy." Fellerman's eyes were slits, and his mouth was compressed into a tight line. "You wouldn't happen to know anything about a hobo named Charlie, either, I suppose?"

Cosmo shook his head. "Never met him."

"But you just happen to know Professor Caplin well enough to be hanging out in his apartment when he's not around. Caplin was a friend of this bum Charlie. He might have been the last person to see Charlie alive."

Cosmo hid his gut reaction to that. Had the local boys found a body since yesterday afternoon?

"The professor interviewed me here less than a week ago for some book he was writing, then he asked me to stay for supper," he told the detective in a low, even voice. "That's how I met Billy. She explained to you about the mix-up with the apartment."

"I hope for your sake you're telling the truth."

Cosmo met the detective's eyes with a level gaze. "What possible reason would I have to lie to you?"

"I wish I knew." Fellerman got to his feet and moved toward the door. He turned and jerked a thumb at the bedroom where Billy was. "You and your lady friend in there are obviously going to be shacked up here till Professor Caplin gets back, so I'd suggest you leave things exactly the way they are until we can hear from the professor what's missing. Right? And we'll be in touch, so don't try any disappearing acts. Also, we've got an inventory of what's here. It wouldn't look good for you if anything else went missing and got blamed on the break-in, would it?"

Cosmo considered punching Fellerman a good one in his overhanging gut but decided it would be a bad move. A very, very bad move. However, when the case was over, he might just have a word or two with this tactless detective.

The door closed behind him, and Cosmo locked it.

Fellerman was right about one thing. Until Max and Amanda returned, there was no way he was going to

leave Billy here alone. He was certain now that somebody had been watching Max's apartment.

Cosmo thought longingly of his .38 police revolver,
snug in its leather holster in the closet at the apartment a few blocks away. Well, he'd have to get along
without it. He glanced at the clock on the wall in the
kitchen. The long day was taking its toll. It was well
after midnight, and he felt exhausted.

Turning out all the lights, he made his way out to the
lanai and scanned the deserted length of Alii Drive.
There was the faint sound of music coming from the
Kona Hilton down the road, but apart from that the
village seemed asleep.

Going back through the apartment, he slid silently
out the door and into the corridor, using the key he'd
located in Billy's back pocket to lock the door after
him. He did a swift and thorough search of the open
walkway and then the stairwell, satisfying himself that
no one was around.

Back in the apartment again, he locked the door and
wedged a chair securely underneath it.

He'd have to get hold of Ema first thing in the
morning and tell her about this latest development;
there was no longer any doubt in his mind that what
had happened here today had everything to do with
Max Caplin's connection to the hoboes. He'd give a
lot to get his hands on the blond man in the sunglasses.

He made his way into the bedroom and, after a
longing look at Billy, asleep and sprawled crosswise on
the narrow bed, drew up the sheet so that it covered
distracting parts of her anatomy and wrestled the other
twin bed together for himself. Inspiration struck, and

he moved the night table that separated the beds to one side, shoving them close together.

The shower was a luxury. A period of hardship sure as hell made a guy appreciate the small luxuries of life, all right.

He washed out his underwear and shirt, the way he'd learned to do whenever hot water was available, hanging them to dry on a chair on the lanai. Then he shampooed and rinsed and reveled in the hot water, the thick towels, the fragrant soap, before making his way back into the bedroom.

Billy slept restlessly, moaning now and then and rolling from one side to the other. He planted a gentle kiss on her mouth, but she didn't awaken. A rueful grin came and went as he remembered his erotic fantasies about being in a real, honest-to-goodness bed with her beside him. It had happened, but not quite the way he'd intended.

He switched out the soft light and lowered his weary body onto the bed. Had a mattress and sheets always felt this soft and inviting? Reaching out, he found Billy's limp, hot hand and clasped it in his own.

He was asleep in an instant, but the sound of splintering glass brought him out of a dream and straight to his feet. The room was black-dark, the door shut. It had been open when Cosmo had gone to sleep; he'd made sure of it. He grabbed his cutoffs and hauled them on, then crept stealthily out into the hall. There was a light in the main bathroom, and he slid along the wall and peered around the corner of the door.

Billy was standing in the midst of a pool of shattered glass and pink lotion, leaning on the sink, her head down in an attitude of utter despondency.

"Don't move, love—you'll cut your feet." Carefully Cosmo bent and picked up the largest fragments. The room was filled with the perfumed odor of whatever it was she'd broken.

"It was Max's lotion for sunburn. I used all mine last night and remembered this bottle in here. Now there's none, and my back's so sore I can't sleep. And my head still hurts—it feels as if it's going to explode. My skin's all sore and prickly and I don't know what to do, Cosmo." She sounded ready to cry again.

Gingerly setting his feet where there wasn't any glass, he picked her up in his arms and carried her back into the bedroom, aware of the incredible softness of the skin on the back of her thighs, the slender feel of her ribs and backbone against his arm. Her hair tickled his nose, and she smelled of talcum and the lotion she'd broken. For all her height, she felt light in his arms.

He put her down on the bed and found his sandals, pulling them on his feet. "I'll be back in fifteen minutes—I'm going to get something for that sunburn. I'm taking a key and locking the door. Don't move till I get back."

"But it's three in the morning. Nothing's open at this hour," Billy all but wailed.

He laughed. "You don't need a pharmacy for what I've got in mind. It's an old Hawaiian remedy."

He checked the corridor and the stairwell again, but there was no one around. Moments later, he was in the elevator on the ground floor. Nothing stirred down here, either, and he made his silent way out the back of the building, using Billy's keys to open the alley door, alert for movement of any kind.

All was still. The moon had set, and everything was black on black. He'd thought to bring a flashlight, but his eyes adjusted and he found he didn't need it yet. He made his way past the adjacent parking lots and over to the overgrown forested area that bordered the apartment on the southeastern side.

Aloe vera grew wild everywhere on the island, and he was certain he'd find the soothing plant in the tangle of tropical foliage.

He slid the flash out of his pocket and was about to snap it on, when something moved in the brush ahead of him. A man's voice muttered a curse as he stumbled and almost fell.

Cosmo's heart thumped and adrenaline coursed through his body as he dropped silently to all fours and took shelter behind a high stand of bushes.

Whoever was there didn't want to be discovered. He moved with stealth through the tangle of undergrowth, and if it hadn't been for the whispered curse, Cosmo might have believed it to be some animal. The muted sound of tiny branches crackling and leaves being moved aside grew gradually closer as the man worked his way out of the thicket, toward Cosmo.

In another minute, whoever it was would see him. Cosmo slid into the underbrush, taking refuge in the deeper darkness created by a huge bush.

The movement nearby stopped abruptly, and Cosmo was certain he'd been discovered. But the man was only making certain the coast was clear before he stepped out of the woods and into the narrow alleyway.

When he did, it was far too dark to make out a face, but the figure appeared to be that of a short and stocky baldheaded man. He set off at a rapid pace along the alley, and when he reached the dumpster near the apartment, he hoisted himself swiftly up and over the edge. There was rustling and more fierce cursing as he rooted around in the garbage. A box loaded with whatever he could find that was edible came sailing to the ground. One more followed, then the shape of the scavenger.

With a furtive look around, he picked up the boxes and hurried back into the cover of the underbrush, following some well-known trail deeper into the thicket. The sounds of his passage grew fainter and still fainter, and eventually there was silence, the eerie, waiting silence of the dark time just before the dawn.

Cosmo didn't move. When his muscles began to knot and cramp from holding the same position, he slowly, cautiously got to his feet. He listened intently, but there wasn't a sound. Whoever it was had gone, losing himself in the bush.

He switched on the flashlight, aiming the beam toward the ground and carefully shielding it with his hand. Within minutes, he located an aloe vera plant and broke off several long, thick fronds. Switching off the light and shielded once again by darkness, he hurried back to the apartment, his thoughts on the discovery he'd made.

Someone was hiding out in the bushes beside the apartment and scavenging for whatever scraps of food he could find.

Cosmo was determined to find out who that someone was before too much more time passed.

"OH, THAT FEELS GOOD." Billy winced each time Cosmo's fingers came in contact with her tender skin, but the medicinal herb was helping already.

"I should have thought of this earlier. China Ben uses pure natural aloe all the time for any cuts or burns the hoboes get. He says it's nature's first-aid kit, much more effective than anything you can buy."

He was smoothing the colorless liquid from the center of the aloe vera leaves over her shoulders and arms, and the prickling pain grew shockingly cool and then began to ease wherever his gentle hands touched.

She closed her eyes and gave herself over to his ministrations. "I can't remember ever feeling as sick as I've felt tonight," she admitted. "I'm so grateful to you for caring for me this way."

"I'm not exactly an expert. In fact, you might just be my first patient." Cosmo's voice was husky. "How does it feel to be a test case?"

"Wonderful," she whispered. "It feels wonderful."

"Billy, there's something I've been wanting to ask you." He moved around so he could see her face. "Why didn't you meet me at the beach yesterday afternoon the way we'd agreed? What possessed you to go off on that crazy bike ride, anyway?"

She dipped her chin down, staring at her bare red thighs. She owed him an explanation, that was certain, but it was awfully hard to put into words.

"Was it because we'd made love?"

She swallowed and nodded. "Partly, yeah." Struggling for words, she added, "I didn't expect...I didn't think I'd feel as, as...involved as I did. After."

He tipped her chin up so he could see her eyes. "You thought it was just going to be some casual roll in the sand?'' There was faint humor in his tone, but there was also a trace of sadness, of vulnerability.

"No, not exactly. I mean, I'm not casual about sex. But it was so...intense...and then afterward, when I was alone again, I felt scared, I guess. And I thought..." She swallowed again, an audible gulp in the quiet of the room. "I guess I thought it might be better if we stopped seeing each other."

"Without letting me in on the decision?" Cosmo said, raising an eyebrow.

Suddenly he looked stern and remote. "I'm sorry. I...wasn't thinking very straight. I was trying to work out how I felt, instead."

"And how do you feel now?" His dark eyes were shuttered, and he stared at her without a trace of a smile.

She looked straight into his eyes, and her hands came up and touched his cheeks, stroking his beard, outlining his lips.

NO ONE HAD EVER cared for her the way he had to-night, selflessly, tenderly. Every moment she'd thought he'd make some excuse and leave her, but he hadn't, even through the humiliating nausea and the awful hassle with the detective. She knew what it must have cost him to go through that with her—she didn't have to be told that hoboes and police didn't exactly seek out one another's company.

The emotions that had frightened her before were still there, more intense than ever, but on some level she'd given up fighting them. She couldn't think right now of consequences, of what the results of loving him might be. Here, in the middle of the warm night, in this untidy bedroom, tomorrow seemed far away and unimportant. What mattered was here and now; what mattered was the man close beside her.

She put her lips on his, a quick, gentle kiss. "Oh, Cosmo. I think it's pretty obvious how I feel." She winced as his rough, wet fingers trailed a path across her burning thigh. "I wish I didn't hurt so much. I could show you."

"I'll take a rain check, for when you're feeling better. Right now, just let me hold you." Utterly gentle, he drew her close to his lean, hard length. "Like this."

She sighed, and soon she slept.

THEY'D BEEN GONE two days already, and every moment was delightful to Amanda. The road they were on meandered through sugarcane fields and rain forests on its way toward Hilo, the island of Hawaii's only real city and the place where Max planned to spend another day or so, doing his research. There was a large museum in Hilo, famous for its realistic portrayal of Hawaiian history.

"There's an old hotel I know of near the center of Hilo town. It's anything but luxurious, but it's comfortable and clean. Shall we book in there?"

"Sounds fine to me." Amanda felt languorous, overwhelmed by Hawaii's opulence and variety, humbled by its beauty. The day had been rich, and she felt she'd remember it always, but most important of all, it had stirred a deep and abiding love for this amazing, various island. She fingered the crystal at her throat and thought again of what Tutu Kane had told her. His words came back to her at odd times: *Your destiny is here in Hawaii, if you have the courage to seize it.*

Maybe it was silly of her to believe him. Billy certainly thought it was. But his words had struck a deep note of truth inside her, a sense of recognition of something she already knew on a subconscious level. Unbidden, the mental picture of Momi's Coffee Shop came into her mind, the way it had several times since she and Billy had stopped there.

As he had the previous night, Max got them adjoining rooms, and they left the connecting door open as they settled in, chatting back and forth and sharing their impressions of the day. They also shared a bathroom, and Max insisted Amanda fill the tub and soak for as long as she wanted. The last part of the drive had been exceptionally hot and humid, and she did as he suggested, closing the connecting doors first.

There was a necessary intimacy to a trip such as this one. During the day, Amanda had often glanced over at Max's handsome profile and marveled that she, a middle-aged woman with what she thought of as a very ordinary life, should be speeding along strange, exotic roads in this lush, equatorial country with this exceptionally good-looking man who made it plain he found her attractive and amusing.

Max's admiration altered her own self-image. She'd looked at herself in rest-stop mirrors during the day and realized that under the same old features was a part of her psyche almost unknown to her, a plucky, lighthearted female who dared to take chances, who welcomed change and excitement, who could quip with a university professor and make him laugh. A woman who didn't just worry and fret over bills and money and the problems of being a widow. Here in Hawaii she was learning that there was much more to life than she'd imagined, a whole wonderful world to be explored if only she dared step forward and meet it.

"Your destiny is here in Hawaii..."

She lay back in the soothing, lukewarm water and let her thoughts wander. She and Max were going out to dinner, then they'd explore the city on foot. She'd wear the strappy sandals that were still respectable looking but comfortable. And the blue wraparound skirt with the open-necked blouse...

And her crystal, of course. She had it on even now, in the bathtub.

IT WAS DARK, but the Japanese gardens where they strolled were softly lit with tiny twinkling lights, giving the grounds an ethereal air. Haunting Oriental music played softly from some hidden speaker, and the moon was rising, a golden crescent that floated in the miniature streams beneath arched bridges.

They were standing on one of those bridges, and Max was holding her hand.

"This is the most romantic place I've ever been," Amanda said in a near whisper.

"Then it's the perfect place to kiss you. I've been wanting to all day."

His arms came around her, drawing her close, and before she had time to think, his lips were on hers. There was a moment of shock, of adjustment to what was happening, then she gave herself up to his kiss. She realized she'd been wishing he'd do just that, wondering how it would feel if he did.

It felt wonderful! He was good at it; self-assured and practiced, knowing how to tease and question with teeth and tongue.

For all her years of marriage, Amanda wasn't very experienced at kissing—how many men had she really kissed in this arousing way, after all? Kissing had seemed to go by the board after she'd been married a while, and besides John there'd been only O'Reilly. But what she lacked in technique, she made up for in enthusiasm. She loved having Max kiss her, and she did her best to let him know.

Max got the message. He made a guttural sound and his arm drew her closer, so she could feel the intimate angles of his body pressing against her modest skirt and blouse. Blood sang through her veins; parts of her that had been long asleep awakened, reaching shyly out to him.

"God, Amanda, I've been wanting to do this. All today, all yesterday, too."

His voice was rough and low in her ear, his breathing as uneven as her own.

"Even before that, if we're being honest here. You feel so good in my arms, Amanda."

He lowered his head and kissed her again, different this time, slower and more exploratory, nipping at her bottom lip, letting his tongue travel in an erotic path to the corners of her mouth, outlining her lips in a hot, wet caress.

They clung to each other, and passion flared and grew between them. Amanda welcomed it, an old friend long absent from her life, one she'd missed sorely.

She could smell the particular scent that had come to mean Max to her, a combination of his after-shave and the clean, male scent of his body. It mingled with the heady fragrance of the millions of flowers surrounding them in the park. The sound of water filled her ears, tinkling streams and fountains and miniature waterfalls making the humid air cool and refreshing. And when she opened her eyes she could see the moon, silhouetted against palm trees, regal in a wide and cloudless sky.

"I'm dreaming. I've got to be dreaming," she murmured.

He drew far enough back to smile down at her. "You have this kind of erotic dream often?"

She wrinkled her nose at him. "Not nearly often enough."

Reluctantly they drew apart and started walking again, hand in hand.

"Amanda?"

"Hmmm?" He'd sounded hesitant. She wondered what he was going to say, sensing it would be important.

"You want to go back to the hotel with me now?"

She turned and smiled up at him, fully aware of what he was really asking. "Yes, Max. I'd like that more than anything."

The Jeep was parked in a nearby lot, and he tightened his grip on her hand and started to run pell-mell toward it, tugging her along behind him.

"Max, you maniac, slow down." Her sandal came loose and fell off, and she could feel the cool grass under her bare foot. "My shoe—stop, I've lost my shoe." She was laughing and stumbling along, her hand still tight in his.

"But if I do, I'm afraid you'll change your mind, and I'll have to wake up tomorrow morning all alone in a strange bed."

She was panting, out of breath from running. "Once . . . I make up my mind . . . nothing . . . in the world...changes it. You just haven't had a chance...to find out...how stubborn and singleminded I can be.''

He had her shoe in his hand now, and he knelt at her feet, fitting her foot into the straps and struggling with the buckle. She steadied herself with a hand on his shoulder and caught her breath, looking down at his silvery hair and broad shoulders, bent over her foot. Tenderness and a great budding joy rose inside her like an opening flower.

Then the shoe was on, but he was still on his knees in front of her, and his hands slid in a slow dance up her calves, past her knees, under her skirt to her thighs and the rim of elastic on the legs of her panties, gentle and caressing, madly arousing. His lips traveled across her knees and above, and she caught her breath in delight.

Voices sounded behind them, the light, breathless sound of a woman's laughter, the deeper tones of a man saying something to her.

''Max, if we stay here like this, there's a good chance we'll get arrested.'' Amanda's voice was uneven. ''This is probably a very respectable place. I'll bet they don't allow older people to make love on the grass. I'm sure I noticed a sign back there...''

Max grinned up at her. ''Somehow I think you're right. It's terribly narrow-minded of them, but when in Rome...''

He was on his feet again, and his arm was tight around her shoulder. ''Control yourself until we get back to the hotel, woman.''

''I'll try, Max. But I won't promise anything.''

''Then we'd better hurry, hadn't we?''

BILLY AWOKE SLOWLY. Her body felt heavy, hot and damp from sunburn and the aftereffects of fever.

Cosmo was still deeply asleep close beside her, his arm looped protectively across her middle. She gently moved it and slid out of bed, aware that her muscles were also sore and tender from the miles she'd covered on the bike the day before.

She was a total wreck.

A moment of dizziness came and passed as she stood upright.

Cosmo's dark hair was spread across the pillow, and her fingers remembered how soft it felt. She studied his face, the strong cheekbones and long eyelashes, the way the almost harsh lines were softened now in sleep. His long, muscular body was naked, barely covered by the thin cotton sheet, and its outlines were familiar and dear to her this morning.

He'd cradled her against him all night, tender and so careful not to hurt her.

She smiled at the memory and slowly made her way into the bathroom, closing the door quietly so he could go on sleeping.

The glass she'd broken all over the floor was gone. When had Cosmo cleaned it up? Green stalks of aloe vera lay on the counter, nearly sliced open to release the healing liquid he'd smoothed over her again and again during the night. It had kept rubbing off all over him.

Despite the healing effects of the aloe, her face in the mirror was a shock. Her forehead, nose, cheeks and chin were a dull and angry red, with white circles around the eye area where her sunglasses had been.

How attractive, Billy.

She grimaced at her reflection and turned on the water in the shower. The warm stream hurt like fury on her sunburn, but after a few seconds she got used to it. It felt wonderful to stand there, letting the water course over her. She rubbed her body gingerly with soap and shampooed her hair, and finally just stood there while the water ran on and on, its hypnotic sound underlining the questions in her mind.

Where do we go from here, Cosmo and I?

The words niggled at her brain. Some barrier had been crossed in the night, some point of no return for her. He'd cared for her with a tenderness and compassion she'd never experienced in a man before, and every barrier she'd erected against him had dissolved in the face of that caring, until she was emotionally naked and new before him, until there was no longer any question of whether or not she loved him.

She did. She loved him. With all her soul.

COSMO CAME AWAKE the way he always did, making an instant transition from one state to the other, immediately aware of where he was and what was going on around him. It felt late to him, later than he usually slept, probably ten or even eleven already.

He could hear the shower in the main bathroom, and he envisioned Billy there, stretching her lovely body toward the water.

His body reacted the way it had over and over again in the night, full and hard and aching for her. Holding her had been both agony and delight.

He slid free of the sheet and sat up, forcing thoughts of Billy out of his head to make room for the other things he was going to have to take care of today.

For instance, he had to make contact with Ema, and soon. She had to be told about the break-in at the apartment, and if Cosmo was right in thinking it was related to the murders, there were any number of possible ramifications that would have to be considered. Billy had to be protected, and when they got back, Max and Amanda, as well. His mouth tightened into a grim line. He wanted a make on the blond man, as soon as possible.

And there was something else he had to tell Ema.

A surge of excitement shot through him when he remembered the predawn excursion to the woods. There was an off chance he'd accidentally located Charlie's hiding place last night. But if he'd found the old man, others could, too. He had to discover a way to contact Charlie without frightening him off, and get him somewhere safe.

Ema would help him with that.

Also, it was going to be harder to find time to do the things he had to do, because of Billy. He wasn't about to leave her alone in the apartment for long, so they'd be spending most of the next few days together—a delightful prospect, but not one that made his undercover work any easier.

There was the added problem of no longer being anonymous. Detective Fellerman was probably going to keep an uncomfortably close eye on him from now on, which could make his job a lot more complicated. If Fellerman really wanted to, he could harass him until life became pretty unbearable.

Cosmo could only hope the detective had too many other things to do.

He got to his feet and headed into the bathroom when he heard the shower stop running. Billy probably needed her back dried. Then, he'd shower and figure out what they needed in the way of groceries, insisting that Billy stay home and rest while he went to fetch them.

That would give him time to contact Ema.

BETWEEN THEM, Cosmo and Ema figured out a plan to find out who was hiding in the woods.

"Billy and I are having lunch together tomorrow," Ema announced. "I'll make sure she's with me most of the afternoon. That'll keep her safe and give you a chance to investigate. I'll meet you later, and you can fill me in on what's happening."

Ema was as concerned as Cosmo about the break-in at Max's apartment. They again discussed the man Billy had seen and the possibility that he was watching the apartment and its occupants. Like Cosmo, Ema felt that whoever it was probably thought Max knew more than he was revealing about the murders.

"You're staying there with Billy until the professor gets back, of course? It's a nasty job, but somebody's got to keep an eye on her. Right, Detective?"

Ema's eyes twinkled and she winked at Cosmo.

Cosmo looked her straight in the eye and without a trace of a smile said, "Right. I'd never forgive myself if something happened to her because of this mess she doesn't even realize she's involved in."

But then he couldn't stop the silly grin that spread across his face. "It's about the best job I've ever had, to tell the truth." He sobered and met Ema's curious gaze. "Billy's a special sort of lady," he admitted softly.

"I think so, too. You in love with her?"

Wryly remarking to himself that Ema wasn't exactly noted for being subtle, Cosmo opened his mouth to tell her his no-nonsense opinions on the subject of love, then closed it again. He stared at Ema, thinking over what she'd asked.

Is this what love feels like?

"Well, are you?" Ema wasn't about to give up easily.

He had nothing with which to compare his feelings. What he felt for Billy was unique in his experience, but he wasn't ready to label it, that was for sure. Still... "Damn, I don't know," he finally said. "How do you ever know about things like that?"

Ema gave him the scathing look she reserved for certifiable idiots.

"It's a feeling you get in your gut."

He thought about Billy. Sure enough, it was there, right in his solar plexus, an aching sort of tenderness, a need to get back to her as soon as possible, an awareness in every pore of his being. A need to protect her so strong that he'd put his life on the line if necessary.

"I'll watch my gut real close and tell you when it happens, Dr. Weiler," he assured her. "Now I gotta get that milk and bread I'm supposed to be after."

He hurried off, but he didn't remember buying the groceries or racing home with them. He was only aware of unlocking the apartment door and seeing Billy waiting for him with a welcoming smile and a kiss.

And sure enough, his gut reacted right away.

CHAPTER TWELVE

THE FOLLOWING AFTERNOON, Cosmo crouched on the roof of the apartment building, a pair of the professor's binoculars trained on the densely wooded vacant area below. Billy had left an hour before to keep her lunch date with Ema, and he'd been up here ever since, scanning the foliage, watching for any sign of movement.

Surely a guy would have to go to the bathroom sometimes, or just move around a little. From this vantage point, Cosmo was reasonably certain he'd see him if and when he ever moved.

But all was still. His arms ached from holding the glasses to his eyes, and he dropped them and mopped at the streams of sweat pouring down his cheeks and dripping off his chin.

It was bloody hot up here. Lawn chairs were set out for people to tan if they wanted, but fortunately for Cosmo nobody in their right mind would try tanning in the oppressive heat of noon. Cosmo felt as if he were frying in the sun.

He was about to stand up and stretch, when he saw what he'd been looking for. A figure stealthily moved through the underbrush, and through the glasses Cosmo could see a blue T-shirt and a flash of bald head before he disappeared again into what looked like a dense growth of bamboo. Cosmo did his best to memorize exactly how far in and in what direction the bamboo thicket lay.

Racing downstairs, he thrust the glasses inside the door of the apartment and took off at a dead run, down the stairs and out the back of the building.

Within minutes, he was deep in the thicket. It was difficult to figure out exactly where the bamboo growth was. He moved as cautiously as he could, taking care not to break branches, moving at a half crouch through the almost-impenetrable underbrush, trying to control even his breathing so he wouldn't be heard.

With shocking suddenness, a ropy arm encircled his throat from behind, pulling him back and off balance. Cosmo's arms went up to break the hold, but a sharp object pricked through the thin cotton of his shirt, and a raspy voice ordered, "Don't try it, or I'll stick ya right through. I got a knife."

Cosmo didn't doubt the man's words for one instant; the blade was even now pressing into his shoulder blades. He turned his head enough to catch a glimpse of a wrinkled face, and in his nostrils was the odor of a sweaty, unwashed body, a smell he'd grown used to because some of the other hoboes weren't fond of bathing, either.

It had to be Boxcar Charlie.

"What ya creepin' through here for like some big-game hunter, tell me that? Who you workin' for, mister?"

Cosmo sighed. There was no point in keeping up the facade, whichever way you looked at it. Charlie had to be taken into custody for his own good.

And for Cosmo's good, the way things were going.

"Relax, I'm not armed. I'm not here to hurt you."

The knife gave a dig that Cosmo didn't care for at all. He raised his hands slowly and rested them on the upper part of the arm clutching his throat.

"Go easy with that knife, old man." Cosmo made his tone slow and soothing, but at the very instant he finished speaking, he threw his hips backward, grasped Charlie's arm in a steely grip and neatly tossed the old man over his head onto the ground.

Cosmo held firmly on to his assailant's arm, controlling his fall. The moment Charlie was on the ground, Cosmo had a knee against his throat and both hands on the arm that held the knife. The weapon wasn't formidable at all; it was a small, multiblade Scout knife.

"Drop it now. And just relax, okay? I'm not going to hurt you, old-timer."

Gradually Charlie's breathing eased.

Cosmo relaxed his hold and moved back, extending a hand so Charlie could sit up. Recovering the knife from where it lay half-hidden in the grass, Cosmo folded the blade shut and handed it over to the hobo. "Put this back in your pocket. I want to have a talk with you."

Cosmo mustered up his official voice. "I'm Detective Antonelli, Cosmo Antonelli. I'm working undercover for Honolulu P.D., and I've been looking for you. I think your life's in danger. As you're probably aware, I'm investigating the deaths of Liza Franklin and your two buddies who drowned. We figure they were murdered. You're probably the only person who can help me catch the people who did it. What about it, Charlie? Were they the same people who did in Liza Franklin?"

Charlie glared at Cosmo. Although his head was totally bald, he had bushy white eyebrows over ferocious pale blue eyes.

"You don't look like no cop ta me. Show me yer badge."

"Unfortunately I don't have it on me. For the moment, you're just going to have to take my word for it. Now, tell me why you're hiding out like this."

Charlie looked away and scowled into the brush. "Ain't none of your derned business. A man's got a right to sleep where he wants ta, ain't he?"

Cosmo sighed and moved his legs into a more comfortable position. This was going to be a long session.

"Look, Charlie, I know you're scared. You've got good reason to be, but you can't hide in here the rest of your life. Tell me what it was you and the other hoboes saw the night Liza Franklin died."

"Nothin'."

"If that's true, there'd be no reason for you to live here like an animal, and Slim and Blackie would still be alive. Isn't that right, Charlie? See, I know the three of you were sharing a bottle that night—Noah told me so. He said Blackie had made some money that day cleaning up trash behind a store in town. He bought three big jugs of wine. Duke and Elmer polished off two and fell asleep. Noah wasn't feeling good, so he didn't drink, and Frisco Joe wasn't around that night. You and Blackie and Slim went for a walk so as not to bother Noah, and you took the last bottle with you."

Charlie stared at Cosmo. "How come you know so much? Old Noah, he'd never talk to the bulls about stuff like that—I know he wouldn't."

"You're right about that. But I've been living with the guys out at the hobo jungle, and they get to talking around a campfire."

"You been foolin' my friends, pretendin' ta be a 'bo? That's the lowest of the low. You gonna be lucky they don't scalp you with a dull knife when they find out who you really are." Charlie gave Cosmo a disgusted look. "Can't trust nobody these days, nohow."

"They're a good bunch of guys, Charlie, and I'm just doing my best to find the people who murdered your friends. Who was it? Who bought the whiskey Slim and Blackie were drinking that night? Who made them drink it, made sure they were too drunk to move when the tide came in? Or did somebody just conveniently dump them into the drink, never mind the tide? What did the three of you know that was bad enough to get murdered for? And, Charlie, hiding here isn't going to work long—you must know that. They're looking for you."

Charlie kept stubbornly silent.

"Professor Caplin's a friend of yours, isn't he?"

Charlie still didn't answer, but his gaze flicked to Cosmo's face and away again.

"I don't know how much you might have told Caplin, but somebody broke into his place yesterday in broad daylight, looking for something. The professor isn't home. They obviously knew that, and my guess is they were after a record of what you might have told him about the murders."

Charlie looked troubled. "He don't know nothin'. I know they're watchin' his place—I saw 'em. But I never said nothin' much to the perfesser. They got no need to—" He stopped abruptly.

"Well, they obviously think he knows something, so I'd guess he's in some danger, too. These are ruthless people, Charlie. Breaking into an apartment is tricky business. These people are pretty desperate. You said yourself they're watching what goes on. They knew the professor wasn't home, and they deliberately tried to scare off a friend of his the other night. And you—they'll find you sooner or later and then what? Your life won't be worth a plugged nickel. So talk to me, Charlie, okay? Between us we can stop this before it goes any further."

Charlie's shoulders hunched forward and he slumped as if the air had suddenly been let out of his body. He crossed his arms on his chest and stared down at the ground. "Truth is, I'm shit scared," he mumbled at last. "I been hidin' out here, waitin', tryin' to catch the perfesser ta see if he'd help me out some. See, I got no money to get clear of here. It ain't like the old days when you could just jump a freight and vamoose. Shoulda thought of that when I decided ta come live on a danged forsaken island. Anyhow, the perfesser, he's had somebody with him, lady friends. And then there's been that dude watchin' the place all the time. Never could seem to get Caplin alone. But I never meant to get him in no trouble, neither."

"You've got every reason to be scared, but running away's no solution. Why don't we help each other out, and I'll do my best to make sure you're safe?"

Charlie shot him a dubious look.

"Tell me what happened that night. Please, Charlie." Cosmo's voice was urgent.

The old man was silent so long Cosmo thought he'd decided not to answer. It was hot, humid in among the trees this way, and the only sounds were the buzzing of insects and the far-off sound of the traffic on Alii Drive. Even the birds were quiet, probably sensibly sleeping in the afternoon heat.

"We was just having us a good time, Slim and me and Blackie, there in the trees." Charlie's voice was subdued. "Blackie, he'd been a 'bo most of his life, like me, and he got to tellin' tales about the early days. It was dark, but the moon was comin' up and there was a high surf that night. It was real nice." Charlie's voice was wistful.

"We was about to go back to camp, when I heard a car comin'. Ain't no real road back in there, ya know, and this car had no headlights on. Stopped real close to where we was, so we hunkered down and just waited to see what was next. Figgered it was maybe some lovers or somethin'."

Sweat was standing out on Charlie's forehead, and the hand he reached up to wipe it away trembled slightly.

"The driver got out and we could see him clear, 'cause the inside light in the car went on. He goes to the trunk, see, and pulled out a bundle, heavy. He grunts when he lifts it, and he staggers when he carries it to the beach and drops it. Then he gets back in, and we get a good look at his face again, see. And he backs up like the devil's after him and drives off." Charlie cast a pleading look at Cosmo. "You got a butt I could borrow, young feller? I ain't had a decent smoke in God knows how long."

"Sorry, Charlie, I don't smoke. But I'll get you a pack later." Cosmo needed to hear the rest of Charlie's story. "So did you guys go and look at what this dude dropped off, Charlie? What did he look like, this guy?''

The old man shuddered at the memory. "We was curious, same as anybody'd be. We waited, and when the car was long gone, Blackie got all het up 'cause he knew who this guy was, recognized him from some newsmagazine. See, Blackie was strange. He made a study of finance—not that he ever had any money of his own to invest. Still, he read all the financial sections of any papers he come across. Knew who was who in the world, Blackie did. He was all excited. Said the man we'd seen was named Harrison Franklin, some big mover and shaker who was deep into real estate. Anyhow, we went over to see what he dumped. We was all a little scared by now. The moon was full up, and we could see pretty clear.''

Charlie's throat worked, and it was several moments before he could get the next words out. "God, young feller, it was awful. It was a woman wrapped in a blanket, and she was deader'n a doornail. Side of her head bashed right in. Little bit of a thing, and somebody'd beat her up bad.''

Charlie was silent again for what seemed like a long time. Finally he sighed and took up the story again. "We hightailed it back to camp, told the other 'boes what we seen. We was all scared. We figgered the bulls would blame us sure as God made green apples. We was all fer runnin', but where the hell can a man go on an island? Like I said, that's the big drawback here. Ya can't jump a freight and take off same as you can on the mainland.

"Anyhow, I figured we oughta tell the cops. Not just walk bold as brass into the clink and announce it, ya understand. Just sorta phone it in, anonymous like.

But Blackie and Slim, they'd both done time fer one thing 'n' another, and they didn't want no messin' with the cops. So we made us a pot of mud. We was all shook up, an' we argued back and forth mosta the night. We finally agreed to phone the bulls and say where that poor lady was...hell, ya couldn't just leave her body lyin' there, not a mile away from where we was camped. Old Noah, he felt like I did, and when dawn came, even though he was feelin' punk, he walked out with me and we phoned the bulls. Put my shirt over the receiver and just told 'em where she was."

"And then, Charlie?" Cosmo was elated, although he didn't show it. He had an eyewitness to Liza Franklin's murder, and it was a good feeling. "What happened next?"

Charlie grimaced in disgust. "Aw, all hell broke loose. Cops everywhere, askin' questions. We all stuck to our story. We was together all night—we didn't know nothin'. When I found out the dead lady was Franklin's wife, though, I figgered we should tell the cops what we saw. I mean, ain't no doubt he did her in, right? Takes a real coward to beat up a little tiny woman like that, and me, I figgered he oughta get his comeuppance, see? But by then Blackie and Slim had other plans."

Charlie glowered at Cosmo. "You get this straight, young feller. I wanted no part a this next stuff, believe you me. See, Blackie and Slim, they got it in their heads to blackmail this Franklin creep."

"And they got themselves murdered for it."

Charlie nodded. "Yup, all of us knew they was murdered, even though it was made to look like an accident." He coughed and spit. "Hell, ain't no hobo gonna get pissed on expensive whiskey and then lay out on the beach like that and drown. They was s'posed to be gettin' their payoff that day. They was all excited. Told the rest of us they'd spring fer a blow-out fer all of us, wine and food and all that. But then they turned up dead.''

"They told Franklin they'd seen him that night, dumping the body of his wife. Charlie, did they tell him you were with them?''

"Hell, no. 'Boes never snitch on their pals. You oughta know that by now.'' But his denial lacked conviction, and a moment later he sighed and added in a subdued voice, "Truth be told, I ain't sure. Maybe they told him there was somebody else there that night, sorta like an insurance policy, see. Blackie, he was real smart about such stuff. Well, I fer one got scared after they died. I figgered nobody gives a shit about us hoboes, so what's to stop this Franklin from rubbing us all out if he wants? And I sorta told the perfesser a little—him and me was friends. I just said that I knew more'n I was lettin' on, and he got real excited and said I oughta go to the cops.''

Charlie became agitated. "But say I did, my life wouldn't be worth diddly squat, 'cause this Franklin, he ain't gonna stay in jail. He's got money. He'd put up bail. And guess who he's gonna come after? So I come here. I knew about a hidey hole in these bushes.''

"You got stuff there you want to bring along, Charlie?'' It was time to leave, and it would be a whole lot easier if Charlie came willingly.

Fear was evident in the old man's piercing blue eyes. "I ain't goin' nowhere. Where you takin' me to? I told you everythin' I know. You got no right ta take me in. I ain't done nothin'....''

"You're an eyewitness in a murder case, and you can either agree to come with me to a safe house, or I'll have you locked up until Franklin is arrested and comes to trial, which could be a fairly long wait. Take your choice."

"Ya got no integrity, none at all, young feller." Charlie bristled and muttered and swore, but in a short while the fight went out of him.

"I gotta go get my pack" was all he said.

MOST OF THE AFTERNOON had slid past unnoticed while Billy was at lunch with Ema. She'd felt reluctant about going at first; she was still feeling wobbly, and anyway she'd thought she'd much rather spend the time with Cosmo. After all, Amanda and Max would probably be coming back tomorrow, and each moment she and Cosmo had alone in the apartment was precious to her.

But he'd urged her to go with Ema. He had some things to do, he'd said.

And she was glad she had. It had been such fun. She and Ema had laughed and talked and ordered more coffee and shared a second dessert, discussing men and clothes and Vancouver and Hawaii and food and art.

Except that it seemed to Billy she had done most of the talking about art. Maybe Ema had some superstitious hang-up about discussing her work, because she said little or nothing about her own painting, even though Billy was full of ideas and prattled on about what she wanted to try.

"I'll walk you back to the apartment—the exercise will do me good," Ema had insisted when they'd finally left the restaurant.

They were in the middle of a discussion about a book they'd both read when they got to the apartment, so Ema followed Billy up in the elevator. Billy had told her about the break-in, and Ema glanced around when they entered the apartment.

Cosmo wasn't home yet.

"This mess is depressing," Billy told her. "I wanted to clean it up, but the police insisted it be left exactly this way till Max gets back.

"I think I'll grab my stuff and do some sketching outside," Billy decided. Ema waited while she found her sketch pad and left Cosmo a note telling him where to find her. Then they made their way out again. Ema left her at the wharf, and Billy settled herself on the seawall.

For an hour or so she caught the images of people around her with sure, certain strokes that gradually began to please her. She kept expecting Cosmo to appear at her shoulder, but then she forgot him, forgot everything except the joy and frustration of having her fingers create almost, but not quite, the effects she was striving for.

It was late afternoon when she finally gathered her messy collection of paper and crayons into the folder she'd brought with her. She stretched her aching back and began walking slowly toward the apartment. She was hungry suddenly, ravenous. She'd make a salad and put some chicken pieces on to fry. But first she'd have to go to the supermarket.

There was a narrow alley Max had pointed out that acted as a shortcut to the market. She headed up it, and she was just coming out the far end, when she caught sight of Cosmo. He was hurrying along some distance ahead of her, and she quickened her steps to catch up to him. But he ducked into a shop door, and when he came out a moment later, a woman had joined him.

It was Ema. She was still wearing the jade green dress she'd worn to lunch with Billy. It seemed obvious that they'd planned to meet.

Cosmo looped a casual arm around her shoulders as they moved through the crowd of evening shoppers, and the two of them walked along, heads close together, talking intimately to each other.

Billy felt as if she'd been punched in the stomach.

She slowed down until they turned a corner and disappeared from view, then she went into the supermarket and mindlessly gathered up groceries, all the while trying desperately to get a perspective on what she'd seen.

They were friends, her rational self tried to insist. Why was she freaking out about this? There was nothing wrong with friends meeting and talking; they were all adults here.

But Ema hadn't mentioned a single word about meeting Cosmo later that afternoon, even though Billy had mentioned him several times. And Cosmo certainly hadn't said anything about making an appointment to see Ema today.

And she knew in her gut that the meeting she'd witnessed wasn't accidental. It was perfectly obvious Ema had been waiting there for him.

So why hadn't they told her?

She pushed the cart into the checkout line and dumped lettuce and tomatoes, chicken, frozen fries and doughnuts onto the conveyor belt.

Cosmo would tell her all about it when he came home, she told herself. There was a simple explanation, and he'd make it. He was probably waiting back at the apartment right this minute for her.

HE WASN'T, HOWEVER. He didn't come in until past nine that evening, long after Billy had given up and put the food away. She'd prepared it and then found she wasn't hungry, after all.

When he did arrive, he didn't mention a single word about Ema. He said he'd had to go out to the hobo camp and was late getting back. He seemed tired and distracted, and he spent a long time in the shower.

Billy tried, but she just couldn't ask him outright. She told him about the luncheon, about the sketches she'd done at the wharf, but she couldn't come out and say she'd seen Ema and him together and ask why. She couldn't bear to confirm the fact that her lover and her friend were betraying her. If she didn't put it into words, it wasn't real.

When silence fell between them, Cosmo yawned and pulled her into his arms, saying it was time for bed.

He tried to make gentle, sweet love to her, and although she did her best to respond, her body felt cold and dead inside. So he cradled her, suggesting that she was tired and still not feeling well, and she agreed.

He fell asleep finally, and she lay in his embrace, listening to his even breathing and to the sound of the surf coming in through the open windows. As of tomorrow, there were nine days left of her holiday. She'd been wishing the time would go slower, but tonight she wanted more than anything to pack her bags and go home.

She fell asleep at some point, but awakened before dawn and slipped out of Cosmo's arms. She showered and dressed, took the case with her watercolors and left him a note saying she wanted to catch the sunrise. She crossed Alii Drive and set up her materials in the tiny park across the street.

He came looking for her not long after dawn, his hair still wet and curling from his shower, a clean T-shirt clinging to his athletic frame. He sneaked up behind her and kissed the nape of her neck. He brought her a mango, two bananas and one of the doughnuts left from last night.

She pretended to be totally preoccupied with the scene she was painting, and after a while, he left her alone.

SHE WAS STARING dejectedly into the pot of spaghetti sauce she'd made when Amanda and Max arrived home.

She hadn't seen Cosmo since that morning, and she wasn't about to go looking for him. But she couldn't seem to bring herself to do anything much but think about him, either. So she'd thrown herself into cooking, a thing she did so seldom it took all her energy and concentration.

She turned to the door when she heard the key, her heart hammering, thinking it might be Cosmo. When she saw Amanda, she had to physically stop herself from rushing over and throwing herself into her mother-in-law's arms, tomato sauce and all.

Max was laughing over something Amanda had said, but the laughter died when they saw the state of the apartment.

Billy had been dreading this moment, knowing it was irrational to feel responsible for what had happened but unable to stop herself. Her voice was strained and thin when she spoke, and she could feel herself trembling. "Max, I...I'm so sorry. Some-body broke in the day you left, and the police wouldn't let us clean it up until you came back. They wanted you to figure out what might be missing. I was out bike riding when it happened...."

"Thank God for that." Max's expression was grim as he walked from one room to the next, taking in the disorder.

Amanda was looking at Billy, taking in the sickly pallor under the sunburn.

"Well, apart from making one hell of a mess, it doesn't look as if anything much was stolen," Max commented when he came back into the kitchen to re-join Billy and Amanda. "My computer's still here, the stereo...I'd have thought those were the things they'd take."

"The detective seemed to think they were after something else. He kept talking about the murder in-vestigation and asking me if I had written proof that you'd invited Amanda and me to stay here." Billy's voice wobbled dangerously, and she swallowed before she went on. "Cosmo was here with me. I was terri-bly sick—I had heatstroke from being out in the sun too long—and this Detective Fellerman was really suspicious that Cosmo and I had done this ourselves. I got the feeling he thought we had most of your val-uables stashed away somewhere."

Max snorted. "That's nothing short of absurd, and I'll tell him so."

Billy found the card the detective had given her and handed it over to Max. "He wants you to phone him right away. He's...he's an obnoxious man." Billy felt on the verge of tears again. "Oh, Max, I feel so awful about this. If I'd stayed home that day..."

"Don't even think about it. If you'd been here, it might have ended up much, much worse. I'd never forgive myself if something had happened to you. There's no real harm done here. Things can always be replaced—people can't."

Max was warmly reassuring, but he seemed distracted, and when he lifted the telephone to call the detective, Amanda gestured briskly to her suitcase.

"Help me get this stuff put away, Billy. Then we can start giving this place a thorough cleaning." She led the way into the bedroom and shut the door behind them as Max began to talk. Her eyes met Billy's, and she clucked her tongue and came over to where the younger woman was standing, reaching up to put a cool hand on Billy's forehead. "What is it, Billy? Are you still feeling sick? You don't look good at all."

The tenderness in her tone, the loving, motherly gesture, were more than Billy could bear. She burst into tears and threw herself down on the beds, still shoved together but neatly made the way Cosmo had left them that morning.

"Amanda...oh, Amanda...I wish...I'd never...come to Hawaii. I wish I'd...never won...this damned trip." She looked up at her mother-in-law with streaming, desperate eyes, her features screwed into a mask of utter misery.

"And I wish...I really wish...I'd never, ever, laid eyes on...Cosmo Menzies."

"What's this about Cosmo? Has he hurt you in some way, Billy?" Amanda's voice was caring and troubled, and she found tissues from a box beside the bed and handed them over when Billy's sobs quieted a little.

"Yes. No. Well, I don't know for sure, but it all seems so suspicious to me. And yet I can't help believing he's honest." Realizing that was anything but clear, Billy haltingly explained about Ema, about how friendly and warm she felt toward the other woman. She told Amanda about having a cozy lunch with Ema and then seeing Cosmo and her together later, when they didn't know Billy was anywhere around.

"They didn't say anything to me about it. Ema didn't at lunch, and he didn't, even later that night when we...see, Cosmo and I...we're...I...that is, he stayed with me when I was sick, and..." Her voice broke. "Oh, Amanda, I feel so betrayed. I feel like such a fool."

Amanda had taken one look at the beds and known instantly what Billy was hinting at. She knew something else, as well. "You're in love with him." It wasn't a question, but a statement of fact.

Billy sniffed and blew her nose hard. "Isn't that the dumbest thing? It's such a stupid cliché—to come to Hawaii and fall in love with the first man who looks at you."

"I don't think it's dumb at all. And men have been looking at you for years now, and you certainly haven't shown any signs of being fatally attracted to any of them before now. There's something powerful between you and Cosmo. I felt it from the beginning. And strangely enough, I'd bet my bottom dollar he's not interested in Ema, not that way. I have no proof, of course, but it's something you can sense about other people. Max likes and trusts him just as I do. We both get the feeling he's a complex young man, that we're not seeing everything that's there."

Amanda was quiet for a moment, pensively smoothing the bedcover with her hand. "I don't mean that you should jump into anything. Cosmo's life-style certainly has its drawbacks. It's just that I've wished so often that you'd fall in love again, dear. I didn't want you to give up because of one bad experience." Her voice was infinitely sad.

For a moment, Billy thought Amanda must be referring to her short-lived affair with Tom Pershell, but at the same time she was sure Amanda didn't know the details of that fiasco. Then it dawned on her that Amanda meant her marriage to Graham, and a shock wave rolled through her.

She and Amanda had never once discussed Graham beyond the usual stories of his childhood or the antics of his teen years or what he liked to eat. They'd never talked, woman to woman, about what it had been like to be married to the adult Graham Reece. How could Billy have talked about her marriage honestly? Amanda was, after all, Graham's mother, and it would have felt like the worst sort of betrayal to tell her how dismal the whole thing had really been.

Billy swabbed at the tears in her eyes and then stared at Amanda, still not convinced. "What...what do you mean?"

Amanda sighed, a deep, sorrowful sound. "I knew my son well, Billy. He had good traits, but he certainly had some bad ones, as well. No one needed to tell me that Graham wasn't the best husband in the world to you. He was spoiled and he was selfish. I knew that, even though it hurts me still to admit it. And he had an attitude toward women that I didn't like. I did my best to change it, with no success."

Amanda's mouth drew into a rueful knot. "It was my own fault, you see. I let John assume a role in our marriage that put me in a subservient position, and I never did anything to change it. So I guess it was natural for Graham to absorb that outlook, as well." Amanda's eyes were tortured when she met Billy's gaze. "I've always felt so responsible for the way things were for you. You never complained once to me, but it didn't take a genius to know that your marriage wasn't right." She shook her head sadly.

"I saw him one day, out with another girl, Billy. I was outraged that he'd do something like that. I did try to talk to him that time, but of course it didn't do any good at all. He'd been trained not to pay attention to me. So I tried to make John see what was happening, but he just got furiously angry—you remember the time he wouldn't speak to me for weeks, when he and Graham went off on that hunting trip?"

Billy did remember. Graham had taken his holidays to go hunting with his father, and she'd been hurt because he'd promised he and she would spend time together that year by themselves. She'd had the mistaken idea that they could somehow patch things up if only they had some time alone.

She'd never known exactly why both men were angry with Amanda, but she remembered how her mother-in-law had taken her out for a fancy lunch, a show and a shopping trip while they were gone. She'd been wonderfully sweet and caring toward her.

Billy reached out and took Amanda's hand in her own. "It wasn't that bad, Amanda, really. You mustn't feel guilty over anything. Graham was supposed to be an adult. He could have—" She stopped abruptly, not wanting even now to hurt Amanda in any way by talking about her son. "You were always marvelous to me. I've felt so fortunate, having you part of my life."

Now Billy wasn't the only one with tears in her eyes. Amanda's large eyes were overflowing, and she reached over and put her arms around Billy, holding her against her soft body in a tight hug.

"I'm the lucky one in this organization," Amanda said as lightly as she could manage, but the tears were dripping off her nose.

A tap sounded on the door, and Max opened it and stuck his head in, obviously taken aback at the sight of them holding each other and weeping.

"You two all right?" he asked, his voice filled with concern. "Is there anything I can do?"

Amanda gave him a wide, watery smile and a wink. "We're just happy to see each other again. Women always cry when they're happy, don't you know that?"

Max grinned ruefully. "It's a concept that escapes me, but if that's really all it is, I'm relieved. I came to tell you I have to go down to the police station and meet Detective Fellerman. I've gone through the other rooms pretty carefully, and the only thing that seems to be missing are two tapes of conversations I had with Charlie. You didn't notice them in here anywhere, did you? They were simply labeled Charlie, 1 and 2."

The women searched the room thoroughly, but the Charlie tapes were nowhere to be found.

CHAPTER THIRTEEN

CHARLIE WAS NOT GOING to be an easy houseguest. That was evident to Cosmo in the first fifteen minutes after he managed to smuggle him into Ema's apartment.

He'd immediately begun complaining about being "cooped up by the cops and left to rot." Cosmo shut him up by giving him a graphic rundown on what his chances were of staying alive outside on his own, but Charlie still wasn't a happy camper.

Ema was living in the two-bedroom suite the department had rented for her and Cosmo to use as a safe house. It wasn't luxurious by any stretch of the imagination, but it was clean and comfortable, and situated on the third floor of a large apartment complex that fronted Kailua Kona's main street, it was ideal for surveillance purposes. And it was air-conditioned, which added a great deal to its appeal.

Ema had the place as homey as it was possible to make it, considering that it was strictly a temporary abode for her. There were a few plants around, and a couple of dramatic batik throw pillows she'd bought at the market. Several of Cosmo's pictures that hadn't sold were tacked to the walls. There were a number of paperback books stacked neatly on the shelves of the bookcase, mostly murder mysteries and romance.

The fridge was well stocked with juices, yogurt, vegetables and fruit, and the place had been shiny clean when Cosmo had brought Charlie in.

Cosmo's art supplies and his sparse wardrobe were stowed in one bedroom. Ema used the other, so Cosmo had fixed up the sofa bed for Charlie.

The old hobo wanted no part of it.

"Floor's good enough fer me. Sleep on one of those and ya get soft in the noodle." The old man unwrapped his pack and spread his meager belongings on the rug, marking out a space for himself. His sleeping bag had long since passed the filthy state. It was indescribably dirty, and it stank. The pungent, gamy smell coming from it and the old man soon permeated the entire apartment, and the air-conditioning didn't seem able to dispel it. Cosmo opened all the windows and turned the air conditioner off in an effort to air the place out, but he didn't think that helped much, either.

Ema wasn't going to be amused at having Charlie as a roommate.

WHEN COSMO ARRIVED the next morning, the situation had disintegrated.

"How's it going, Charlie?" he asked when he let himself in.

Charlie barely nodded at him. He was sitting on the floor three feet from the television, his jaw hanging slackly as he watched Geraldo interview an ax murderer inside a prison. The volume was turned up almost full. The smell from the day before had grown more pungent.

Ema appeared from the bathroom, looking as immaculate as ever, but she rolled her eyes and pulled

Cosmo into the bedroom, shutting the door so Charlie wouldn't hear.

"He's a disaster and he's all yours for the day. I may never come back. I'm considering handing in my badge. What ever made me think I wanted to be a cop? This guy stinks so bad I can hardly stand it. I suggested he have a bath, but he says he can only wash in saltwater or his skin itches, can you believe that? And he hawks and spits all the time—in the sink, in my plants, out the windows."

Ema used her hands to punctuate her words. "He won't sleep on the sofa—insists it's too soft—so he spent the night on the floor, and this morning he burned a hole in the rug with those damned cigarettes you got him last night. He smokes one after the other, and he's already asking for more. The only good thing about it is that the stink of cigarettes covers up the other smell a little."

Ema turned to the door, then whirled around as she remembered something else. "And he snores, Cosmo. I've never heard anything like it. Besides that, he won't eat one lousy thing I've got in the fridge. He says he's had enough fruit to last him a lifetime and now he wants beans." Her voice rose an octave. "Beans, for God's sake! Can you just imagine what that'll do to the atmosphere in here? And he's had the television on full blast since five this morning. He loves game shows and he can't sleep past dawn, so naturally neither could I. And he's gone through four pots of coffee already, so there's hardly any left. Boy, I hope the department's going to pay for all this. I'm putting it on my expense sheet. In fact, they oughta kick in for hardship allowance."

The litany should have been funny, but Cosmo's sense of humor wasn't working well this morning. He was pondering the way Billy was acting. There was something wrong with her. He should have figured it out last night, but he'd been too beat after finding Charlie and settling him in here to notice much. And this morning, when he had noticed, there wasn't time to get into anything serious with her. He'd promised Ema he'd be back here to relieve her before she left for work.

"Want me to go back down and get him beans and cigarettes?" he asked.

Ema shook her head. "I'll get them and drop them back up to you. I've got to make contact with headquarters this morning, then I'll shut up shop early this afternoon and take over here."

She shuddered at the thought. "Actually, I don't think we need to keep a constant eye on him, do you? He's pretty rational about staying here, but there is the real problem of him setting the place on fire with his cigarettes—the smoke alarm in the hall went nuts last night. I had to disconnect it, so see if you can get it adjusted again."

She hurried out of the apartment, returning shortly with a bag of groceries and three cans of aerosol air freshener.

"Spray this around once every hour. Good luck."

The morning dragged past. Charlie watched game shows and news broadcasts and grunted when Cosmo tried to talk with him. It was obvious that the old man was adjusting well to civilized living, thanks to the television.

At noon, Cosmo heated up several cans of beans and one of spaghetti and scraped them onto plates.

Charlie devoured his share plus half a loaf of bread, finishing off with six of the doughnuts Ema had thought to add to the list that morning.

His table manners left a great deal to be desired; he ate with his mouth wide open and made a lot of noise. He didn't bother with niceties like napkins and belched loudly when he was finished. Cosmo could see what Ema meant. Charlie as a roommate left a lot to be desired.

Cosmo washed up the dishes while Charlie sat on the floor in front of the television again.

Cosmo was working on a plan. He and Ema had talked it over, and she was bouncing it off their bosses at H.Q. today, but there were details he still needed to figure out. He'd need Charlie's help with it, but if it worked, the case would soon be history and there'd be no problem convicting Franklin of all three murders.

The trouble was, he needed the department's approval as well as Charlie's full cooperation. He figured his boss would go for it all right, but getting Charlie to agree to help was going to be the tough part.

He dried his hands and went into the living room, switching the television off.

"Hey, I was watchin' that, young feller. Ain't you got no manners?"

Cosmo held his tongue and settled down in an armchair, wishing he had a cigar. Not that he smoked cigars; it was just that a cigar might muffle the other odors in the room, and that wouldn't be a bad thing at all.

"Listen up, Charlie. This is what I figure we ought to do."

But before Cosmo had gotten three sentences out, Charlie was shaking his head vehemently. His eyes were wide with fear, and the stench of sweaty terror coming from his body mingled unpleasantly with the other smells in the room.

MAX WAS GONE for several hours, and while Amanda and Billy tackled the job of putting the apartment in order, they talked.

They'd always talked, but never like this. Their conversations had always been interesting but never deeply personal. Now some barrier was down between them, allowing a more intimate relationship to form.

Under Amanda's gentle prodding, Billy had finally admitted her deep anger toward Graham, and the guilt she'd felt about that anger after he'd died.

"I've never talked much about how I really felt after John died, either," Amanda was saying as she methodically cleared the floor of clutter and dusted shelves before replacing items. "The truth is, if he hadn't already been dead, I'd have wanted to kill him when I found out what a mess he'd made for us financially."

Billy was shocked at that, but she couldn't suppress a tiny smile at Amanda's feisty choice of words.

"He was an accountant, for Pete's sake," Amanda went on, her voice full of scorn. "And yet any idiot could have done a better job with our money than he did. I don't know what he thought was going to happen to us after he retired. Still, the fault wasn't all his. I went along like a mindless sheep, never asking enough questions, just trusting him to take care of it all." Amanda plopped two heavy books back in place and shook her head in disgust. "I can't believe now how stupid I was. I'd certainly never be that trusting again."

Billy was uncoiling the cord from the vacuum. She hesitated before she plugged it in. "Speaking of trusting, I've wondered how come you haven't freaked out at the idea of me falling for a hobo. Most people wouldn't consider it very acceptable, and yet you've been supportive all along."

Amanda was silent for a long moment. "I learned many years ago not to judge a man by the label society hangs on him. One of the finest men I ever knew was a hippie." She met Billy's curious glance and smiled. "The true hippies were before your time, but they weren't unlike hoboes."

"Did you—" Billy stopped abruptly. "Sorry, Amanda, I don't mean to pry."

Amanda's gaze was inward, and far away. "Did I have an affair with him? Yes, as a matter of fact, I did. He got me over a particularly bad spot in my life. I'll tell you about it some other time."

Billy had to stifle the urge to question Amanda right now. It was astonishing to find out that Amanda, who'd always seemed the soul of propriety, could have such a delicious, unexpected secret. If the man had been even remotely like Cosmo, she was fiercely glad for her mother-in-law. She plugged the vacuum in, and for a while its racket made conversation impossible. When she unplugged it, she asked, "Think you'd ever get married again, Amanda? Or would you just live with somebody?"

Amanda gave her a strange look and then she turned a becoming shade of pink. "Until the past couple of days, I would have said either situation was pretty unlikely, because there weren't any men in my life and I didn't foresee any coming along. But..." She stopped what she was doing and stared down at the duster in her hand. The silence stretched on and then she said, "Well, you'll probably guess on your own, anyway. Max and I...on this trip we took, we didn't exactly have separate bedrooms."

Amanda's face was scarlet, and Billy couldn't help teasing her a little. "I certainly hope you practised safe sex," she said sternly, then she erupted into giggles at the shocked expression on her mother-in-law's rosy face. Amanda looked for all the world like a shy teenager caught out in a clandestine love affair.

"Oh, you." Amanda flicked the duster in Billy's direction and then she laughed too.

"Jokes aside, Amanda, I think that's fantastic," Billy said after a moment. "Max is a great guy. He's got that air of virility about him that intellectual men sometimes have." Done with the vacuuming, she sprawled on the couch. "But how are you going to feel about leaving here? We've only got the rest of this week and part of next week left. Although," she added thoughtfully, "Max lives in Vancouver part of the year, so you'll see him again, anyhow."

"That's true, and it would be nice to see him. But I don't ever want to make a man responsible for my happiness again, regardless of our relationship. That's what I did with John, and once was enough."

Her mother-in-law's words made intellectual sense, but Billy wasn't sure they were applicable emotionally. Being in love with a man made reason impossible—in her experience, anyway. And Amanda wasn't under any pressure here, either. Max might live in Vancouver, but not so with Cosmo.

Billy got to her feet and went to stir the spaghetti sauce she'd started earlier that day, her thoughts still on her ill-fated romance. Once she left the islands, that would be that. Hoboes couldn't afford flights to Vancouver, and she'd probably never make it back to Hawaii, at least not for years and years. The idea of not seeing Cosmo again made her feel physically sick.

So why was she getting herself tied in a knot about Ema and Cosmo and spoiling the time she did have with him? It wasn't as if she and Cosmo had a lifetime thing going, anyway. Why couldn't she take one day at a time, the way she'd planned to do in the beginning?

She stirred the sauce and sniffed in the rich tomato aroma, then put a huge pot of water on to boil for the pasta.

The trouble was, she admitted with reluctance, she'd brought along a lot of emotional baggage on this trip, all the distrust and betrayal and hurt feelings that had resulted from her marriage. And from Tom, as well. She'd been packing the whole mess around for a long time. So maybe she was far too ready to see duplicity everywhere.

The other mistake she was making was waiting around for Cosmo to entertain her. What was wrong with her? Amanda's comment about not making a man responsible for her happiness had struck home.

All in all, talking with Amanda had helped immeasurably. Rather than centering what was left of her holiday around Cosmo, she'd make plans of her own. She dropped the long strips of dry spaghetti into the boiling water and began gathering the ingredients for a salad.

She'd finish the two sketches that she'd been working on that morning and take them to Ema. Then there were several sight-seeing bus trips she could take. And there were still places right here in the village that she hadn't explored. She'd just have to get over feeling desolate because Cosmo wasn't around—that was all there was to it.

THE SPAGHETTI WAS half-eaten by the time Cosmo arrived that evening. Billy greeted him with a warm smile, and Amanda had him sitting at the table with a heaping plateful within minutes.

Max had just spent an entire afternoon answering questions, filling in forms, then being asked the same questions all over again. He wasn't any more impressed with Detective Fellerman than the others had been. He told Cosmo about it, mentioning the tapes that were missing.

"There wasn't anything on those tapes that would interest anyone else. They were just stories of Charlie's wandering days. But this Detective Fellerman seems to think now that I know more than I'm telling him about Charlie. He grilled me about you, as well, Cosmo."

Cosmo didn't say so, but he'd just spent forty uncomfortable minutes in the detective's car himself. Fellerman had stopped him on the street shortly after he'd left Charlie in Ema's reluctant hands that afternoon. He'd asked detailed questions about the caricatures Cosmo did, how much he sold them for, whether he had a business license, whether he was paying income tax.

He'd asked pointed questions about Cosmo's citizenship and noted that he had no visible means of support. He'd made it plain he was watching Cosmo's every move and wouldn't hesitate to run him in on the slightest provocation. Just as Cosmo had feared, the detective was determined to make life difficult in every way he possibly could.

Cosmo didn't tell Max and Amanda about the encounter, but he needed to tell Billy. After the meal, he asked if she'd go for a walk with him. They strolled hand in hand down the darkening streets, and Cosmo told her about Fellerman's thinly veiled threats.

"I'm going to have to keep a low profile for a while," he told her gently, hating himself for using this as the excuse he needed for not spending the next few days with her. He was uncomfortably conscious that her holiday was fast drawing to an end.

"I'll probably hang out at the hobo camp for a couple of days, until this thing with Fellerman blows over. I won't be able to see you much, not for a little while."

Her voice was falsely bright. "Oh, sure, I understand, no problem. There are a lot of things I want to do, anyway, and I'm working on those drawings for Ema."

They were nearing a small park, and Cosmo tugged at her hand, drawing her under the dim canopy of a huge tree. She held back, and his hands closed tight on her upper arms. He drew her roughly into his embrace. He could feel her resistance, strong at first. Then bit by bit she relaxed, her hands searching out and touching familiar parts of him, sliding around his torso and stroking his back, her breasts softly pressing against his chest. Her hair smelled sweet, and he buried his nose in it.

He simply held her that way for long moments. When at last he spoke, his voice was raw with emotion. "Don't play-act with me, Billy. Don't pretend you don't care about this. I care, and I know you must, too. It isn't okay—none of it is. It's not the way I want it to be for us. But for the moment, there's not a hell of a lot I can do to fix it. When I can, I will. Can you trust me on that?"

She hesitated for what seemed a long time, but at last she nodded against his neck. He tipped her head up with a thumb under her chin and kissed her, loving the sweetness of her mouth, the instant response that flared between them.

"I'm gonna hate sleeping without you beside me tonight," he growled, catching her mouth again and losing himself in the feeling.

"Billy. . ." He wanted to tell her how she made him feel, but it wasn't the time. He had to get out to the hobo camp now; he'd been away too long, and he and Ema had agreed that it was essential they keep up the whole facade for just a little longer.

Charlie hadn't agreed to the plan yet, but he would by morning. Ema could be very persuasive when she chose, and they already had a go-ahead from the boss.

Not much longer. If only he could get this wound up before Billy had to leave Hawaii.

"ALL YOU HAVE TO DO, Charlie, is tell Franklin on the phone that you and I were there the night his wife died. Tell him you know about Blackie and Slim and that the police are after us because they figure we know something we're not saying. But all we want is money. We need to disappear, and that's gonna be expensive. Twenty-five thousand dollars, Charlie. Tell him we want twenty-five grand and then he'll never hear from us again."

Cosmo had been over and over the story. Charlie was terrified. Even talking about making the call made him tremble uncontrollably. Finally Cosmo got out a bottle of whiskey and a glass, and the liquor brought on a false bravado.

"Twenty-five big ones," Charlie reiterated, taking a hearty gulp of the amber fluid in the glass Cosmo had just refilled for him. "In small bills, stashed in a coin storage locker out at the airport, with the key taped to the bottom of that big mailbox on Palani Road over by the post office."

He narrowed his eyes at Cosmo. "Too bad Slim and Blackie never figured it all out this way. They coulda gotten on a plane right then and there, been long gone. What makes you think Franklin won't figure we're gonna hop a plane when we pick up the money?"

"Like everybody else, he figures hoboes are drunks, and not very bright ones at that," Cosmo explained. "He'll figure on us buying booze and having a party with the guys before we leave town. He'll likely have somebody watching us from the minute we stop and get that key, anyway."

"But he might try 'n' blow us away right at the airport, ain't that right?"

The thought had crossed Cosmo's mind, but he was counting on Franklin wanting a lot more privacy for it. He told Charlie so.

"Yer smart, ya know that? You got a hell of a mind fer crime, young feller. Good thing yer a cop 'stead of a crook." Charlie took another sip and squinted at the phone on the counter as if it were a rattlesnake about to bite him. He made a trip to the bathroom and clicked the television on and off half a dozen times. "Hell's bells," the old man finally said unhappily. "I may as well get it over with—it's eatin' away at my gut. He did in Blackie and Slim. I owe 'em this, I reckon. You dial the number fer me, okay? I got the shakes."

Cosmo dialed, and after a delay in which a secretary relayed a message guaranteed to raise Franklin's blood pressure, the smooth, unctuous voice of the developer came over the phone line.

Cosmo nodded at Charlie and gave him a reassuring wink as he handed him the receiver.

AMANDA'S HAND WAS shaking as she dialed the number she'd found in the book for Momi's Coffee Shop.

Don't be so silly. All you're going to do is ask the price, she told herself. Which was a pretty ridiculous thing to do when you came down to it, considering the state of her bank account. She had no money to spare.

Unless she sold her house.

The woman who answered quoted a price and added that there were living quarters above the café—three modest rooms and a bath.

Amanda talked to her for some time, asking questions she'd never dreamed she knew to ask, about profit margins and operating costs and assuming mortgages. She'd learned more than she'd realized by having to put John's affairs in order.

When she hung up, she took a deep breath and placed another call to a Vancouver real estate agent who had an office near the bookstore in which she worked. She charged the call to her home number, and when it was over, she knew that all things really were possible if one only had the courage to set them in motion.

The crystal at her throat felt warm, much warmer than her skin, and when she put her hand up to it, she imagined she could feel it pulsing with energy.

And approval.

"THEY SOLD? My drawings of the fishermen actually sold? For this much money?"

Billy was unable to believe it, even holding the substantial amount of cash Ema had just handed her.

"Darned right they did. And some tourists from Germany have been back twice to look at several of the other ones—the one of the little boy in particular. My bet is they'll come back today and buy more." Ema looked smug and just as pleased as Billy felt. "Too bad we didn't get you busy drawing the day you arrived. You'd leave Kona a wealthy woman."

Billy felt dazed and utterly delighted. The drawings hadn't been in Ema's booth for long at all. Her unexpected success made her want to run out and draw fifteen more pictures immediately, but there wasn't time.

"How much longer before you have to leave, Billy?"

"Only two more days, after today." The thought sobered her, taking a little of the pleasure of the sale away. There really wasn't much time left for drawing pictures . . . or for anything else, for that matter.

The anything else, of course, was Cosmo. She longed to race off this minute and tell him about her success, but he was nowhere to be found. She'd watched for him in the park, maybe doing caricatures in the square. She kept expecting him to walk up behind her or appear on the street, but he never did.

He just wasn't around much anymore.

She'd filled this last week of her holiday with frantic activity, but nothing took away the loneliness she felt for him. She'd seen him only twice in four days, and the encounters had been brief, rushed and somehow strained. He seemed distracted, and they couldn't think of things to say to each other. She was beginning to wonder if she'd have any more time alone with him before she flew home.

Maybe it was for the best, she tried to convince herself. Parting might be easier if they weren't on the intimate terms they'd established so early on. But it was cold comfort, because she missed him with a steady, penetrating loneliness that seemed to pervade her very soul.

The thing to do was keep busy.

"How about having lunch with me, Ema? I've wanted to try that fancy little French restaurant here in the village, and seeing as how I'm suddenly rich..."

It was a way of thanking Ema for selling the pictures, but it would also help fill a lonely afternoon. Billy felt that Amanda and Max needed time to be alone these days, and she tried her best to stay away from the apartment, but the long hours seemed to stretch out indefinitely.

"Oh, Billy, thanks for asking. I'd just love to, but I can't today." Ema sounded genuinely regretful. "I have things I absolutely have to do this afternoon."

"How about tomorrow, then?" Billy was sure the other woman would accept.

But Ema shook her head again. "I'm afraid the next few days are impossible for me. I'm really sorry."

Billy forced nonchalance into her tone. "Well, then, I'll just go and pig out on my own. Thanks again, Ema."

"Be sure to come by before you leave and say goodbye, won't you?"

Billy agreed and hurried off as if she actually had somewhere to go. When she came out of the market into the blazing sunshine, however, her steps slowed and she wandered aimlessly up the busy street. She'd buy something nice for Max, she decided, as a small thank-you for all his kindness. And a T-shirt for Amanda with a gaudy I Love Kona message across the front.

That would take about an hour, and she could dawdle through lunch somewhere for another hour. The days she'd spent with Cosmo had gone past in the blink of an eye. Now the afternoon stretched out ahead of her like an abyss that had to be filled with endless, sluggish drops of time.

THREE STORIES ABOVE the street, Cosmo caught sight of Billy, moving slowly along below him, her silvery curls gleaming in the sunlight. He clenched the windowsill and something in his gut contracted into a hard knot and wouldn't let go.

It was agonizing, seeing her this way and not being able to go to her. He studied the way she moved, the loose, easy sway of her narrow hips, the pleasing shape of her body beneath the green cotton minidress she wore, and slowly he began to understand the depth of his love for her.

He'd wondered if something was wrong with him all these years, never having truly loved a woman. He'd thought at times in the darkness of his soul that perhaps he'd been born without the capacity to love a woman this way.

He knew now that wasn't so. He'd never loved before simply because he was waiting for Billy, and she hadn't come along till now.

Some men might need practice at this, need to experiment with falling in love again and again before they found the one person they were searching for. Not him. She was it for him, now and always, and at last he was smart enough to recognize it.

"Whatcha starin' at out there?"

Charlie came to stand beside him, the ever-present cigarette drooping from one side of his mouth. They were both on edge. This was the day they'd planned for, the day the trap was in place.

They'd arranged to call Franklin this afternoon at one o'clock to verify that the money was at the airport waiting for them. Franklin had stalled for the past couple of days, insisting he needed time to get cash. Cosmo was sure the delay was simply an attempt to launch one last effort to find Charlie and get rid of him.

Once the call was made today, Cosmo would notify Ema and confirm the fact that their backup system was in place and ready to go on a moment's notice. Then things would move along at speed. The pickup was tentatively scheduled for four this afternoon.

It was twenty to one now, and the minutes dragged past as if they wore lead boots.

"See that blond-haired woman down there, Charlie? The one in the green dress?"

Billy had stopped to look at T-shirts in an open-sided shop.

"Yeah, I see her."

"I'm going to marry that woman, Charlie."

Charlie was shocked. The cigarette tilted dangerously in his open mouth. "Holy Murphy, young feller.
Why would you be wantin' to go do a thing like that
fer?"

"Look at her, Charlie. She's the most beautiful
woman in the world, and I intend to ask her to marry
me first chance I get."

Charlie moved closer to the window and studied
Billy carefully. "She's fine lookin', I'll grant ya, but
marryin' is serious business."

Billy had disappeared up a side street, and Cosmo
left the window to glance at the clock again and pour
himself and Charlie a coffee.

"You ever been married, Charlie?"

"Nope. Never lit in one spot long enough, I
reckon."

"You ever wish you had married?"

Charlie looked pensive for a moment. "Last coupla years, maybe. Gets kinda lonely as ya get older,
bein' a hobo. Ya get to thinkin' about takin' that
westbound freight to the big jungle in the sky, an'
wishin' there was somebody down here who gave a
damn about ya."

"You been a hobo all your life, Charlie?"

The old man nodded and took a long slurp of his
coffee. "Most all. I was born in Portland, Oregon,
back in June of 1926. My mother wasn't married, sixteen years old, some school kid. Never knew her myself. Back then they took illegitimate babies away and
put them in a state-run orphanage, an' that's what
they did with me." Charlie's face screwed into a gri-
mace. "Hell of a place. I stuck it till I was fourteen,
then I up and run away. Met up with a coupla 'boes,
and they took me under their wing, so to speak. Kept

me outa trouble, took care a me till I could do it myself. Real good guys. Steam Train and Bullfrog was their names.''

The story touched Cosmo. He thought of his own happy childhood, growing up in a big old noisy house with his brothers and sister, secure in his parents' love and his place in the family. Knowing even now there was always somewhere to go home to, a group of people who were his flesh and blood, who accepted and loved him no matter what.

Like Charlie, Billy had never known that kind of security.

"Did you ever find a place you wanted to settle, a place that felt like home, Charlie?''

"There was one town, a little place in the mountains back in Washington State. Nothin' special, but it called ta me. I worked there two years, in a mill. But then one night I heard the whistle of a freight train, an' I had to go. Always planned on goin' back, but I never did.'' Charlie gave Cosmo a bashful look. "There was a girl there I sorta liked, but she was way too good fer the likes a me. I still think about her sometimes. Gladys, her name was.''

"You ever take her out or anything?'' Cosmo knew he was prying, but Charlie didn't seem to mind. It kept their minds off the clock.

"Yeah, took her to a picnic once. The mill had this big picnic each summer for all the people what worked there. Gee, we had us a good time that day.'' Charlie's blue eyes were misty as he remembered. "She had on this yeller dress. We won the three-legged race, her 'n' me.''

He smiled, and there were gaps in his teeth, but for the first time Cosmo could see a glimmer of a younger, good-looking Charlie. Then the smile slipped away and resignation took its place.

"Two days after that I hopped the freight."

"You just left? Without saying goodbye? Without even giving her a chance to tell you how she felt? Why the hell would you do a thing like that?"

Charlie gave him a long look, as if it ought to be evident to any idiot. "That way she never had to let me down, see. Ain't no way it coulda worked. She came from a real nice family an' all. Me, I wasn't nobody."

The words were said with such conviction, such acceptance, that Cosmo looked at the old hobo and felt a lump gather in his throat. How much happiness was lost because people were afraid to try, because they felt unworthy of love? How much terrible damage was done to a child who had no one of his own to care for him, who went through life feeling undeserving?

His thoughts went to Billy, and his heart ached for her. The moment, the very instant he was able, he was going to tell her exactly how he felt. He was going to make sure that for the rest of her life, she had all the love she could handle and then some.

The hands on the clock had finally moved along. It was one.

"C'mon, partner," Cosmo said with a cheerfulness he was far from feeling. "Let's make the call and get this show on the road."

CHAPTER FOURTEEN

ACCORDING TO FRANKLIN, the money was waiting. Cosmo dialed Ema's number to confirm backup, but there was no answer at the booth. He tried again five minutes later, and again in another five minutes, with no luck.

Where the hell was she? Adrenaline was pumping through his veins.

"I gotta sit in the toilet fer a while. This thing's givin' me a gut ache," Charlie announced in a weak voice, clutching his stomach. Fear had turned his normally ruddy skin a sickly yellow. The bathroom door slammed behind him.

Cosmo decided to go and see if he could find Ema. Charlie was safely occupied for at least fifteen minutes, and he could hurry to the market and back by then.

Locking the door carefully behind him, he made his way to the street.

BILLY HAD DAWDLED as long as she could over lunch. The restaurant was nearly empty by the time she left. She turned toward home, thinking that maybe she'd spend the rest of the afternoon by the pool at the apartment.

The street was exceptionally busy. A cruise boat lay at anchor in the bay, and the excited passengers had taken the village by storm, cameras and wallets much in evidence. A laughing, chattering group came barreling toward her. She stepped into an open-fronted shop to let them pass, and staring out over their heads to the other side of the boulevard, she saw Cosmo. Ema was close beside him. They were hurrying along, shouldering their way through the crowds, obviously intent on getting somewhere fast.

Disbelief was Billy's first reaction. She'd been with Ema only an hour ago, and once again, Ema hadn't mentioned a single word about Cosmo or admitted that he was the reason she couldn't have lunch with Billy.

"I have things I absolutely have to do this afternoon," she'd said.

Why couldn't she have admitted that those things involved Cosmo?

Slowly, incredulity gave way to the wrenching pain of betrayal, then came the first stirrings of anger. Within seconds the anger escalated into fury as the pair moved away.

How dared they treat her this way? How dared they lie and cheat and make a fool of her?

Billy was trembling, her entire body reacting to the rage pulsing through her body. She wasn't going to allow them to think they'd fooled her this time. She was going to confront them, tell them exactly what she thought of both of them.

They were more than half a city block ahead of her by now, and she pushed her way frantically through the crowd, running hard, dodging startled pedestrians, her eyes intent on Cosmo's tall, dark form.

She was only ten steps behind, when they turned into the doorway of an apartment building. She raced for the door and caught it an instant before it closed, shoving her full weight against it and bursting into the foyer just as Cosmo and Ema were stepping into an elevator.

"Cosmo. Ema." Her voice reverberated through the small lobby, echoing again and again.

They whirled around, and the look of alarm and amazement on their faces as they turned toward her should have given her satisfaction, but it brought only renewed pain.

"Billy?"

Cosmo took a step toward her. Ema was still standing in the door of the elevator, one hand holding it open.

"Honey, what are you doing here?"

"Maybe I should ask you two the same thing." Her throat constricted, and she could barely force the words out. Suddenly she was perilously close to tears.

"How could you two do this to me? I thought we were . . . I thought . . ."

Cosmo turned and exchanged a look with Ema, then he hurried over to Billy and took her hands in both of his. She tried to snatch them away, but he was incredibly strong.

"C'mon, we can't talk down here. Come upstairs and I'll tell you what's going on."

Billy's entire body was trembling. For an instant, she continued to resist the steady pressure of his hands, but then she allowed him to pull her, like a wooden marionette, into the elevator.

Ema's dark eyes met hers in a long, silent exchange, then the other woman reached out and gently touched Billy on the arm. "It's not at all what you think," she said in a soft tone as the elevator lurched to a stop. "Give him a chance to explain, okay?"

Cosmo led the way down a hall and fished in his pocket for a key, and the three of them went in.

Billy was prepared for the worst. One wild conjecture after another flitted through her mind, and now she wished with all her heart that she had never started this. She'd rather not know; it hurt too much.

Did they live here? Together?

Ema had moved with easy familiarity into the kitchen and was pouring juice from the refrigerator into three glasses. A shirt Billy recognized as Cosmo's was tossed carelessly across a chair, and his backpack was nearby.

"Charlie?" There was anxiety in Cosmo's tone, and he called again, louder this time. "Charlie? Where are you?"

"In the toilet." The aggrieved bellow came from down a hallway, behind a closed door. "I told you—I don't feel none too good. Belly's aching."

Cosmo let out a relieved sigh. He still had Billy's hand firmly in his own, and he tugged her toward the living room and pulled her down onto the sofa beside him. She deliberately extricated her hands from his grip, first one, then the other, clasping them tightly in her lap.

"Honey, don't look at me like that, please." His words were low and his expression somber. "Billy, Ema and I are police officers, detectives with Honolulu P.D. We're working undercover here in Kona on the murders of Liza Franklin and those two hoboes."

Police officers? Billy heard the words, but she couldn't seem to make sense of them. She stared at

Cosmo, her expression blank, her hands still clasped tightly in her lap, every muscle in her body rigid.

"There's nothing personal between Ema and I except a business friendship, believe me. The department rented us this apartment, and Ema's been living here. For the past couple of days so have I, because we've got Charlie in protective custody. That's why I haven't been able to be with you."

"You're... a policeman?" Her voice was thin and high. "So you've been lying to me all along about being a hobo?"

He sighed and rubbed a hand wearily across his face. "Yeah, I have been, and I hated doing it. But it was necessary, Billy."

His dark eyes met hers, full of appeal, but she ignored it.

"Don't you see I had no choice? This thing doesn't just involve me—there's the whole operation. Other people are vulnerable. And things like this are always on a strict need-to-know basis."

The extent of his deceit was more than she could take in all at once. "So everything you ever told me was a lie?" She groped for solid ground, anything to hold on to. "Is...what about you...is your name even Cosmo? All that stuff about your family in Seattle? About..." Small details came back to her clearly. "About the friend you had who was Indian? About riding boxcars to Mexico? It was all a lie?" She looked at him, and she thought of Graham and Tom. The awful lies they'd told her tumbled about in her head like stones.

Excruciating pain filled her chest. How many times in her life would she have to face the fact that once again she'd been lied to by someone she thought she loved? What was it about her that attracted dishonesty?

Cosmo shook his head in frustration. "My name's Cosmo, all right. It's just not Menzies. That's my cover name. I'm Cosmo Antonelli." He tried for a crooked smile, and failed. "Real good old Italian handle, huh? And my dad's a cop as I said, in Seattle." A pleading, desperate tone came into his voice. "Billy, most of the rest of what I told you was true. As much as possible I was honest with you."

He was aware that Ema had left the kitchen and gone into her bedroom to give them privacy, but Charlie appeared in the doorway now and stood, stomachache apparently forgotten, avidly watching the two of them, not even pretending he wasn't listening.

"Billy, all the really important things I told you were true," Cosmo insisted, wishing to God they were alone so he could do a better job of this, take her in his arms as he longed to do and show her with his lips what the really important things were.

"So you've always been a policeman? You never did the other things you said, the things you told me about being a hobo?"

"Some of them were things I did. Some were fiction, a necessary part of my cover."

This was rotten, far worse than he'd imagined it would be. He caught a glimpse of the wall clock. On top of everything else, he was going to have to leave before they had time to get this settled. "Most of them happened, but a long time ago, before I joined the force. I've been an undercover detective for four years now, working in the Seattle area. I only transferred to

Hawaii a few months ago. This is the first case I've worked on over here."

Ema came quietly into the room. She was dressed in dark slacks and a loose shirt, and Billy realized she was wearing a holster and a gun. It was a shock, and it brought home as nothing else had done the reality of what Cosmo had confessed.

"Cosmo, I'm sorry, but we've got a schedule to meet," Ema said. "I've called the guys to send the cab for you and Charlie. It'll be here in a minute."

Cosmo cursed under his breath, a vicious, frustrated stream of words. He got to his feet. "Billy, I can't explain right now, but I've got to go to work. Things are finally coming together in this case. If everything goes the way we plan, this whole damned mess could be over with tonight, but it might be late before I get back. Can you stay here and wait for me? I need to talk this out with you. It won't wait till tomorrow—I need to get it straight tonight. You can call Amanda and tell her where you are. My bedroom's down the hall on the left. Go and sleep there if it gets too late."

She began to shake her head, but he bent over and took her face in his hands, forcing her to look into his tortured eyes. "Billy," he said intently. "Billy, I love you. Do you understand that? I love you, and I need to talk to you, so wait here for me. I want to know you're here, safe. I'm still concerned about that guy you saw, the one who followed you that night. Promise me you'll stay here, that you'll be here when I get back."

"*I love you.*"

The beautiful words she'd longed to hear him say were impotent now in the face of all his other lies.

Sadness came over her, heavy and bleak. What difference would talking make? And yet...

"Promise me, Billy." There was something so compelling in his tone that she couldn't refuse him.

She nodded reluctantly.

"Thank you." It was a fervent whisper, and he bent swiftly and pressed a hard kiss on her lips. He turned then and hurried into a bedroom, leaving Billy alone with the hobo called Charlie.

"There's lotsa stuff ta eat in the fridge, missus," he volunteered. "There's a pot a mud on the stove, too, fresh this mornin'."

She tried to smile at the strange old man. "I'm sure I'll be fine."

He sidled closer to her, and she caught a whiff of his odor, sweaty and thick. "Don't be too tough on the young feller. He's a good sort, even if he ain't a 'bo like he pertended ta be."

Ema came in just then. "Charlie's right, Billy. Cosmo's an honest guy and a good cop. I've felt rotten, too, because I couldn't be straight with you, but this job's like that sometimes." She grimaced. "It's the reason I'm having trouble with my man. Remember I told you? He doesn't understand all this undercover stuff. I think when this is over I'm probably going to request a transfer back to regular duty. I mean, how many great guys are there left running around loose?" She gave Billy an understanding smile. "Besides, I've about had it with pretending to be an artist. You really had me on the spot a couple of times, you know that?"

"You didn't paint any of those canvases, then?" Billy realized she should have guessed before now. The style of the drawings and that of the oils had puzzled her, because they were similar. And Ema had been the most reticent artist she'd ever met. "Did Cosmo paint them all?"

Ema gestured to a painting hanging on the wall. "He sure did. That one's his, too. He's good, huh? And he made a bundle doing it, as well, which was a nice bonus. See, the booth was a good cover for me—the market's the best place around to hear whatever's going on, and it made it easy for Cosmo and me to keep in touch. But we never imagined his paintings would get so popular."

Billy thought of the primitive dramatic power of the landscapes she'd believed to be Ema's work. Cosmo was incredibly talented and versatile.

Nothing was quite what it had seemed to be. There was so much she still had to learn about the man she'd thought she knew so well. There was something else disturbing here, too, an aura of tension and urgency in the air that bothered her.

"Is this job you have to do tonight... is it very dangerous, Ema?"

Charlie answered before Ema could. "Dangerous? Hell, it's suic—" he started to say.

But Ema cut him off quickly. "It's mostly routine," she said in a soothing voice. A buzzer sounded. "There's the cab. You all ready, Charlie?"

Cosmo hurried in, wearing a loose denim shirt over his habitual cutoff jeans. He'd exchanged his worn sandals for equally worn running shoes. He leaned over to kiss her, and Billy saw the shoulder holster he was wearing beneath the shirt.

Suddenly his transition from hobo to policeman was real to her, and frightening. She wanted to tell him to be careful, but he was already going out the door with Charlie.

Ema waited a few moments after they left, tension evident in every line of her body as she watched from the front window until the cab pulled away with Cosmo and Charlie in it.

"Show time for me, too," she said then, deliberately casual. "Make yourself at home, Billy. I'll see you a bit later."

The door clicked behind her, and Billy was suddenly alone.

FOR THE FIRST HALF HOUR Billy's thoughts were stormy and unfocused, beginning and ending always with the colossal hoax of Cosmo's identity.

How could he have deceived her so thoroughly? She went over and over the conversations they'd had, looking for clues, trying to remember if there were hints she'd ignored, but even now it seemed to her that his cover had been totally convincing.

She felt tricked, as if he'd somehow made a fool of her. She'd thought of him always in the context of what he pretended to be, a hobo, a free spirit, a man who'd chosen a life-style that, extreme as it was, had endeared him to her partly because it seemed such a courageous, even romantic, gesture. And now she had to try to see him in a totally different way, see him as a policeman, a man with a life-style diametrically opposed to the one he'd pretended to have. His job was stressful and dangerous, demanding and difficult.

Graham's responsibilities as a fireman had not been dissimilar to a policeman's. How many of the problems between them had been a result of his job? She remembered the nights alone when he was on duty,

Christmas and Thanksgiving dinners without him, the anxiety she'd felt, knowing his work could be dangerous. She also remembered the stag parties he'd gone to, the amount of time he'd spent drinking with his friends, other firemen, but policemen, as well. They were both careers that seemed to draw men closer to one another while at the same time driving their women away.

Cosmo had said he loved her. Did that mean he wanted to spend his life with her? And if he did, what would that life be like for her?

Her marriage to Graham had been miserable, a trap she'd entered willingly enough, and all too soon had found heartbreaking. Would life with Cosmo be any different?

After a while she realized that she was pacing around the apartment like a caged animal. She forced herself to stop, to go into the kitchen and make some tea, but the hot liquid did nothing to calm her or make sense of what had occurred.

She called Amanda and told her only that she was at Ema's apartment and that she'd be late getting in. Then she took her cup and stood in front of the unframed painting on the living-room wall.

Unlike the dramatic landscapes Ema displayed in her booth, this one was a study of hoboes around a campfire at night. Cosmo had captured the essence of the scene in a few bold strokes of his brush.

Four men sat huddled in a tight group, their craggy, worn faces reflected in the flickering firelight. They each held enamel mugs, and a pot of coffee hung suspended by a crude tripod over the flames. One of them was obviously telling a story, gesticulating with one arm, and the others were hanging on his every word.

In the background, dark palms were silhouetted against a darker ocean. There was a kind of magic to the scene, an intimacy that drew the viewer in and made him long for simple pleasures like the one portrayed.

She felt admiration and respect for such ability. They shared this fascination with art, her and Cosmo, this need to take mental snapshots of the world around them and transfer them to canvas. But what should have been a bond between them had instead been one more area in which he'd deceived her.

Quicksand. Her relationship with Cosmo was like a house she'd built on quicksand, its foundation shifting and untrustworthy.

The awful unrest inside her quieted after a time, and she became still and cold, sitting immobile in an armchair and staring unseeing at the hobo picture.

She'd wait for him as she'd promised she would, but words couldn't mend what was irrevocably broken.

THE KEY AND THE MONEY were just where they were supposed to be, and Cosmo knew the hidden video surveillance on both mailbox and locker would have documented evidence of the person who'd placed them there.

So far, so good.

Cosmo opened the top of the plain brown grocery bag he'd just retrieved from the locker at the airport and glanced inside. Neat stacks of bills, tens and twenties, were held in place by rubber bands.

"Looks like it's all here, Charlie."

The old hobo was close beside him, and he kept swiveling his head nervously, searching the bustling crowds surrounding them for anything that would spell a trap, but it seemed no one was paying any attention to the two scruffy hoboes.

"I gotta go to the toilet agin," Charlie moaned, clutching his belly and scuttling toward the door to the men's room.

Cosmo smothered a groan and hurried after the old man, praying nothing would happen here. He hadn't counted on a delay like this.

Boxcar Charlie was almost hysterical with fear, even though Cosmo had assured him again and again that the airport was far too public a place for Franklin to try anything. That was the very reason Cosmo had chosen it for the drop. All his reassurances did little to calm the hobo, however. Charlie was still shaking with fear when they came out of the men's room a few moments later.

"Let's go, old-timer." The bag in his hand, Cosmo casually led the way out the airport doors and back toward the taxi waiting in the shade of the buildings. He was acutely aware of Charlie scurrying along beside him, still peering around suspiciously in all directions.

Cosmo couldn't see Ema's car, but he knew she was somewhere nearby, monitoring their every move and relaying it over her radio to other plainclothes detectives, some stationed along the route and others disguised as hoboes, waiting out at the campsite. The trap was in place, and all he could do now was pray that it would spring tight around Franklin's neck the way he and Ema had planned.

Cosmo knew there were others watching them, just as Charlie feared. He was certain they'd been under surveillance from the second they'd entered the airport, and that at this moment, dangerous men would be scrambling into a nearby car, waiting with motor idling for their cab to pull away.

Once inside the taxi again, Charlie collapsed in a corner, his eyes closed, his hands cradling his stomach. "I'm too old fer this kinda stuff," he whined. "I got a bellyache..."

Cosmo's eyes met those of the cabdriver in the mirror, and a silent spark of amusement traveled between them.

The cabdriver was, of course, an undercover policeman.

Charlie peered anxiously out the back window every three seconds on the ride back into town, trying to figure out which cars were following them, with no success.

They were soon in Kailua-Kona. Cosmo told the driver to take them to the liquor store, then he settled back in the seat, his thoughts not on the job as they should have been, but on Billy.

In the past, this stage of a job had been filled with tense anticipation and a high excitement that forced all other thoughts from his mind. Today, the job took second place to the emotional turmoil inside him. The look on Billy's face when she'd learned the truth a few hours ago haunted him.

If only he'd had a chance to do things differently, to tell her in his own way, instead of having her find out the way she had. If only she'd wait at the apartment as she'd promised.

Charlie touched his arm and he jumped.

"We're here. You okay, young feller?"

Cosmo realized the cab had pulled to a stop in front of the liquor store. He and Charlie went inside. They bought a number of large bottles of wine.

One more stop, to pick up quantities of cold cuts and bread and pickles from a deli, then they were on the road north that led to the industrial park near the hobo camp.

At the playing fields Cosmo made a show of paying off the driver, before he and Charlie loaded the things they'd bought into their backpacks and headed off across the parking lots to the overgrown road. Cosmo had the paper bag with the money tucked inside his shirt, leaving his hands free in case he had to get the snub-nosed revolver out of his shoulder holster under his denim jacket.

His back prickled and adrenaline surged through his veins as they hurried along the rough pathway. The low shrubbery wasn't adequate cover, and this was the portion of the journey that was the most dangerous. Every nerve in his body was on edge.

Here, despite the officers Cosmo knew were stationed in secluded spots all along the route, he and Charlie were still out in the open, most vulnerable to attack. Sweat broke out on his forehead and trickled down the small of his back as he tried to sense danger in the seemingly placid scene around them.

The sun was hovering over the ocean, almost ready to slip beneath the watery horizon, and Cosmo prayed they'd second-guessed Franklin correctly. They'd figured he and his thugs would wait until dark, until the hoboes had partied themselves into oblivion and were easy targets for ambush.

Charlie also sensed the danger they were in. "I don't like this one bit. I feel like a sitting duck out here in the open like this," he muttered, shuffling along at Cosmo's side and trying to look in every direction at once. "Never shoulda said I'd take this on. My belly's hurtin' again," he complained bitterly. "You get paid fer this sorta stuff, but what the hell do I get, I'd like ta know, 'cept fer a sore gut and a case of the trots?"

"You get a story to tell for the next fifty years to every 'bo in the country—that's got to be worth something," Cosmo said in an attempt to tease him out of his fear.

Finally they were within sight of the depression that housed the hobo jungle, and Cosmo felt immensely relieved and grateful that they'd arrived safe and sound. The responsibility for keeping Charlie safe through this operation weighed heavy on him.

The four officers disguised as hoboes ambled out to meet them.

"Nothing doing yet," one of them said to Cosmo.

"Okay. Have you tested the loud-hailer?"

The man nodded. "Earlier on. The sound's plenty loud enough. The guys out in the bushes have both it and the flare guns."

"Good. Has everybody been briefed on departure procedure if tonight turns out to be a no-show?"

"Done." He handed Cosmo the small hand-held portable radio. "The signal to release the flares is three consecutive pumps on the transmitter button."

"Great. Then there's nothing else to do except build up the fire and fake a party," Cosmo said. *And hope Franklin shows,* he added silently.

"Let's face it, how often do we get paid to have a party?" he added in an effort to ease the growing tension.

FULL DARKNESS HAD FALLEN a good two hours before, and the moon was up, a huge golden orb in the clear sky.

Still they waited. Even Charlie had finally gone beyond fear to boredom, and his trips into the underbrush had slowed considerably. He'd spent the past hour telling stories of his traveling days, making the officers laugh at his outrageous tales.

The campfire was only embers now, and they'd eaten most of the food. Charlie had made inroads on one of the wine bottles and was now half asleep, his back against a log; every now and then he'd mutter something under his breath.

All at once the earphone Cosmo wore came alive and Ema's voice said quietly, "Car with unidentified male passenger approaching the beach, a quarter of a mile to the south."

The pounding of the surf muffled the sound of the car's engine. Cosmo relayed the message, and the men arranged themselves on the sand, pretending to be sleeping off the drunken effects of a party.

Cosmo's heart was beating hard and fast. He'd been afraid all along that Franklin wouldn't come himself, that he'd hire a henchman, instead, to do his dirty work. He and Ema had spent hours discussing it, and they'd finally concluded that the odds were Franklin would show. It was a calculated risk, but they thought Harrison Franklin would want to tie up the messy ends of his wife's murder once and for all, this time doing away with all the hoboes himself.

Still, Cosmo had been certain Franklin would bring others along with him as backup. Franklin's type weren't usually long on guts. So what was he doing—if it was him—alone in that car a quarter mile away?

The radio receiver crackled again. "Suspect appears to be waiting inside the car."

Another fifteen minutes passed, and the same message was relayed once more. Tension was high around the campfire.

"It's probably some tourist taking telephoto shots of the moon, for heaven's sake," one of the policemen commented in a whisper.

Charlie had come fully awake at the first radio warning, and by the time the second had come, he'd groaned and announced that he once again had to head into the bushes. Cosmo swore and warned him to be quick, and the old man scurried off.

"Shoulda bought him a bottle of Kaopectate instead of that wine," one of the cops remarked, and the others laughed quietly. It helped ease the strained atmosphere, but Cosmo couldn't shake his anxiety over Charlie.

He should have figured out a way to keep Charlie right out of this, he reproached himself. The other hoboes were safely stashed away for the night in Kona, at the department's expense, and he should have managed to send Charlie with them. It wasn't fair to the old man, having him here.

With a suddenness that made him jump, the radio earphone announced urgently, "Four subjects arrived by small boat and are now approaching from the beach. The subject in the car is still not moving."

Where the hell was Charlie? There wasn't time to go searching for him. Cosmo sent up an urgent prayer that the old hobo was flat on his stomach, hiding in the bushes.

Minutes later, four men armed with what appeared to be short-barreled rifles materialized on the shadowy periphery of the hobo enclosure.

"Okay, nobody move. Keep your hands where I can see 'em," a voice shouted. "Which one of you bastards is Charlie?"

The voice was the one on the tape, and Cosmo could dimly see the man doing the talking. It was Franklin, and a feeling of immense relief swept over him. The trap had attracted the prey.

"I guess that's me." Cosmo did his best to sound like Charlie.

"I believe you have some money that belongs to me. You've got two seconds to produce it, greaseball, or you're history."

"Then you're gonna murder us all like you did your wife, huh?" Cosmo tried for a nasal whine.

Franklin snorted. "A few more dead hoboes won't make a hell of a lot of difference, right?"

It was all Cosmo needed; he pressed the button with his finger.

But before he'd finished the signal, a terrified voice from behind the four men trebled, "Don't shoot him. You got the wrong guy. That ain't Charlie down there. I'm Charlie. Don't shoot..."

The flares roared high into the darkness as Franklin whirled and fired. In an instant the scene was bright as day. A voice from the loud-hailer boomed, "This is Hawaii P.D. Put down your weapons. You're completely surrounded.

Three guns dropped to the sand, but Charlie's body had already hurtled up into the air. Instinctively Cosmo reached for his revolver and fired, though afterward he didn't remember doing so. In slow motion, Cosmo saw Franklin's body jerk, jerk, jerk and then slump to the ground. Instinctively Cosmo reached for his revolver and fired, though afterward he didn't remember doing so.

Suddenly the camp was alive with police officers.

"This one's dead," someone hollered, kneeling over Franklin.

Cosmo hardly heard him. All he could think of was Charlie. His legs wouldn't move fast enough. He clawed his way up the embankment and over to where the old hobo lay.

The blue eyes were filled with agony, and blood poured onto the sand. Cosmo gripped Charlie's gnarled old hand and spoke desperately into the radio. "Ema, get on the main channel and get a helicopter out here. Charlie's been shot."

CHAPTER FIFTEEN

COSMO'S KEY TURNING in the lock woke her. Billy had been slumped over in the armchair for the past two hours, sound asleep, and she felt crumpled and stiff as she straightened up.

The light in the kitchen was on, and she squinted over at the wall clock. It was twenty to four. Her brain felt sluggish, and the conclusions she'd reached during her hours alone were now all jumbled together in an unruly mass inside her head. All she could think of was how glad she was to see him, how ridiculously happy it made her feel to have him in the same room.

"Billy?" He stood just inside the door. "You should have gone to bed instead of waiting here."

His shoulders were slumped and the usual lithe grace was absent from his body. His voice was filled with weariness, but there was tension in it, as well.

"I have to put on some clean clothes. Excuse me a minute."

He disappeared into the bedroom and she heard drawers opening and closing, water running in the bathroom sink. Soon he reappeared, wearing clean cutoffs and a fresh gray T-shirt. His beard was damp and his hair had been brushed and tied back neatly, but he didn't look refreshed. He came over and sank down on the sofa across from her.

"I'm sorry I've kept you waiting here so long," he said in a peculiar, formal sort of way. "I've been at the hospital. Old Charlie was...injured tonight."

"Badly hurt? Is...will he be all right?" Billy's voice was still husky from sleep and she couldn't seem to think straight.

Cosmo shrugged laconically. "He was shot in the abdomen. They've removed a good portion of his bowel and most of his stomach. He hasn't regained consciousness yet, and it doesn't look too good. Ema's with him—she stayed so I could come to you."

Billy waited for him to go on, but he didn't. He fell silent, his head bowed, shoulders hunched.

The silence lengthened. Billy began to feel uncomfortable, as if she were with a stranger, trying to make polite conversation.

"The job you had to do tonight—is...was that how Charlie got shot, Cosmo?"

He raised his head and looked at her, and even in the dim light, she could see the closed expression in his eyes, the hard set of his mouth.

"Yeah," he said without emphasis. "He got himself in the wrong place at the wrong time. He's a stupid old man." His voice was suddenly harsh, and he turned his head away from her.

"I'm sorry." She shuddered, wondering how much danger Cosmo himself had been in tonight. Into her sleepy brain came the eerie echo of Tutu Kane's prophesy: *"There is death all around him."*

She shrugged it off. Cosmo was here; he was obviously safe and unharmed. "Did anyone else get hurt?"

A strange smile came and went, a cold, hard smile that had nothing of humor in it. "One other guy. He died."

Silence again.

Billy sat up straighter and ran her fingers through her hair, trying to tidy it. She found her sandals and slipped them on. She stood up, uncertain what to do or say. Cosmo was acting decidedly strange.

"Do you want me to make some tea? Or a sandwich? Are you hungry?" This was ridiculous, this nonconversation. If he'd come back in the middle of the night for the express purpose of talking to her, why didn't he do it?

He shook his head at her offer of food, but he still didn't look at her. Finally, after a long moment, he sighed and got wearily to his feet. "I've got a patrol car outside. Maybe I ought to drive you home."

Billy swallowed her shock and disappointment and tried to ignore the spark of anger his words evoked. She'd waited here alone for this man, doing as he'd asked her—begged her—to do, agonizing over what to say to him, what decisions to make. Had she waited for hours and hours so that now he could walk in and offer to drive her home? It didn't make sense at all.

She made a supreme effort at being understanding. "Cosmo, what is it? What's wrong?" The words sounded ludicrous, because of course everything was wrong between them. Anyway, it should have been him asking her that question, shouldn't it?

He looked at her at last, but there wasn't any change in the frozen expression in his eyes. "Wrong? Nothing's wrong. I'm just kind of tired. It's been a hectic night and it's far from over."

She nodded encouragement, but again he was quiet.

"Well, I guess I'm ready to go home, then." There was nothing else to say.

As polite as any chauffeur, he escorted her down in the elevator and settled her in the car. She'd never been in a car alone with him; he'd never driven her anywhere before. He handled the vehicle with all the offhand assurance of a man who'd spent hours behind the wheel, and in a short time the car drew up in front of Max's apartment building.

Cosmo got out, opened the car door, took the key from her and used it on the street door of the building. He came inside, walked her to the elevator. "By the way, one of the men we arrested matched your description of the guy you saw here that night. You don't have to worry about him anymore." He put out a hand and touched her hair for a moment. Again she waited for more. But that was all.

"Good night, Cosmo," she managed to say after an interminable silence.

As if he were returning from some distant dream, he looked at her, and a shadow of feeling crossed his face.

"Billy, I'm sorry about tonight. I'll see you tomorrow."

Before the elevator door closed, he'd already turned and was making his way across the lobby, away from her.

And this was the same man that only hours before had told her he loved her?

BILLY CREPT into the bedroom she shared with Amanda. Confusion and despair made her wish with all her heart that her mother-in-law were awake, that she could confide in her, tell her all the things that had happened tonight, perhaps cry on her shoulder a little and ask her advice. Everything was in such a mess.

Amanda *was* awake. She sat up and switched on the small bedside lamp. Her hair was tousled, her green eyes wide and shining with excitement.

"Billy, I've been lying here hoping you'd come home soon. I'm so excited I can't sleep. Oh, Billy, the most wonderful thing has happened! I can hardly believe it myself."

Amanda drew up her pajamaed knees and clasped them with her arms, her voice trembling as she talked. She was far too exhilarated to notice Billy's distress.

"You're not going to believe this, but I'm buying a business here in Hawaii. Can you imagine that? You remember the little café where we stopped on the way to the flea market, Momi's Coffee Shop? That's the one. I thought and thought about it, and decided to try to do it. I phoned Dunbar Realtors in Vancouver and put my house on the market. I'm going to stay over here and work in the café until my place sells. The agent felt it wouldn't take long at all—I'm pricing it very realistically." Amanda's words tumbled out of her, and waves of energy seemed to emanate from her body as she talked.

"There's no reason really for me to go back to Vancouver until then, and the café needs so much done to it—paint and new curtains and everything. There's the nicest little apartment upstairs, so I'll move in there right away. Max is helping me get it all in order. He's showing me how to arrange for interim financing—he knows this wonderful lawyer." Amanda tossed the sheet back and sprang to her feet, wrapping her arms around Billy in an exuberant hug.

"Darling, it's a dream come true for me. I'm scared to death, but at the same time I'm determined to make a success of it. And I'd never have had the chance if it hadn't been for your winning this trip and inviting me along. I'd have gone on for the rest of my life, working in The Book Bin, living my ordinary little life, never daring to dream of anything like this. Oh, Billy, I'm so very grateful to you."

Billy's cheek was wet with Amanda's tears. She held her mother-in-law close, using the time to compose herself, to try to absorb this latest occurrence. So many things she'd thought were stable had changed tonight. She felt dazed by them all.

Groping for words, trying to dredge up excitement and enthusiasm, she asked Amanda questions and listened to her eager answers, inwardly astounded at how many dreams her mother-in-law had concealed. Billy thought she knew her, but she'd known only a tiny part of the person who was really Amanda.

Was it always this way? Did one person ever truly know another? Were there always hidden secrets, even with those who were closest to you?

She thought about it as the flow of words from the other bed gradually slowed, then stopped altogether as Amanda fell asleep between planning a luncheon menu and deciding on the color for new tablecloths.

Billy lay awake as the hours passed. She felt icy cold and infinitely alone in the tropical warmth of the dawning Hawaiian morning.

Inevitably her thoughts turned to Cosmo.

They'd been close, he and she, as close as two people could be physically, and Billy had believed they'd shared a mental and emotional intimacy, as well.

Well, she'd been wrong, colossally wrong. She couldn't begin to figure out what he was really like in the midst of all the dishonesty, and she no longer had the energy left to try.

When she heard Max stirring at half-past six, Billy got up and crept into the shower. It wouldn't take her long to pack, and she was sure she could catch one of the hourly flights to Oahu without worrying about reservations. She'd try to get a standby seat on a plane back to Vancouver this afternoon, but if she couldn't, she'd stay in Honolulu tonight and fly out tomorrow the way she and Amanda had originally planned.

Either way, there'd soon be miles of ocean between her and Cosmo. Maybe it would help.

MAX MEASURED COFFEE into the filter and filled the container with water. He'd been awake for hours, listening to the muted murmuring of the women's voices in the other bedroom. When they'd grown quiet at last, his own thoughts had kept him from sleep.

He'd waited until the clock signaled that it was past dawn, then he'd gotten up and shaved and showered.

He'd guessed that Amanda had been telling Billy about the café, about the changes she was making in her life, and he wondered if the news surprised Billy as much as it had surprised him.

Surprise, hell. The truth was, Amanda's plans had come as a huge shock to him. It was amazing that he'd been able to disguise his reaction when she'd first told him.

The problem was, he'd been making plans of his own. Ever since their trip around the island, he'd been toying with the idea of asking her to stay on in Hawaii with him. She was a delightful companion, funny and bright and quick-witted. She was warm and passionate and incredibly sensual in bed; she was a tremendous cook; she'd simplified his life enormously by holding the Matrimonial Brigade at bay.

And, he'd finally concluded, he was more than half in love with her.

But there was plenty of time to make major decisions about their future without having her stay on. He'd be going home to Vancouver before many more months passed. She'd be there, and they could continue their relationship at a sedate pace.

What an ass he'd been, egotistically believing the whole matter was his decision. Being on his own with only himself to think of all these years must have made him incredibly selfish.

Certainly it had made him arrogant.

Half in love, indeed. He realized now that he was head over heels in love with Amanda. Like a fool, he'd been biding his time, waiting for the perfect moment to tell her. But before that moment had come, she'd dropped her bombshell about selling her house and buying the business over here.

"You gave me the idea, you know, Max. Remember that night you took me to dinner at the Spindrifter and talked about the hoboes and how they allow themselves to be free? You said that too often we let our possessions and our houses own us, we forget how to dream, we set our expectations of life and ourselves much too low."

The lovely color in her cheeks had been heightened by her excitement, and all he could think of was the silky texture of the skin on her full breasts and how it flushed that same way when he made love to her. He'd imagined again the delightful weight of those lovely breasts in his hands, and suddenly he'd known the awful irony of having his own ponderous words come back to haunt and destroy what might have been.

"Well, I thought about what you said a lot," she'd added. "And I decided it was high time to be a bit of a vagabond, to dig up my roots and at least try to do the things I've dreamed of all my life." She'd looked at him with those eyes that reflected her soul and said softly, "Dear Max, you don't realize how very much you've done for me in these past few weeks. You know, I feel almost sympathetic toward the Matrimonial Brigade. Heavens, if I were a marrying woman, I'd propose to you myself."

Her eyes had twinkled with that special mischievous gleam he liked.

"Aren't you glad I'm a modern career gal, instead?"

He hadn't been glad at all, but he couldn't have told her that.

Instead, he'd helped her every way he could with her complex business dealings, and he'd go on helping her as long as she needed him. Maybe this time *he* was the one who'd have to make adjustments. He had enough material about hoboes to finish his book, his research projects were done and his sabbatical year would be over in a matter of months. He'd just have to find a way to make their lives work together before then. If he knew anything at this point, it was that he wouldn't ever let her walk out of his life now that she'd changed it forever.

The coffee gave one last gurgle, and the light came on to indicate that it was ready. He poured a cup and was about to take it outside, when Billy came out of the bedroom, closing the door quietly behind her. She greeted Max with a strained smile, and he noted the dark circles under her eyes. Obviously she hadn't slept any better than he had.

He got another mug out of the cupboard and filled it for her. "You're looking very dressed up this morning, Billy. You off somewhere special?" She was wearing a pair of tailored brown trousers and matching vest over a white short-sleeved shirt.

Her eyes didn't quite meet his. "Actually, Max, I'm leaving Kona today. This morning, as soon as I get my stuff together. I thought I'd fly over to Oahu and take a tour of Honolulu before my flight leaves tomorrow. Amanda told me last night she's staying on here, so I might as well play tourist and see some of the rest of Hawaii."

"You're going alone?"

"Yes." She'd tried to sound bright and confident, but her voice had come out sounding forlorn, instead.

Max gave her a long, steady look. "I don't mean to sound nosy, Billy, but are you leaving early because of something that's happened between you and Cosmo?"

She stared down at her coffee cup. "Yes, I guess I am." She took a long, steadying breath. "Cosmo isn't at all what he pretended to be, Max. I found out last night he's not a hobo at all. He's an undercover policeman. He's been working on the murders that happened here."

Things that had puzzled him all along slipped into place for Max, and he accepted the news easily. "Well. That doesn't surprise me at all. Cosmo never did fit the typical hobo persona."

Before Max could say anything else, Billy added, "There's something else you should know. Last night that hobo friend of yours was shot—the one you called Boxcar Charlie. There was some sort of meeting, and all Cosmo would tell me was that Charlie was in the wrong place at the wrong time and that he's seriously injured. He's in the hospital."

Max set his cup down in slow motion and stared at her. "You don't know exactly what happened?"

Billy shook her head.

"The murderer? The person who killed Liza Franklin and the two hoboes? Did they catch whoever was responsible?"

Billy felt like a fool. She hadn't even asked; she'd been entirely obsessed with her own problems and hadn't thought to ask the most obvious question of all.

"Cosmo only said that someone else was injured," she said miserably. "He said whoever it was died. But he didn't say who. He . . . he wouldn't talk to me at all when he got back."

Max got up and hurried over to the television. "Maybe there'll be something about it on the early news."

The screen flickered to life.

"An unidentified man is reported in serious but stable condition this morning. Dead is Harrison Franklin, well-known land developer and prominent social figure throughout the islands. Latest news reports indicate that Franklin was a primary suspect in the recent bludgeoning death of his wife, Liza Franklin, and also in what was previously believed to be the accidental deaths of two homeless men discovered drowned a month ago in the vicinity of Old Airport Beach Park. Three other suspects are in custody."

"Sounds like Cosmo and his friends did a good job, and it couldn't have been easy. He's a fine young man, Billy, hobo or policeman."

Billy knew it was true.

"Are you in love with him?" Max's voice was gentle.

"Yeah. Yeah, I am." Tears welled in her eyes and overflowed. She wiped them away with her fingers.

"Then tell him so."

"He...hasn't given me the chance. And he lied to me about who he was. How could I ever trust him again?"

Max sounded sad and tired. "Words aren't all that count, Billy. There are other ways of communicating that are more honest than words. You know that— you're an artist."

"Trust in your heart. Listen to the still, small voice that speaks truth."

Where had she heard that before?

COSMO KNEW Charlie was going to die. He'd known from the moment he'd knelt beside him on the sand and looked at the damage Franklin's bullets had done. A man, an old man like Charlie, couldn't live with that sort of injury.

And yet Charlie was holding on. He'd survived the operation, the doctors had said he was holding his own, but reason dictated that the end was coming soon.

Cosmo hurried back to the hospital after he'd taken Billy home, steeling himself as he walked toward the waiting room where Ema was, certain that she'd meet him with the news that Charlie was already gone, that he, Cosmo, had killed the old man as surely as if he'd held his own gun to Charlie's head and pulled the trigger.

Cosmo could taste coppery fear in his mouth as he moved along the hospital corridor. He was afraid in a way he'd never been before, held in the grip of a different sort of fear than the high, keen edge that came over him in the midst of a crisis like the one earlier tonight. That sort of apprehension sharpened his wits, but this was immobilizing, crippling dread that made his belly feel sick, that usurped his energy and drove everything else from his mind.

He entered the small room where Ema waited, watching her intently for a sign of Charlie's passing. Instead she got to her feet when she saw him and stretched and yawned. There were dark smudges beneath her eyes, but she smiled reassuringly.

"He's just regained consciousness. The nurse said you could see him for a moment or two if you want. She's the blonde over there at the desk. Then we're going to have to go over to the Police Office and start on the reports."

Moments later, Cosmo stood beside Charlie's bed. It was surrounded by tubes and bottles and monitors all hooked in some fashion to the shriveled form of the old man lying deathly still between the sheets.

"Charlie?" Cosmo's voice was hoarse, and he cleared his throat before he spoke again. "Charlie, you awake, partner?"

Cosmo didn't know what it was he wanted to say. "Sorry" didn't begin to make up for taking what was left of this old man's life. There was a lump in Cosmo's throat, and he reached out and grasped Charlie's hand in his own, unable to form the right words.

Slowly the blue eyes opened, disoriented at first, then slowly focusing on Cosmo's face. It took a long time to get any words out, but Charlie was determined.

"We...get...Franklin?"

Cosmo had to bend close to catch the whisper. "Yeah, Charlie, we got him, thanks to you. He's dead. He . . . got shot."

Some of the strain seemed to disappear from Charlie's pinched features. "I . . . did . . . good," he breathed, and closed his eyes again.

"You sure did, Charlie. You did great, just great."

The nurse was nearby, and she said quietly, "I think you'd better go now, Detective."

But Charlie opened his eyes once more and he gripped Cosmo's fingers in a surprisingly firm clasp. "You . . . ast . . . yet?"

It took Cosmo two tries to catch the words, and then he couldn't figure out their meaning. Charlie's eyes conveyed his impatience with Cosmo's stupidity, and the nurse grew more insistent that the visit end.

Charlie was determined. "Yer . . . lady. You . . . ast her . . . yet?"

Billy. Charlie was talking about Billy.

"No, old-timer, not yet. I haven't really had a chance."

Disgust was plain on Charlie's face. "What's . . . keepin' . . . ya?"

The nurse had her hand on Cosmo's arm now, urging him toward the door, and she wasn't amused.

He resisted for one more second. "If she says yes, you coming to my wedding, old-timer?"

It took a moment, but Charlie opened his eyes again. There was fiendish determination in them this time, and his smile revealed all his missing teeth. "Damned tootin'," he said, then his head fell to the side and he was asleep.

Cosmo wasn't aware of the nurse's displeasure or the door closing behind him or even Ema's sympathetic questions about Charlie's condition.

He felt as if a heavy cloud were lifting from around him, a black mantle that had settled over him when he'd seen Charlie's body lift into the air with the force of the bullets from Franklin's gun. From that moment till just now, he'd been certain Charlie was going to die. He'd been convinced that it was his fault, that he'd been responsible for another human life and allowed that life to be destroyed. That awful knowledge had weighed on him like lead.

He knew now that he'd been mistaken about Charlie dying. Boxcar Charlie was as tough as an old rope, and he was going to live. Cosmo couldn't have said why he was so certain of it, but he knew all the same— he'd known in that moment when Charlie had smiled at him. There was cockiness and assurance and the will to survive in that smile, and it gave Cosmo hope.

It changed everything. It made him aware of the bone-deep fatigue in his body, aware that he hadn't eaten for far too long. Most of all, it reminded him of Billy and of the things left unfinished between them.

"We have to get over to the station right now. The boss is going to have our heads if we don't get those reports in," Ema was insisting. "The doctors have promised they'll get hold of us if there's any change in Charlie."

"I need to make a phone call." Cosmo dug for quarters and was heading for the pay phones at the end of the corridor, when he caught a glimpse of the large clock on the wall. It was still only six-fifteen in the morning. Because of him, Billy had been up most of the night. Undoubtedly she'd be sound asleep right now, and so would Max and Amanda. They wouldn't appreciate being awakened by a phone call from him.

Reluctantly he shoved the change back in his pocket and loped back down the hall to join Ema at the elevators.

He'd call in another hour or so.

"WELL, WELL, you sure had me fooled there, didn't ya?"

Detective Fellerman was holding a cup of coffee in one hand and a huge Danish in the other. It was eight-fifteen, and he'd arrived at the police office only moments before. He'd already heard reports of the stakeout on the early news, but it had obviously been a nasty shock to him to find Cosmo sitting in his office, slouched in front of his computer, typing up reports of the operation. Another officer introduced them, and Cosmo nodded coolly without getting up.

"Really had me going, thinking you were nothin' but a tramp." He took a huge bite of the Danish, and jam dropped down on his tie. He talked with his mouth full. "You done much of the undercover work before, Antonelli, pretending to be a bum like that?"

Fellerman's jovial manner didn't match the open resentment that showed in his narrow eyes, Cosmo saw at once. "'Hobo,' Fellerman. I wasn't a bum or a tramp—I was a hobo. There's a difference."

"Oh, yeah?" Fellerman smirked and winked at Ema, who'd just come in with more sheets of paper. She ignored him.

"They all look pretty much the same to me. So what's the big difference?"

Cosmo softly repeated what Max had told him was Charlie's definition. "Hoboes work. Tramps can't. Bums won't."

Fellerman guffawed as if Cosmo were making a joke.

"Actually, they do all have one thing in common, Fellerman, and it's a damned good thing to remember." Cosmo's voice was quiet and lethal.

"Yeah? And what's that?" Fellerman's grin had slipped a little at the menace in Cosmo's tone.

"They're all just as human as you are, and they all deserve to be treated like human beings. You should work at it."

It was satisfying to watch Fellerman's bloated face turn bright red. He glared at Cosmo and marched out of the office.

At ten-thirty, most of the paperwork was finally done, and the steady stream of officers coming by to ask questions or comment on the success of the undercover operation had slowed to a trickle.

Cosmo dialed Max's number. When Amanda answered, he asked for Billy.

There was a moment of silence, then Amanda said, "Oh, Cosmo, I'm so sorry. I'm afraid she's gone. We've just come back from taking her to the airport. She caught the nine-thirty flight over to Oahu this morning."

BILLY WATCHED the Big Island grow small beneath her as the crowded commuter plane gained altitude. She refused the coffee and biscuits the lovely Hawaiian stewardess offered, and she wondered dully if she'd ever feel hungry again. She hadn't eaten since yesterday at lunch, and for the first time in her entire life, the thought of food made her nauseous.

Saying goodbye to Amanda had been agonizing, yet it was a relief to be alone, not to have to smile or pretend any longer that she was all right.

She fingered the quartz crystal at her throat. At the last moment, tears running unheeded down her cheeks, Amanda had taken it off and slid the chain around Billy's throat, settling it inside the neck of her blouse. The stone still felt curiously hot against her skin, as if it had absorbed and stored some of Amanda's warmth and love and was radiating it, trying in vain to warm the icy-cold misery sitting like a lead weight inside Billy's chest.

The truly awful part of leaving was the niggling feeling somewhere deep inside her heart that she was making a terrible mistake. From the moment she'd boarded the plane, she had an overwhelming urge to turn back, to find Cosmo and force him to put into words whatever he'd been going to say to her the night before. Instead she was running away. She was allowing pride and anger to overcome the still, small voice inside her heart.

But the plane had taken off, and she knew it was too late. She'd set out on a course of action, and she'd carry it through.

CHAPTER SIXTEEN

THE FLIGHT to Honolulu took less than an hour. Billy deplaned and followed the signs to the departure area, hurrying down the long corridor. All her cheerful talk about exploring Honolulu had been a smoke screen for Max's and Amanda's sake. She wanted nothing more than to crawl back on another plane now and fly home. Surely there'd be a cancellation and she could catch a flight back to Vancouver today.

She didn't pay any attention to the security guards until they were right beside her, one at either shoulder, a polite distance away but close enough to grab her if she ran. She slowed and then stopped, and they did, too. She looked from one to the other, unable to figure out what was going on.

"What is it? I think you've made a mistake..." she started to say.

But a tall man in a gray suit materialized out of nowhere and said politely, "Ms. Billy Overton Reece?"

Dazed, she nodded.

"We're with airport security, Ms. Reece," he said. "We've been instructed by the Hawaiian Police Department to detain you for questioning. Would you come this way, please?"

"But... but I haven't done anything! What do you want with me? Questioning about what?"

His smile was meant to be soothing, Billy realized, but all it did was reinforce his authority.

"I really have no idea, ma'am. If you'll just come with me, someone will be along shortly."

BUT NO ONE ARRIVED.

For over an hour Billy waited. She was left alone in a small, gray-walled room with two hard chairs and a scarred table. There was a calendar on the wall with a picture of an angry-looking swordfish and the words "Oahu Security Systems, Where Your Investment Brings You Peace of Mind."

Peace of mind was the last thing Billy had.

The door was closed, and a guard sat outside. He wouldn't answer any questions, but he brought her coffee she couldn't drink and asked politely if she wanted something to eat. She didn't. She wanted an explanation, but when she asked again what she was being held for, he shrugged and shook his head.

"I don't have any idea, ma'am. But someone will be along soon, don't worry."

She almost laughed at that. Don't worry when she was being held prisoner with no clue as to what crime she might have committed?

Apprehension began to give way to outrage as the minutes passed. What on earth was going on? Should she call a lawyer?

But she didn't know any lawyers. She didn't know anyone in Honolulu. She didn't know what to do. She hadn't done anything against the law, had she?

Finally someone appeared in the doorway, and slowly she got to her feet. She'd been sitting so long one leg had gone to sleep, and she lurched a little and grabbed for the table. A rapid succession of emotions coursed through her as she stared at the tall figure that came through the door.

"Cosmo?" Her voice was out of control, and so was her heartbeat. She gaped at him, taking in the worn cutoffs, the same shirt he'd put on last night in the apartment. "Cosmo, I'm so glad you're here. No one will tell me..."

A slow and awful suspicion began to form in her head.

He stood immobile and simply looked at her for a moment, his expression intense and unreadable. It was obvious he hadn't slept recently; his eyes were red rimmed, and harsh lines of fatigue showed on his face.

He reached behind him and shut the door with one firm shove. "Billy. Billy, I'm sorry I had to do it this way, but I couldn't just let you walk out on me like that." He moved toward her, and in another moment, he had her in his arms. "Billy, my dearest love..."

He was trembling. His huge body was trembling, holding her, and it shocked her. He was always so strong, so much in control, yet now she could feel his tension, his terrible need of her, in every pore in her body.

The feel of him overwhelmed her, the dear, familiar warmth and bulk and scent that was Cosmo, and automatically her arms circled him, drawing him closer, tighter.

"Last night...Billy, I had to shoot a man last night." His voice was quiet, close to her ear. "He shot Charlie, and I shot him."

She drew away enough to look into his face. "Franklin?"

He nodded. "He was a murderer, but he was a human being. I've never killed a man before. Then I thought for sure old Charlie was going to die on me, as well, and it did something to me. I felt responsible. I should have taken better care of him. I couldn't think of anything else, and I went a little crazy for a while. And because of that, you nearly got away on me." There was raw emotion in his voice, an edge that spoke of exhaustion and heartsick despair. "This damned job of mine, Billy. I've always enjoyed it before, but this time—this time I nearly lost you, and part of myself, as well. Max figured you were going to try to get a flight back to Vancouver this afternoon."

"I was. So you had me arrested just to keep me here?" Her voice was still unsteady, but any anger she'd felt was gone. She couldn't think beyond the momentary delight that came from being in his arms.

"Well, not arrested, exactly. Just detained for questioning." He looked at her, a little sheepish now, trying to gauge how she'd react to what he'd done.

She couldn't pretend to be angry, even to tease him. She looked at him, certain that what her heart was saying must be showing in her eyes.

His next words seemed to burst from him. "Billy, why the hell didn't you wait for me today? Why did you run away from me like this? I know I haven't given you much reason to trust me, but surely you understand that I couldn't be open with you about who I was or what I was doing until now. I give you my word I'll never lie to you again."

He drew away from her and, gently urged her back into the chair she'd been sitting in. He groped behind him for the other chair, dragging it close enough so he could hold both her hands in his as he talked.

"I felt absolutely rotten having to mislead you. And those things I lied about—my last name, my hobo disguise—they were superficial, Billy. But this thing between us, this feeling I have for you . . . it's stronger and more honest than anything I've ever felt before. You must know that—you must feel it, too.

"Damn it all, I know you do. I know you care for me," he added passionately. "So why couldn't you wait a few more hours for me to come to you? I told you how I felt. I told you I loved you." He waited a moment, and when she didn't respond, he added more gently, "I do, you know, Billy. Love you."

She dropped her gaze to their hands, intertwined on his knees, and for the first time she knew exactly what the answer was, the real reason she'd had to leave him the way she had.

It wasn't for the reasons she'd thought at all. Deep inside her, where everyone recognizes truth, she knew Cosmo was an honest, good man. She understood the necessity of what he'd had to do.

The real answer was rooted in the ghost of a small girl who still lived somewhere inside her, a little girl nobody ever wanted enough to keep.

"See, nobody's ever really wanted me around for long," she said in a small voice. "Graham actually left me long before he died." There was a lump in her throat, and she could barely hold the tears back. "I guess . . . I guess I thought if I went away first, this time it wouldn't hurt quite so much."

She raised her gaze to meet his. The tears that had threatened moments before had dried. There was an awful desolation inside her, an aloneness so profound and deeply rooted she could scarcely bear to confront it. But it was time she did. Past time. Understanding could heal. Love would heal.

"I was wrong, you know, Cosmo," she added softly. "It hurt like hell leaving you. I'll never do it again—I promise."

He heard what she said and he thought of Charlie, and the girl named Gladys: *"That way she never had to let me down, see. Me, I wasn't nobody."* In different words, Billy was saying the same thing.

A hard lump formed in his chest, and he had to struggle hard to keep from weeping. This woman he adored tore at his heartstrings, and the depth of her vulnerability touched him in ways he'd never dreamed of.

All the verbal reassurances in the world would never erase the insecurity she'd lived with all these years. He'd have to show her; he'd have to make his loving visible for her, every hour of every day, until she knew, deep in her soul, that she was the center of his world, that he'd love and protect her for the rest of this life and beyond.

He slid forward off the edge of his chair to his bare knees. "Will you marry me, Billy?"

Her eyes were wide and very dark, the way he'd seen them when she was just waking up from a dream to answer his kisses.

She only nodded at first, a hesitant nod, and he understood how much courage it took.

"Yes, Cosmo, I will," she whispered finally.

He drew her head down and kissed her.

He was going to have to buy a new suit, not only for himself but for Boxcar Charlie, as well.

It would last him the rest of his life, though.

He planned to do this only once.

Following the success of WITH THIS RING, Harlequin cordially invites you to enjoy the romance of the wedding season with

BARBARA BRETTON
RITA CLAY ESTRADA
SANDRA JAMES
DEBBIE MACOMBER

A collection of romantic stories that celebrate the joy, excitement, and mishaps of planning that special day by these four award-winning Harlequin authors.

Available in April at your favorite Harlequin retail outlets.

THTH